MARINA BAY SINS

MARINA BAY SINS

An Inspector Low Novel

Neil Humphreys

**MUSWELL
PRESS**

First published by Marshall Cavendish International (Asia)
Private Limited in 2015
This edition published by Muswell Press 2022
Copyright © Neil Humphreys 2015

Neil Humphreys has asserted his right to be identified as the author of this
work in accordance with the Copyright, Designs and Patents Act, 1988

This book is a work of fiction and, except in the case of historical fact,
any resemblance to actual persons, living or dead, is purely coincidental

A CIP catalogue record for this book is available from the British Library

Typeset by M Rules
Printed and bound by CPI Group (UK) Ltd, Croydon CR0 4YY

ISBN: 978-1-83834-014-8
eISBN: 978-1-73987-947-1

Muswell Press
London N6 5HQ
www.muswell-press.co.uk

MARINA BAY SINS

Chapter 1

MADONNA pushed her cleaning trolley along the corridor and cursed. She hated one-night stands. They rarely left a tip and always made a mess. They knew they were only staying for one day. The sordid filth left behind wasn't their concern. Swearing in Tagalog, she stopped outside room 4088. An *ang moh* and a prostitute had checked in the night before. She had seen them, giggling and fiddling, as they fumbled for the room key beneath the soft lighting. It was always the same with *ang mohs* and prostitutes; empty mini-bars and soiled sheets. Those girls let them do things that their wives never would. And they did them on Madonna's sheets.

Biting her inner lip, she knocked on the door.

"Hello, housekeeping."

She waited, listening for a response. She stood back impatiently. At her previous hotels, she always had an ear to the door. She knew immediately if the room was empty that way, but the Marina Bay Sands management did not tolerate such vulgar behaviour. Housemaids squeezed up against hotel room doors was an unseemly sight, unbecoming of such a reputable establishment. What guests got up to inside the rooms was of course their business.

"Hello, housekeeping. Is there anyone inside?"

Madonna had to call out three times before being allowed to enter. She looked at her watch. Check-out was an hour ago. These guys were not over-stayers. They were not even gamblers. They hadn't dashed downstairs to the casino. He had obviously dashed home to the oblivious housewife and she had returned to the street. The last place they wanted to be seen together was inside a Marina Bay Sands hotel room.

"Hello, housekeeping. I'm here to clean the room. I'm opening the door now."

Madonna swiped her card key and waited for the click. She pushed open the door. The room was only Deluxe, the cheapest available. She had 45 minutes to clean each room. She expected this one to take at least an hour.

The carpet was littered with empty mini-bottles, room service plates, bed sheets and underwear. But the smell was something else. Madonna sniffed. The odour wasn't the usual leftover chicken rice and flat champagne. Eager to press on and forget about the stench, she busied herself with the carpet. Madonna picked up the stained duvet from the cluttered floor, rolled it into a ball and turned towards the sheets on the bed.

She opened her mouth, but her voice cracked. She dropped the duvet and covered her mouth to block the silence as tears ran over her fingers. She tried to move, but her frozen legs betrayed her. Finally she stepped forward, completely forgetting about the duvet. As her foot got tangled with it, she lost her balance and tripped, falling towards the bed. Her face brushed against a leg. She flew backwards in horror, crying hysterically, crawling blindly on her hands and knees towards the door. When she found the corridor, she found her voice. Madonna screamed and didn't stop screaming until the police arrived.

*

Detective Inspector Stanley Low flicked the fake rubber plant. He loathed fake plants. They summed up his fake country. He lived in a fake country with fake plants in phony psychiatrists' offices. He was supposed to get to his real feelings, find his real core. How the fuck was he supposed to do that sitting beside a fake plant?

Dr Tracy Lai watched Low flick her IKEA plant. She adjusted her skirt, checking that it still covered her knees. She was Chinese, an attractive woman for her age. With her long, straight, silky black hair and fondness for dressing for the boardroom, Lai had once been labelled a "MILF" by a patient with a colourful history of sexual deviancy. She was disturbed that she had found his description strangely comforting. She smiled at Low and spoke softly.

"You don't like my plant, do you?"

"No, I don't like your plant."

"Why?"

"Why? Because it tells me you're lazy *lah*, that's why. It tells me you *heck care* about the environment. It tells me you cannot even take the time to water a plant once a day. It tells me this is why Singapore is so fucked up. We're a plastic country now, *basket*."

"It's interesting that you lapse into Singlish when you get excited, animated or aggressive. Why do you think that is?"

"Oh, I don't know, because I'm Singaporean? I mean, really? Is this where we're at now? My speech patterns? If I speak standard English, I'm cured. If I speak Singlish, I'm fucked up? Is that the general psychiatric diagnosis?"

"No, you know your diagnosis. You have mild bipolar disorder with aggressive tendencies and we're working on that through the treatment and these sessions."

"No, you say I have bipolar. I say my job makes me angry

3

sometimes and I get pissed off when people around me are always talking cock. Come on *lah*."

"You have violent, episodic mood swings. You have detailed periods of prolonged energy and creativity and . . ."

"That's what gets me through a case."

"And you have admitted that there are days when you refuse to get out of bed or talk to anyone."

Low smiled. "I'm an old-school detective *what*. You think my job is easy, is it? You think you could do my job is it?"

"No, I'm not saying that at all. I cannot begin to imagine what your job must be like."

"No, you can't."

"But I am saying that your condition both helps and hinders your line of work. I agree it must help the investigative process, but you were referred to me because your superiors felt your relationships with your colleagues were being compromised by your behaviour."

"*Wah lau*, you don't listen is it? Look at me. I'm a skinny Chinaman. I look like a gangster, so I play the gangster. My bosses give me greasy hair, a white vest and some money and I go play Chinese gangster for six months. My *kakis* are pimps, prostitutes, gamblers, *ah longs*, *kelong* match fixers and a mad bastard with a knife."

Low lifted his shirt to expose a line of ragged stitches across his torso. He glared at the psychiatrist. She chose not to speak, but the slight shuffle in the chair told the inspector all he needed to know.

"I know about your injuries. I read about them when you were referred to me," Lai said firmly, sitting up straight, reasserting control.

"So what do you want me to say?"

"I don't want you to say anything if you don't want to."

Low's smile came out like a snarl. He sat back in his chair

4

and opened his legs wide. Wearing shorts and a scruffy T-shirt, his physical belligerence was a practiced performance, but Lai had seen the routine too many times before. Low then sat up and leaned forwards. He stared at his psychiatrist.

"Look, I know that you're only doing your best for me, OK? And if you say I have bipolar, OK, I have bipolar. I will say to you that I am a First Class degree holder, a government scholar from the London School of Economics who has spent much of my working life pretending to be an illiterate gangster, but OK, I have bipolar. What would you like me to do now?"

"What would *you* like me to do?"

Low slumped back into his chair, sighed and examined Lai's office. The clean, sparse room was practically lifted from an IKEA catalogue.

"Well, you can get rid of that fucking plant."

Detective Inspector James Tan nodded to a pair of uniformed officers as he passed them in the grand, opulent lobby of the Marina Bay Sands Hotel. The police presence was minimal, presumably at the hotel's request. Like Singapore, the integrated resort was obsessed with calm exteriors. Little publicity was second only to no publicity. The casino buried within the bowels of the island's biggest ATM machine planned to generate around 0.8 per cent of the entire country's GDP in the near future. Police and publicity were bad for business. Marina Bay Sands courted neither.

As Tan passed beneath the baffling post-modern stainless steel installation that looked to him like a million wired coat hangers tied together, he thought about the recent cases around the resorts. There were always one or two, more around Chinese New Year, obviously, but this one was different. This one was messy. He was in no mood to lead another investigation and planned to palm this one off as soon as possible. But there were drugs involved. There always were in these glitzy, grotesque houses of hypocrisy.

Standing outside room 4088, Tan grunted a hello at a couple of plain-clothes officers he didn't recognise. Hearing his boss' voice, Detective Sergeant Charles Chan made his way through the crowded hotel room to join Tan in the corridor.

"There are drugs everywhere, boss, everywhere."

Tan gestured for his breathless colleague to keep his voice down. A couple of hotel housemaids hovered nearby with their cleaning trolleys.

"Hello, ladies, don't you have somewhere to be?" asked the portly policeman, kindly but firmly.

He straightened his crisp white shirt, making a point of smoothing the sides and tucking them inside the waistband of his freshly pressed black trousers, then followed his younger colleague.

Everyone in the hotel room was staring at the naked body. The Caucasian male was spreadeagled across the bed. Tan thought of that da Vinci drawing, the man stretched out with extra arms and legs. The corpse's arms and legs almost reached the corners of the double bed.

"It's an *ang moh*, boss," said Chan.

"Yes, I can see that, Charlie."

"It's Charles, sir, please call me Charles. The other officers make fun of me when you call me Charlie."

"*Wah lau*, not now *ah*, Charlie?"

Tan sidestepped the rubbish on the carpet to move closer to the bed. The cocaine was everywhere, on the bedside table and across the bedspread. The pillow and sheets had damp stains, certainly saliva on the pillow, possibly semen on the sheets. Two empty pill bottles were on the carpet beside the bed, next to an empty vodka bottle. Four other uniformed officers lingered in the background, waiting for their instructions. Tan sighed. They were typical Singaporean civil servants, always waiting to be led. Chan scribbled notes in a pad, writing furiously, always opting for quantity over quality.

Tan leaned over the bed and examined the corpse. The *ang moh* was obviously in his late thirties and had worked out. His biceps and pecs were well defined. Tan looked down at his own protruding stomach. His beer belly had appeared shortly after National Service and he made little attempt to conceal it. He was well-fed and contented. His plump gut was a sign of affluence.

The dead man had been vain, too. The pubic hair beneath his belly button had been shaved, as had his testicles. It wasn't the first corpse with waxed testicles either. Tan struggled to understand his own world. He reached the foot of the bed and grimaced.

"Hey, Charlie ... DS Chan."

Chan cringed as the other officers chuckled.

"It's Charles."

"Where is that smell coming from?"

"From the guy *lah*."

"Don't talk cock. Cannot smell like that so fast."

"Can *what*, after suicide. He's dead already."

"*Wah*, did you work that out all by yourself? Go get me the maid who found this guy and the hotel manager."

"Yeah, I tried already. But the hotel staff said he's very busy at the moment. They are at full capacity. Got the Singapore Grand Prix coming."

As he crouched over the corpse, Tan glared up at the box-ticking rookie. The image was an incongruous one for the younger detective as his boss was still examining the dead man's genitalia.

7

"OK, OK, I try again, I'll ask him to hurry."

The inspector stood up suddenly.

"No, no, don't ask him. Get him. We're the Singapore Police Force, I'm the investigating officer and I want to go for *makan* already. Tell him to come now or I'll conduct the interview at the police station. And I'll issue a press release. OK or not?"

"Yes, boss."

"Hey, where are these guys' details?" Tan shouted after the departing detective.

"Oh, I left them on that table by the balcony."

The inspector pointed towards the closed sliding door that led to the balcony. "Has that been opened at all?"

"No, boss, locked when we came in."

"Well, that's a possible point of entry."

"We're on the 40th floor, boss."

"Eh, don't be a smart arse, OK. Balconies can climb one. Check who was staying in the rooms along this floor and maybe above and below this room. Now, where's the *ang moh*'s stuff?"

"On that table."

Tan ignored the wallet, phone and keys and went straight for the passport. Through the balcony door, he watched the cranes piece together the new developments to the right of Gardens by the Bay. Imperious monuments to money, they all jostled for a place in the South-east Asian sunshine. Manufactured gardens of today squeezed alongside glassy cash cows of tomorrow all built on reclaimed land. The only thing natural about the sweeping vista was the South China Sea, but Tan admired the view nonetheless. He couldn't afford a view like that, not on his salary, but he was proud of it. It was a uniquely Singaporean view; modern, micro-managed and artificial.

He was surprised that the passport cover was Australian. With the shaved testicles, the inspector expected the corpse to be European—French or Italian perhaps. He found the ID page. The poor bastard was handsome. He was actually almost 40. His name was Richard Davie.

Tan pointed at the nearest officer, jabbing the passport in his direction.

"Hey hello, call CPIB. Get me Detective Inspector Stanley Low. Now."

Chapter 2

LOW watched the ERP gantry crawl towards him on the East Coast Parkway. The ERP. Singapore's electronic road pricing system set up to introduce congestion charges and minimise traffic. It didn't minimise traffic, but it maximised revenue for the Government. Even the other police officers openly called it 'Everyday Rob People'.

The three towers of Marina Bay Sands crept closer, moving across the left side of Low's windscreen. Three packs of cards standing tall and ready to deal out fortunes for the country. Low had been there before, but as Ah Lian, never as himself. He went with Tiger. Someone owed the old *ah long* money. Someone always owed Tiger money. Low smiled at the memory. He enjoyed playing the gangster, the *blur* apprentice loan shark, far more than he would ever care to admit.

A BMW cut across the front of Low's Toyota Prius, barely missing the paintwork along his right wing. Low honked loudly and repeatedly. The young Chinese driver gave him the middle finger. That was just what Low needed after the exorbitant session with Dr Lai—proper therapy.

Taking advantage of the traffic jam, Low cut into the

left-hand lane before pulling up sharply beside the BMW. He put down his window and grinned at the Chinese guy, who was at least 10 years younger than Low and earned 10 times the salary, judging by the obvious car and the outsized horse prancing across his left nipple.

"Hey, man, what's with all the aggression and the middle finger?"

The BMW driver lowered his front passenger seat window.

"Fuck you," he hissed in heavily-accented English.

Low laughed. The driver was from Mainland China.

"Is that the best you can do, really? Has your English not improved at all since you arrived? OK, shit head, we'll do it your way."

Low applied the hand brake, stepped out of his car and strolled brazenly across the expressway. He tapped his police ID card on the window. He watched the man shrivel before him, disappearing into the leathery seat.

Low gestured for him to lower his driver seat window. Other cars honked their horns continuously. He turned and waved his police ID card at them all.

"Sit still, be patient and shut the fuck up," he said, smiling. He was really enjoying himself now.

"OK, OK, sorry, *ah*," replied the driver. "Sorry *ah*, officer, very stressed one, late for meeting already."

Low leaned into the window. "*Wah*, your Singlish not bad, *ah*? Yes, I understand that. I can see why you did that. You think you damn *garang* one, cut across lanes, go past me, but the finger thing, that was too much. You are basically saying 'fuck you', and then, you actually said 'fuck you', which you really cannot do, not to a Singaporean police officer. This isn't China, or Malaysia, or Indonesia. You can't give me the middle finger. You can't make this finger and then give me 50 bucks. This is Singapore. And here, I fuck you."

Low called a colleague at CPIB, gave the driver's personal and car registration details and asked for a complete background check: visa status, employment, property, investments, everything. He'd find something. He always did.

Chan struggled to get a word in with Pierre Durand. The hotel manager intimidated the young detective. Tall and handsome, the grey-haired Frenchman had a neutral Eurozone accent that was impossible to pin down but spoke of confidence with every crisp consonant and narrow vowel. He made box-ticking Singaporeans like the perspiring officer nervous, and he knew it.

"Look, I understand you have a report to complete, officer, but we are running at full occupancy and we really need to clear this room and prepare it for our new guests this evening," Durand said, rudely peering over Chan's shoulder to examine the horrid mess the other officers were making in his hotel room.

"Someone died in your room last night."

Durand decided to look at the naive detective, if only to patronise him.

"People die in hotels all the time, every day. We have more than 2,500 rooms here. They are usually always occupied and the guests change frequently. We have more than 90 per cent room occupancy; it's 100 per cent around major events and conferences. So we have tens of thousands of people going in and out of these rooms all the time, people of all shapes, sizes and ages. Of course, people die in hotel rooms."

"Well, this gentleman died in here last night—or possibly this morning—and we need to find out how he died."

"Judging by the empty pill bottles and the substances found around the bed, I should have thought that was obvious."

Tan had heard enough. He had listened to Chan's soft

interview whilst examining the empty pill bottles on the coffee table. There had been 14 in each bottle, Valium, 10 mg, more than enough to kill a man, more than enough to kill a mammoth. He avoided the clothes, bottles and plates strewn across the carpet and joined the two men in the hotel corridor.

"Shall we leave the deductive reasoning to the police officers?" the investigating officer interjected.

Durand stared at the tubby, unkempt Chinese inspector. He often thought that the worst aspect of running a Singaporean hotel was dealing with bumbling Singaporean officials.

"I'm sorry, we haven't been introduced. My name is Pierre Durand. I am the manager of Marina Bay Sands. Would you like my name card?"

"No, I'd like you to answer our questions."

"I'm trying to be as helpful as I can."

"Please *lah*, don't waste my time. You are trying to get us out of your hotel room, so you can squeeze more gamblers into your hotel tonight."

"No, I would like to settle this matter as quickly as possible so, yes, I can offer the new room guests the discretion and privacy that they value at Marina Bay Sands."

"*Wah lau*, you guys really are full of shit."

"I beg your ..."

"You've got a dead *ang moh* in there with cocaine everywhere. So please, don't bullshit me with your talk about privacy, luxury, quality. My narcotics guys come here so many times, I should put my desk inside your casino. Now, answer his questions, before I cordon off the corridor for the rest of the day and get my uniformed officers to knock on every one of your 2,500 stylo-milo rooms."

Chan cleared his throat and said, "Now the maid said she

saw two people go into the room yesterday—a Caucasian man and a Chinese woman—some time yesterday afternoon, but you say Richard Davie checked in alone."

"That's according to the staff on the counter. They are reasonably sure that he checked in alone."

"Reasonably sure?" enquired Tan. "You just said you've got 10,000 people in and of this place every week. How can they be certain?"

"He ... er ... he wanted to pay by cash. He insisted on it. You see, the girls on the counter remembered that because you know, well, because ..."

"He didn't want his wife to see the credit card statement and realise he'd been sleeping with a prostitute. Yeah, yeah, yeah, yeah, but he had to give a credit card for anything in the room right?"

"For the incidentals? Yes, of course."

"Right, give us all the credit card details please."

Durand shifted the weight between his feet uneasily. He was aware that a couple of Filipino cleaners were lingering in the background, pretending to inspect the plush, leaf-patterned brown carpet in the corridor. As he caught his reflection in one of the corridor's subtle mirrors, he felt a bead of sweat trickle down the back of his neck, which irritated him. Perspiration was an unprofessional image, even in Singapore's equatorial climate. He was annoyed a little with himself, but more with the fat, sweaty inspector.

"Can't one of my staff do that? Why do you need me to collect the man's credit card details?"

Tan took a step towards the fidgety Frenchman.

"Because I can and because you are very irritating. Just as I can also say you're not having anyone in this room tonight."

Schooled in hospitality at Paris' finest hotels, Durand

found their lack of civility and extraordinary ignorance exasperating. Who paid these imbeciles their derisory salaries every month? Where did they think the money was coming from? The Frenchman had a greater grasp of Singapore's basic cash flow than these bumbling *gendarmes*. He stared, open-mouthed, at both men, waiting for a sign; a reaction to suggest that this was all a misunderstanding; some earthy humour to distract from their distressing job.

"Now, look, you can't do this. I don't want to do this, but if necessary I will have no choice but to call . . ."

Tan's mood changed suddenly. He looked menacingly into the Frenchman's flawless face.

"Call who? Who are you going to call? Ghostbusters? Were you going to drop names then? You think you can drop names because you work for MBS, is it? Cannot be so *blur* right? You cannot be crazy to drop names to a detective inspector at the Central Narcotics Bureau. You weren't going to do that? Cannot be right? But it's OK. I can drop names also. I can say Singapore Police Force. Maybe it's not as sexy as your name, maybe you know a *towkay*, very big gambler one, maybe you know some politicians, maybe even a minister. But they will not support you now, not when it involves the casino . . ."

"We are not the casino," Durand interjected quickly.

Tan's eyes bulged. "Did I look like I was finished? You are right. Your name is a big name. Marina Bay Sands is a big name. But my name can issue a press release in one hour saying you got a dead body with illegal substances all over your nice hotel room facing Marina Bay, OK or not? You want to drop any big-shot names?"

"No, no, I was just going to . . ."

"Get me the credit card details and then bring me your eye in the sky."

Tan pointed at the round, black orb discreetly placed on the ceiling over Durand's shoulder. Without looking up at the CCTV camera behind him, the Marina Bay Sands manager scuffed his polished loafer against some fluff on the carpet and nodded. The camera was far too close to room 4088 for his liking.

Low squeezed his hybrid into a VIP parking space between a Bentley and a Ferrari and slammed the door shut. A hefty concierge wearing an ill-fitting dark uniform shuffled towards the inspector. Shimmery metallic flaps on a sculpture fluttered behind him in the breeze, offering an incongruous sight. There were 260,000 of these flaps, knitted together by an artist to provide a facade, to deflect attention, to hide the resort's unsightly bits. They defined Marina Bay Sands. The glamour was an illusion. Everything was flaps and mirrors.

"Hey, you, cannot park there *ah*, cannot, that one reserved for . . ."

"Me."

Low turned and flashed his police ID card at the puffing hotel employee.

"Ah, you police, is it?"

"No, I'm a children's entertainer. I just forgot the balloons. How do I get to the 40th floor?"

"Which tower?"

"The Tower of London. Don't talk cock now, which tower."

"Got three towers, sir."

Low sighed and checked the message on his phone. "I want room 4088, it overlooks the gardens, not the city."

The concierge's spotless white gloves pointed towards some sliding doors where a tour party from China were listening impatiently to a guide explaining in Mandarin where

16

the underpass to the casino was. "Go through there," the concierge said. "Walk straight to the other side of the lobby, past the gift shop. Take the Tower 1 lift, the one next to the concierge counter. Get off at the 40th floor. But must need hotel room key to press button, one."

"You think I'm staying here, is it?"

"But lift will not open without hotel room key."

"OK, I'll speak to security inside. Thanks man, you've been really helpful. Make sure no one steals my car, *ah*."

The concierge swore under his breath, pulled his white gloves tighter and then abused some children for running across the taxi stand. He felt better.

Low spotted his old friend Tan speaking to a couple of hotel maids in the corridor. The old inspector had gained weight. That was the trouble with CNB work in Singapore; too much paperwork and not enough drugs. The CPIB was different. Corruption was a treadmill. Match-fixing alone kept Low on the streets. And then there were the internal cases, former bosses, the stat board tenders, the religious groups siphoning church funds and the sex-for-grades and the sex-for-tenders and the sex-for-contracts. He was buried in sex. No one had babies in Singapore because they were too busy having sex. And then there was the internal investigation, the undercover work to find the corrupt within the Corrupt Practices Investigation Bureau. He was ordered to clean out his own house. He lost sleep, friends and dignity in one case. He couldn't remember the order. He didn't want to remember the order.

"*Wah*, you very fat *ah*," Low shouted, rubbing Tan's stomach. "Too much desk work, is it?"

Tan gestured for Chan to escort the maids along the corridor and ushered Low away from room 4088 and prying eyes.

"Are you sure it's him?" Low asked.

17

Tan's voice was low and controlled. "Yeah, definitely, his passport is there, his IC. It's Richard Davie, your Australian guy."

Low checked again that no one else was listening. "He's not my guy, *lah*. He was just giving me data, insider stuff, betting patterns, he wasn't one of them. He was a straight, typical *ang moh*, loved the expat life, shagged some Singaporeans, but he wasn't one of them, didn't have the balls for that."

Tan chuckled. "*Wah*, how you know *ah*? He definitely never had the balls. Come and see."

The elder inspector guided his old friend past the uniformed officers outside the door and into the hotel room. The police were chatting and squinting through the balcony door, looking down at the container ships dotting the Singaporean skyline, queuing up for the port that never slept. They were obviously bored, no longer interested in the corpse. Low walked around the bed slowly, stepping across the sheets that were draped around its four sides. Davie's body was already turning blue. His Christ-like pose was unusual, but not disturbing. He was still in one piece at least. When he encountered fresh corpses, Low always thought of his illegal bookie found on Pulau Ubin. By the time he was discovered by one of the island's residents at the back of her kampong, his remains were covered in red ants. Most of his face and torso had been eaten by wild boars. His arm was found weeks later in the boggy Chek Jawa swamp by a honeymooning couple from Germany.

Low pointed at Davie's scrotum. The other officers in the room laughed.

"You see, I told you, right," Tan cried. "He shaved his balls."

"Well, I did not expect that. And he was Australian."

"That's why."

"Unbelievable. The Aussies are shaving their balls now?"

Low squatted beside a sofa opposite the bed and scanned the room. He took in the empty pill bottles, Valium, the usual escape route, the vodka empties, the half-finished chicken rice, the semen stains, the shorts, the T-shirts and the underwear on the carpet. They obviously had sex immediately.

"What's this?"

A piece of red silk was poking out from beneath a sheet hanging off the end of the bed. Low gently lifted the sheet.

"So no one saw these then?" The red silk knickers had a frilly black trim and were soiled. "Why would she leave without her panties?"

"Hey, come on, you know these girls *lah*," Tan said. "These ones not Geylang girls, these are MBS girls. These ones always have extra panties, must change each time, cannot meet a new client with dirty panties from the last one, right or not?"

"Yeah, maybe."

Low wandered into the spacious, marble-covered bathroom. The smell was stronger nearer the bathroom. Tan watched him go as a breathless Chan shouldered his way past the two officers at the door and waved his notepad at his boss.

"Sir, we've found the CCTV footage of them going into the hotel room. We haven't found the footage of her leaving yet, but I've got them checking for it now, sir. We'll find her."

"She's in here," Low muttered.

All the officers in the room hurried past the forgotten corpse of Richard Davie. Standing in front of a storage rack between the bathroom and the bedroom, Low held up the top cover of a suitcase. A crumpled woman's body was curled up inside. For a moment, Chan thought she looked peaceful

19

in a foetal position. Then he saw her eyes, still open and frozen in terror. Her tongue was hanging out. And then he saw her bloodied and bruised neck.

He just made it to the sink before throwing up.

Chapter 3

PROFESSOR Chong was furious. He had missed both the end of the musical and the gin and tonic that he had ordered earlier at the Sands Theatre bar during the intermission. Marina Bay Sands had been a godsend to the pathologist. The musicals took him away from all that murder and suicide and sleaze.

The sleaze was the most nauseating aspect of his work. His Singapore crime scenes were rarely ghoulish or calculated. They were generally haphazard, spontaneous and clumsy. Serial killers were the stuff of CSI and American gun-nuts. Singapore specialised in decapitated motorcyclists and drunken Bangladeshis killing each other with beer bottles in puerile arguments over who should pay for the beer. And suicides. Singapore had so many suicides; more than most if truth be told. The island of rat racers laughed off their lowly position in the annual happiness index. Straw polls in the mainstream media usually disputed the research, but Chong's findings were more scientific. He counted their body parts in the car parks beneath apartment blocks.

When the casinos went up, the bodies came down. Chong couldn't prove that of course. He had no intention of trying, but he had examined them all—heartlanders who left their

HDB flat on a baccarat table, love-struck Filipino helpers who handed their money over to disreputable boyfriends, the mainlanders who blew their savings over Chinese New Year—Chong had examined all their corpses back at the lab.

He heard Tan's booming voice, so he moved quickly along the rows of mortuary drawers before stopping at a tray with "R. Davie" written on a white card. He pulled out the tray and then moved to the tray beside it; the one without a name scribbled on a white card.

"Well, fat man, what have you got."

Chong ignored Tan's rude greeting. They had worked together for years. Their paths had first crossed at Toa Payoh Block 11 back in 1981. Tan was still in uniform and Chong was a student shadowing the forensic pathologists. They were kids back then, rookies largely ignored by their superiors, but their attention to detail impressed each other. They became firm friends, and traded insults at crime scenes and mortuaries to underline that fact.

Tan was a strait-laced family man, a Chinese conservative and a fiercely proud patriot. Chong was gay and an effete socialite, but Tan was extraordinarily proud of the success of his oldest professional friend. Chong was the most respected pathologist in Singapore, if not the region, a highly sought-after public speaker and a bon vivant beyond compare. Tan treated him like a brother. His squad members knew not to make archaic homophobic jokes in either man's presence. They waited for both men to leave the room.

"I'll tell you what I haven't got," hollered Chong, his voice echoing around the cold, bleak mortuary. "I haven't got a gin and tonic in my hand after giving a standing ovation at the Sands Theatre. You've dragged me away from a musical for this, you know. And it wasn't a bad musical either, very good costumes, the book was patchy—didn't come close to *Jersey Boys*—but the lyrics were top notch."

"How does it compare with *Oliver*?"

"Oh, don't be silly, man. Nothing compares to *Oliver*. There'll never be a song as jaunty as *Consider Yourself* and there'll be never be a performance that'll make me weep like Nancy belting out *As Long As He Needs Me*. I watch it every Christmas and cry every time. Who's this skinny chap?"

Chong prodded a manicured fingernail towards the officer standing beside his *kaki*. He was tallish and ruggedly handsome for a Chinese guy, Chong thought, but far too skinny to be taken seriously. He looked like a trainee gangster, the sort of scrawny runt that usually ended up laid out on one of Chong's trays with his name scribbled on a white card.

"This is Inspector Low and this is Professor Chong."

The two men shook hands quickly.

"I know all about your work, it's an honour," Low said sincerely. "You've been involved with every major case since I was in National Service."

"And now you immediately make me feel like an old man. It's strange that you've reached the rank of detective inspector and we've never met before. Which is it? Drugs like my tubby friend here? Vice? Murder?"

Low grinned and took a step towards the two corpses beneath the two sheets. Tan gestured towards the younger detective.

"This one *ah*, doesn't like to blow trumpets. He covers all three. He's CPIB, mostly undercover; not bad this one, thinks he's a gangster. Look at him."

"Yes, he does look rather malnourished."

"You remember the Tiger case; destroyed the gambling syndicate."

"Of course."

"That was this one *lah*."

Chong nodded approvingly. "That was a big corruption case wasn't it?"

"Not bad *ah*," Tan continued. "Anyway, I ask him to come down because he knows one of these guys."

"Which one?"

Low stood over Richard Davie. "This one."

"Ah, please do not touch the sheet, we cannot risk contamination. Keep your gloves on and touch nothing."

"This isn't my first rodeo."

Chong drew back the sheet slowly and glanced up at Low. "Don't those cowboys wear gloves when they take the bull by the horns? He's touchy isn't he?"

"You've got him on one of his good days," Tan sighed. "What have you got so far?"

"Well, if you look, there are no visible marks or bruises on most of his body. He had been dead for several hours before the maid found him, around 12 in all likelihood. He's all stiff from rigor mortis."

Chong pointed at the torso as Low and Tan both made notes.

"The tox report has yet to come back of course, but the condition of the body and the absence of any distinguishable marks or features ... oh, apart from the shaved scrotum, did you boys pick that up? He was Australian, right? You wouldn't think that of Australian men would you? There appears to be some slight swelling there, which may well suggest drugs."

"Yeah, there was enough cocaine around," Tan interrupted. "But you're thinking heroin as well?"

"Maybe. Anyway, at this very early preliminary stage, it does look like suicide, judging by the empty Valium bottles that were found beside his bed. How do they get hold

24

of such quantities? I don't know. OK, now for the good news ... look at this."

Chong lifted Davie's right arm. There were scratches and light bruising on his hands and forearms.

"The other arm is just the same." Chong sighed. "She was brave. She put up a fight. Even though she might have been drunk, she still tried to put up a fight. She did not go quietly. She was one brave lady. But the scratches are all centred around the hands, wrists and forearms, suggesting that was all she could reach."

"She was strangled from behind," Low commented.

"Quite possibly."

Chong brushed past the two inspectors, his body language making the hierarchical structure clear; his mortuary, his kingdom. He pulled back the sheet of the female victim. The swelling around the woman's neck had increased; it was black and blue and bulging. Her eyes were still open and staring at Low, yearning, pleading. She was not granted the peaceful, controlled death of Davie. She died scared and in heartbreaking pain.

"I say she was probably drunk, or at the very least mildly intoxicated, because of the empty bottles found in the room obviously, the strong smell of alcohol and because the poor girl didn't have the strength to put up that much of a fight. In similar cases, stranglers are found with deep wounds in their forearms, fingernail marks like train tracks from here to here." Chong ran his finger along his forearm. "The most depressing aspect of this job is discovering the inner strength that poor dying souls find when they are desperate to cling on to life. I have seen teeth puncture wounds reach the bone and chunks of flesh ripped from the arm."

Chong placed his hands around his own neck and mimed biting his wrist. "But this girl tried, she really tried, as you could see from his arms, but she tired very quickly. I suspect he got her drunk first."

Low cleared his throat and nodded towards the victim's vagina. "Was she raped?"

Chong pulled the sheet back to the corpse's ankles. He pointed at her genitalia. "On the contrary, no, but they certainly had sex, possibly more than once. There were traces of semen around his penis and in her vagina, mouth and anus. That, along with the injuries being sustained exclusively around the neck, would suggest at this stage that she was a willing participant in the sex acts. She was not coerced."

Low was puzzled. "Couldn't he have raped her whilst he was strangling her?"

"It's possible. Anything can be just about possible. But how do you get someone to perform oral sex whilst you are strangling them?"

"Fucking hell," Low muttered. "I knew this guy. He wasn't . . . I can't believe it. I mean, I don't even know why."

"Even anal sex rape can be difficult without pinning or tying the victim in some way. There are no physical marks to suggest that any excessive force was applied to the arms, the wrists, the hands, the thighs—the areas commonly vulnerable in rape attacks. Though I have to say, I'm at a loss to explain why it always seems to be the anus these days."

"Too much pornography," Low said. "I meet these girls all the time. They all say the same. The locals and the expats all want the same thing. They want what they see in the videos. They want what their wives won't give them."

Tan was eager to leave. He liked Low and really admired his work ethic. He swam deep inside Singapore's underbelly, but at times sounded like he was drowning. Tan always kept his head afloat, always kept kicking. He refused to stop treading water. At every mortuary, every crime scene, his head stayed above the stench. He wouldn't sink into the abyss. He loved his country and didn't want Low's downbeat pessimism to convince him otherwise.

"So, Chong, what do you think?"

"What do I think? I think I'm going back to where I should be in the first place, have a couple of gin and tonics at Ku De Ta and savour that cool Straits breeze. I think I've got to buy another ticket to catch the last act properly, without my bloody phone buzzing repeatedly, and I think you already know what I'm thinking. They had sex several times and got drunk and high. This one strangled this one and then this one, still in shock, killed himself with a Valium overdose. He obviously didn't have the shaved balls to do what you're going to have to do."

"What's that?"

"Tell his wife and daughter that he was booking hotel rooms at Marina Bay Sands to have anal sex with a Singaporean prostitute."

"But why stick her in the suitcase first? What's the point?"

"He panicked," Low reasoned. "Remember the body parts killer, late nineties, *ang moh* from the UK, chopped up the tourists and stuffed the evidence in a suitcase? You know how many body parts have popped up in the Singapore River over the years. Davie was going to dump her body. And then he changed his mind. It might have been the family. He could've thought about his family and panicked, taken the coward's way out. I'm not sure if that's a good enough reason to kill yourself though."

Tan nodded solemnly. "It would be if you were married to my wife."

27

Chapter 4

LOW read the sign behind the pretty counter girl's shoulder. *Sports Watch. We specialise in sports data and analysis.* The detective had to agree. They really did. Richard Davie hadn't so much found a gap in the market as he had found the market itself. Every dodgy expat and loud-mouthed local was fighting for every shrinking dollar in the event management industry, but the casinos and the illegal bookies were printing money at a time when online gaming was exploding. A surveillance technocrat was the Rockefeller of the digital age. Snowden was a rock star, Assange a celluloid hero. Data decoding devices were the pickaxes and online information was the gushing oil well. People would be willing to pay top dollar for the world's gaming and betting habits. As gullible punters cashed out, Sports Watch collected. Right now, Sports Watch CEO Richard Davie was the wealthiest man in the mortuary.

"Mr Viljoen will see you now." The stunning Malay receptionist didn't look up. She was too attractive, and Low too skinny and too Asian for him to be worthy of her interest.

Low took a seat in the office of the new acting CEO of Sports Watch. The room was typically bare to accentuate the unblocked view of Marina Bay. Commercial units didn't come cheap at the Marina Bay Financial Centre, but the prestige was priceless. As with most sports offices and bars, the obligatory framed print of a fuming Muhammad Ali standing over a diving Sonny Liston adorned the white wall behind Leonard Viljoen's desk. Some saw the iconic image as a sporting titan humiliating a lesser mortal. Low always saw the shot for what it was: a naive young man ordering an older cynic not to take a dive.

"Thanks for seeing me, Mr Viljoen."

"Not at all, and please call me Lennie."

With freshly-trimmed hair and a crisp, tailored shirt, Viljoen exuded confidence. Low recognised the unmistakable accent from his years studying at the London School of Economics. Viljoen had that clipped, narrow South African accent that betrayed a history of a white man's privilege and supremacy. The black man had slowly found his voice in South Africa. But in Singapore, the brash white voice could still shout the loudest.

"Thanks, Lennie. Look, I'm really sorry to hear about your loss. I had gotten to know Richard reasonably well and I know he was a popular guy around this place."

"He was, he was, there's no doubt about that. Richard was the life and soul of any party. He was the party. They loved him here. He built this company from scratch, from nothing. No one knew what sports data analysis was, or what the point of it was, and now look at us. We're the market leader in Asia and that's all down to Richard. He was such a great guy."

Low felt the anger rising. Davie wasn't a great guy. He was a post-colonial prick treating Singapore like the final days of Rome, sticking his dick into any local hole he could pay for. He was the wolf on Shenton Way; a proud, paid-up participant in the expat exploitation number; the chimps' tea party with Rolex watches. But Dr Lai had warned the inspector.

He could hear her voice. *Count to 10 and start again. Be master of the bipolar. Don't let the bipolar be master of you.* So he tried counting. *One* ... He saw the dead woman lying on that cold tray with her tongue hanging out ... *Two* ... He saw Davie shagging her from behind ... *Three* ... He saw Davie throttling her to stop her spoiling his Singaporean dream ... *Four* ... *Ah, fuck this.*

"Yes, I understand he was a great guy, Mr Viljoen."

"Lennie."

Low gritted his teeth. "Lennie ... I understand that he was a decent guy, and I'm sorry that he has died, but the circumstances of his death are unusual and they are now the subject of an ongoing investigation."

"I thought I read in the paper that he topped himself."

"Then I'm sure you read he was not alone."

"Yeah, he was with a whore, right?"

"No, no, not a whore ... not a whore," Low tried to keep his voice level. He thought about counting again, but pictured punching Viljoen instead. "She wasn't just a whore, she was a Singaporean woman and now she's dead. So your friend might have been the toast of the trust fund babies at all the best parties, but I need to find out why two people died, not just one."

"You're right, I apologise. That was unacceptable."

Low took out his notepad to avoid glaring at Viljoen. "Now, can you tell me what Richard was working on before he died."

"Directly? Nothing much. He didn't actually do much of the analysis himself; I don't either, most of that is delegated now. Generally, we've been monitoring betting patterns in Australia for the Victoria Police over there. Europol is still keeping us busy with their investigations. You boys ask us for a few things occasionally."

Low stopped writing. "You boys?"

"You know, your mob. You've asked us to look at gambling links between ..."

"I know what the CPIB do. That's our name. We do have one. And I trust any enquiries are handled discreetly and not discussed with Russian models at DOM Lounge."

Viljoen's face turned puce. He reclined in his leather executive chair, somehow hoping that the extra distance between his face and the inspector might hide his embarrassment.

"No, no of course not. But you would know more about that than me, right? I've seen you around the office a few times talking to Richard, meeting with him late at night."

"And I'm sure he filled you in, so there's no need to play Columbo," Low retorted. "I was looking at a couple of match-fixing syndicates in Singapore, small-scale stuff, some strange score-lines in the region and down in Australia. It was low-level fixing, nothing to get excited about. He must have been working on something else, something that got him in trouble, or got him worried, or blackmailed. Was he under pressure? Was anyone leaning on him?"

Viljoen sat up and straightened his tie. "That wouldn't be possible. Our clients are FIFA, UEFA, the IOC, Interpol and, yes, very occasionally, governments too, but I am not at liberty to disclose the governments involved or what their interests might have been."

Low laughed and leaned across Viljoen's mahogany desk, moving aside a family photo showing the South African cuddling the wife and doting toddler; the loving father and husband for naive visitors to see, a positive image of respectability for potential clients and easy to brush aside when escort agency clients needed to use the top of the desk.

"Please *lah*, don't get your dick out and wave it at me. I work with the CPIB. I know exactly what you do, who you do it for and why. And you know why I know? It's my job. You mention the government to show off the size of your dick? I am the Singapore Government. I know who your clients are: the rival syndicates, the illegal bookies, the big-shot *towkays* looking for insider information on sudden market changes before betting big, so you can take that family to a spa retreat in Bali and the wife temporarily forgets that you've been shagging every hostess from here to Bangkok. I know how it works here and we've had an amicable relationship. I need the maggots to catch the big fish. We allow you to operate only because you provide us with what we need, when we need it. But don't start thinking you're Julian Assange or we'll shut you down tomorrow and I'll personally throw you and your family back to the tribal gangs of Cape Town."

Viljoen suddenly felt parched. He sipped from a glass of water slowly, stalling for time. He raised his glass to Low. "Hey, you haven't got a drink. Were you offered one when you came in? What would you like?"

"I'd like a fucking answer."

Viljoen sipped his water again and cleared his throat. "Yue Liang," he whispered.

Low eyeballed the South African. "What?"

"Yue Liang."

"Who's Yue Liang?"

"The singer, the really sexy one, the one who makes all those videos, she's very popular in Asia."

"The one who's married to the self-guru guy? The one with the silly shoe name?"

"Yes, Jimmy Chew, calls himself the master of motivation."

"Yeah, what about them?"

"That's who Richard was looking at—Jimmy Chew. No one else was, only Richard, he never delegated anything with this one. She gave him all their bank account details. She thought that Jimmy Chew was gambling too much online, losing thousands, maybe hundreds of thousands. She thought their whiter-than-white reputation might be tarnished, you know."

Low put down his notebook, sat back and folded his arms. He needed a moment to absorb the information. He leaned forward again.

"So ... Yue Liang, the singer worth a fortune, gave all her husband's personal bank accounts details to Richard Davie so he could trace the spending and betting habits of her husband, who's a millionaire."

"Richard told me he was a multi-millionaire. He saw the accounts. The guy has got money coming in from everywhere, from conventions, seminars, corporate shows, books, everything. But it seems like he was a shit gambler, he was spending it almost as fast as he was earning it, so the wife asked Richard to help her out."

Viljoen felt his confidence returning. Low was paying attention. All that unnecessary talk about closing the company and deportation had been forgotten now.

"But why would he?" Low asked.

"Have you not seen photos of that singer? Have you seen what she looks like in a bikini? Have a look at her music videos on YouTube. Got tits like pneumatic drills. I wouldn't mind hanging out of that."

Lau Pa Sat was Tan's favourite *makan* place. The old Telok Ayer market was built for merchants, bankers, dockers, stevedores, labourers and the trishaw boys. The food was good, cheap, plentiful and messy. Even after the renovations, the place was still scruffy, decaying and held up by rusting cast-iron supports. The inspector knew how the old market felt. He stirred his *teh-c* and watched the Singaporeans go by, balancing trays of chicken rice, *char kway teow* and *nasi padang*. Mostly, he tried to ignore Chan.

"Sir, would you like something to eat? You haven't eaten since breakfast. You want *bao*? *Siew mai*? Curry puff?"

Tan found the arse-licking truly grating. *Kiasu* scholars were always the same—eager to please but unwilling to get their hands dirty. The kid was willing to run errands on duty, but when the time came to clock off, he was always the first to run home to the dinner prepared and cooked by his maid. Tan had read that this was symptomatic of the softer strawberry generation. They bruised easily. Chan's lot didn't bruise easily. They didn't bruise at all.

"No, thank you."

"You sure? They make very good samosas at that stall."

"Hey, I said already, right? What did you find out about the hotel rooms?"

Chan opened his notepad and found the relevant page. "OK, room 4088, one of the basic rooms, around \$400 a night. The suites are all on higher floors."

"I don't want to spend the night there."

"Yeah, right, room 4088, such a lucky number, right? Must buy 4D this week. On the left side, there was an old American couple celebrating their golden wedding. *Wah*, not bad *ah*, married for 50 years. He was stationed in Singapore after the Second World War and they wanted to come back because ..."

"*Yah lah*, *yah lah*, and next to that one?"

Chan flicked the page. "Past that one was housekeeping. There's no balcony on that side. We're checking the CCTV to see which maids went in and out of housekeeping and who accessed the room."

"And on the other side, the right side?"

"On the right side, that one was a Chinese couple from Shanghai, said they came down for the casino."

"Promising?"

"Er, not really, boss. They spent all night in the casino. Never returned to sleep until early morning, the victims were dead upstairs already."

"You believe them? You check their alibi?"

"Er, yes, boss. A fortune teller told the girl some shit about her fortune star shining brightly."

"Eh, don't joke. My wife believes that stuff, OK."

"Right, right. Anyway, she thought it would be unlucky to, you know, wash in case she wash away her good fortune, so she stayed at the casino all night with her husband."

"How are you so sure?"

The young officer shifted uncomfortably in his seat. "It was her period. She was wearing a skirt and bled onto the carpet. The other gamblers complained about the smell, but she wouldn't move. In the end, security had to take her away. Apparently, the stool had a lot of blood stains. She sat there the whole time, playing blackjack."

Tan sighed. "Bloody gamblers, always the same ... OK, check the other rooms on that floor."

"But they'd have to climb across other balconies. The other guests would see them."

"Just do it. And the floor above and below."

"But boss ..."

"Yes, I know it was the 40th floor. Go through all the CCTV on the corridors above and below as well. That'll do for now. Call Stanley Low again, see what time he can make it."

Chan took out his phone, then paused. "Hey, why do we need him on this case? This is a murder enquiry. He's not part of your narcotics squad, he's CPIB. They don't cover murders. They cover loan sharks, ministers who get caught having sex at East Coast Park and their own people who steal too much money. He's never covered a big murder case before."

Tan stirred his *teh-c* again. He saw the words coming out, but he only heard greed and ambition. Fast-tracked scholars always thought that the travellator through school and university continued through life. But he said nothing. The young officer was about to be put in his place.

"Hey, never mind. He's here now."

Tan felt a hand on his shoulder as Low joined them at the table.

"Go and get the inspector a *teh tarik*, and bring over some of those curry puffs and samosas you keep talking about. You would think this kid's father ran the samosa stall."

Low grinned, watching the eager officer as he snaked his way through the early dinner crowd. On a neighbouring table, a family gleefully ripped a chilli crab apart and laughed as the red, oily gravy splattered onto the table. No one looked up from their food. The experienced policemen knew that Singaporeans usually minded their business as long as their business was eating. He glimpsed a final time at the chilli crab-eating family before leaning across the table.

"Richard Davie was checking out Jimmy Chew," he whispered.

"Aren't they shoes?"

"No, the other Jimmy Chew, the *dua kang* one, the one who writes all those books about becoming a millionaire in five minutes."

"Ah, the one with the sexy wife always on TV."

"Yue Liang. She went to Richard about Jimmy's gambling, wanted him to find out how much he was spending online with the bookies."

"How much was it?"

"Don't know yet. I've asked his colleague to check. A South African. Lennie Viljoen. Typical *ang moh* over here, you know—big mouth, small dick. He will help. I told him I will deport him if he doesn't."

"Can you do that?"

"Of course I can. I'm the Government."

Both men laughed. Tan gulped his *teh-c* and wiped his mouth on his sleeve. "Well, I've got good news for you, man. They want you on this case. The Ministry."

Low turned away from watching a small, plump boy suck on a chilli crab claw as the sauce dribbled down his chin. "Eh, come on *lah*, I only come down to check Richard Davie as a favour to you, OK. Why do they want me?"

"Why do you think? Got a rich expat and a murdered Singaporean in a Marina Bay Sands room, *what*. Look around. Ask these people to talk about MBS and they'll say what? For the rich only, rich foreigners some more, they cannot afford. MBS is like the rest of Singapore, built in Singapore but not for Singaporeans. And there's an election coming some more. All that talk on Facebook and Twitter. And now you got an *ang moh* killing a local after sex and drugs? No one likes foreigners anymore in Singapore, not even *ang mohs*. They beat up taxi drivers, they make page one. They ride bicycles and give our drivers the finger, they make page one. They make fun of our public transport, they make page one. They have anal sex with our women, they make page one. So this one definitely cannot. This one cannot make it outside, OK? No bull in a china shop. We want duck rice."

"Duck rice?"

"Yah, you know, duck. On surface, duck is calm, no one can see anything. Under the water, he paddles like crazy. That's you, you are our duck."

"*Wah*, your mixed metaphors still fucked up, eh?"

"Balls to you, *ah beng*. Look, I will still lead the investigation on my side, but you do your thing, work on your people, take as much time as you need. The Ministry told SPF and CPIB, no bullshit, no more bad press, in fact no more press releases. Just work together, do whatever to finish this one quietly, CPIB style. So find out all the connections and let me know."

"And you take all the credit?"

"Hey, I helped you with Tiger last time, right?"

"Yeah, true, true."

Chan returned to the table juggling a cup of *teh tarik* and two plates of curry puffs. He dropped the plates on the table, spilling the *teh tarik* across the table. The two inspectors jumped up quickly to avoid being splashed.

Tan held Chan's arm as he struggled to mop up the mess with a small packet of tissue. "And this is the best news of all. Charlie Chan has been assigned to work with you, help you with the filing, paper work and routine interviews, while you do what you have to do."

Low stepped back from the table and watched Chan inadvertently push some of the spilled tea onto his own trousers.

"You're joking right?"

"It's Charles, sir," the younger man mumbled as his sleeve dipped into the *teh tarik*. "My name is Charles."

Tan raised his hands towards the clumsy kid. "He's all yours, inspector. And his *teh tarik* is damn *shiok*."

Dr Lai caught herself staring at the clock. She suspected he would notice. He usually did. She pretended to scribble something in her notepad. In the facing armchair, Low smirked.

"You see, I know you didn't write anything there. I know

that. That's what I do. That's my job. I observe people and I'm pretty fucking good at it. Sometimes I bully people. Sometimes I bluff people. But I push whatever pressure point it takes to get the job done. And if I start taking these lithium tablets then I'm going to neutralise those skills; you're going to take away the only thing that I'm any good at."

Lai handed her patient a leaflet across the desk. He ignored it. She rested her notepad on the lap of her black trousers and smiled sympathetically. "As I've said before, the basic information is in that leaflet. I'm not here to try and take away anything. I'm here to make you healthy."

"You said it yourself. The medication will have me flat-lining, the highs won't be as high and the lows won't be as low. I'll be everyman, boring Joe Public, shuffling along through life and boring people about property prices and the cost of a new car. Is that healthy?"

"But you will reduce the likelihood of more manic episodes."

"But I need those ... I mean, I cannot function without ... look, what we say here is strictly confidential, right?"

"Whatever is said is here is strictly confidential. That ethical code applies to anyone in the medical profession, from a psychiatrist to a local GP."

"Yeah, and I'm only supposed to protect and serve. Are you going back to the CPIB with any of this?

Lai forced a smile to hide the grinding of her teeth. "No."

"Right. I met a South African guy who pissed me off. I mean I took an instant, irrational dislike to him, hated everything about him—his good looks, his arrogance, his attitude—he was an arsehole. The sort of annoying expat that fuels the xenophobes in this country, OK?"

"OK." Lai brushed some hair from her face. Her beauty often overawed her patients, but not this one.

"I wanted to punch him, as a matter of principle, for no other reason. So I tried your counting nonsense, and that was a waste of time. So I channelled it."

"Channelled what?"

"Channelled 'it'. This shit here," Low tapped the side of his forehead so hard the unexpected outburst shocked his psychiatrist. "The stuff in here that we waste hours talking about. I used it. I spat it out all over the guy's table until he shit himself, until he gave me exactly what I wanted."

"And did that make you feel better?"

"Yeah, it did."

"Do you not think such outbursts will take their toll on you emotionally? You have said in the past that there are days when you refuse to get out of bed. Those are the lows that nearly always follow such euphoric highs. You drain your batteries each time. The highs always come at a heavy emotional cost."

"That's not a low, me feeling sorry for myself. That's not a low. I'll tell you what a low is. Do you read the papers? A woman goes to an MBS hotel room, gets fucked every which way, stuffed in a suitcase to rot, no dignity for this poor woman, not even in death."

Lai's curiosity suddenly trumped her professionalism as she heard herself say, "The woman was found in a suitcase? Oh dear, I never read that anywhere."

"No, well, these are some of the lows that we hold back from the rest of you. We don't put these lows in the press releases, not good for the squeaky-clean image. These are the lows that only I get to see. I decide what kind of fucked-up depravity my pampered countrymen can endure. So it's not actually people like you, but people like me who decide how far the lows can go for everyone else. I decide the lows for other people, not you. But I'll do that, no problem. I'll take

40

all those lows, ball them up and shove them in here." Low jabbed his forehead hard again, leaving a red mark. "And then I'll unleash them on any shit head who helps me find out why that poor woman died. And then I'll have my high. Then I'll have my fucking high, if that's OK with you."

Low got up from his armchair and headed for the door. Lai called after him.

"Hey, we haven't finished the session yet."

"No, we're done."

Low slammed the door behind him.

Chapter 5

THE Minister of Home Improvement waved to the crowd. They waved back half-heartedly. He hated this part of the job now. He used to love it, looked forward to the public speeches. He won every debating prize at Catholic High School. He became national debating champion without really being challenged. The competition practically insulted his intellect, as did his own school when they brought in an *ang moh* public speaker to hone his oratory skills. The Minster, still a teenager at the time, took on the British instructor in a mock debate in the school auditorium and humiliated him. The victory was a point of principle. The stubbornly persistent perception that the white face was an inherently superior teacher offended his Singaporean sensibilities. No one shouted him down then. No one shouted down the Government now. They were made for each other.

But Singapore was changing far too rapidly for the Minister's tastes. As he continued to wave to the restless crowd at Toa Payoh's HDB Hub, he registered the silent dissent. Even in Singapore, the eyes never lied in front of a minister. In the past, the heartlanders attended the family fun days out of warmth for the Government's achievements, a genuine sense of collective commitment, the last vestiges of the kampong spirit in all its glory.

Now they came for the free goodie bags.

But the Minister would make them wait. He was in no hurry to be harassed by the wolves waiting for him with the voice recorders. The rise of online news sites had emboldened the mainstream media. They asked far too many questions now. The Government still shaped the national conversation, of course, but the reporters occasionally butted at the parameters of the discussion. They had been told before, more than once. With this sordid business at Marina Bay Sands, they would have to be told again. The retired editors–turned-online crusaders were already probing into darkened corners beyond both their confidence and their pay scale when they were employed within the mainstream media. Now they were independent. Now they had ideas. And no one was allowed to have a monopoly of ideas in Singapore, not unless it was their job.

"I would like to thank you all for coming," the Minister began. He always sustained eye contact, highlighting the absence of a script or prepared notes. The shocking demise of parliamentary oration in recent years had deeply upset him. Politicians had become prisoners to their typed papers. He was appalled. Public speaking was a treasured aspect of his job description and never an afterthought.

"Family days like this one at Toa Payoh are an integral part of who we are as Singaporeans. We always put our family first. It's no longer fashionable in some parts of the world to do so, but that is who we are, that is what we are. We rely on our families, and the Government relies on your families. Self-help, resilience, determination, financial independence—these are our core values. They underpin our success and we must safeguard them at all times to ensure future economic growth."

The Minister spotted a number in the crowd gazing across at the two-for-one bakery sale at BreadTalk. Even the national debating champion could never compete with a discounted pork floss bun. When he singled out a fidgeting kid kicking his maid's shins, he figured it was time to wrap things up. Maids being physically abused on a Sunday by a parent-less brat sent the wrong message at the annual family fun day.

"So may I finish by saying, we must never neglect our responsibilities to our families. We should cherish our Asian values and take care of one another and not delegate our duties to third parties. You are always telling me you don't want to live in a nanny state. I agree. Nor do I. So please do take away that family-first message today. Enjoy the activities, I hope the kids like the free face painting and, no, I will not be getting my face painted to look like a clown. Some say I don't need the face paint for that."

No one in the crowd laughed. They had already made their way over to the goodie bag counter.

Low and Chan watched several families argue at the goodie bag counter, accusing the other of pushing in. Low continued to eat sweet corn from a polystyrene cup.

"Do you think I should go over there, sir?" Chan asked.

"What for?" The CPIB inspector never looked up. He loved his cups of buttery sweet corn.

"They are getting quite loud sir, quite troublesome. They are starting to push each other. I think the security guards are coming."

"Then they will handle it."

"But other families are getting involved now, sir."

"So what would you like to do, *ah*? You want an inspector to arrest some *sotongs* for fighting over a goodie bag, or shall we continue our murder investigation?"

"Yes, sir."

"Anyway, the Minister is coming over. You might as well play reporter while he's here. Make notes of what he says."

The reporters, clustered outside Burger King, stopped the Minister as he made his way past the stall promoting Mandarin enrichment classes. The voice recorders and phones were immediately shoved under his nostrils. Chan shouldered his way through the crowd to stand beside the Minister, and took out his notepad. His senior officer rolled his eyes and returned to his sweet corn.

"Minister, could you please give us an update on the Marina Bay Sands murder?" an enthusiastic young reporter enquired.

Lights came on above the video cameras. The Minister instinctively flicked the hair away from his forehead. Pushing 50, his lean frame and unblemished skin made him one of the most handsome members of the Cabinet. Within parliamentary circles, he knew he was featured in the most group selfies posted up on Facebook and Twitter pages. A couple of scholars within his department were employed to count the number of group selfies with government ministers on social media sites every day. He always came out on top.

"Yes, of course, the Singapore Police Force is working around the clock to bring this terrible case to a satisfactory conclusion. We are working closely with the Australian Embassy, who has been extremely co-operative in what is a sensitive case, one that must be handled sensitively, out of respect for the families involved."

"The Corrupt Practices Investigation Bureau is said to be assisting the police. Does that suggest that this might be another corruption case?"

"*Another* corruption case?"

"Well yes, the CPIB itself has not been without its scandals. There was the recent jailing of . . ."

"*Another* corruption case?"

The Minister scanned the crowd to find the questioner. He knew it. A white face in an Asian crowd. It was always an *ang moh*, hiding behind their passports and taking pot shots from their BBC or Reuters bunkers. But there were ways. There were always ways.

"Why do you say another corruption case? Firstly, this isn't a corruption case as far as I understand. Our law enforcement agencies often work together to share information; it's a mutually beneficial relationship between the CPIB and the police force and there's no reason why that shouldn't continue on this particular case. And secondly, the question suggests we have had a spate of corruption cases. I must point out that Singapore remains the least corrupt country in Asia. We are in the top five of least corrupt countries in the world and when we do come across a rare example of corruption, the culprits feel the full force of law. Just as those involved with this terrible case will when they are apprehended."

The Minister paused to smile. He had to take back control.

"And that's probably all I can tell you at this stage, but I'm sure the police will provide you with regular updates."

The Minister made his way through the crowd, shaking hands and hovering long enough for shy folks to ask for selfies with him for their Facebook pages. As he passed Low, he nodded a brief hello to the CPIB underling and headed for his car waiting outside at the front of the HDB Hub. The journalist had irritated him, but every foreign professional deserved the chance to learn from a mistake made in an unfamiliar culture. The Minister would give the *ang moh* a chance to learn his lesson by cancelling his employment pass in the morning.

Chan squeezed between two children face-painted as lions. He brushed past their cheeks, which left a streak of wet

46

yellow paint on either side of his trouser legs. He waved his notepad at Low.

"He didn't say much, sir."

"I heard. You've got yellow paint on your pants."

Chan pulled at his trousers at the sides.

"*Wah lan eh.*"

"You look like an idiot."

"Can I go back to the station to change my trousers, sir?"

"No, we both need to be here."

"What for?"

"The main event."

Low lifted his plastic cup towards the stage.

Yue Liang stepped onto the stage and savoured the applause. She stretched out her arms, Christ-like, absorbing the adoration. She closed her eyes and tilted her head towards the sky. She heard the phones click, not to mention the incessant whirring of paid snappers. That was their front-page photo tomorrow, Singapore's messianic Madonna in a shimmery dress acknowledging her god. The Minister of Home Improvement had relegated himself to a head shot on an inside page by leaving. Yue Liang was pissed off that he had left before her performance, denying her a photo opportunity and a subtle call for cash. She was recording her album in LA for a cause, and anyone who thought otherwise could go screw themselves. Singapore needed her spreading the word in the US. She wasn't doing it for herself. She was spreading a positive message for Singaporeans, all Singaporeans.

"Hello Toa Payoh, are you ready to make some noise!" she screamed into a microphone.

The crowd of mostly *kaypoh* aunties, dirty *ah peks* and impressionable teenagers shuffled towards the makeshift stage of the Toa Payoh HDB Hub. Yue Liang crouched down and posed for photos with a gaggle of kids. She always went for the kids. They had the smartphones. They kept her trending on Twitter.

"I just wanted to say how honoured I am to be here today and I thank the Minister of Home Improvement for those kind words earlier. Well ... both me and my husband!"

The crowd erupted. Yue Liang kissed her husband warmly on the cheek after he had bounded across the stage. The kiss hid her reddening cheeks. The sleazy uncles and hormonal boys came for Yue Liang and her slinky cocktail dresses which accentuated her long legs and covered her small-ish breasts. The perverts reading the papers, the perverts working for the papers; they were only interested in what she wore. She accepted that. But everyone came for Jimmy Chew. She promised them songs and sex appeal. He promised them wealth. She had no chance.

Jimmy kissed his wife on both cheeks. As they separated, her long, dyed, rusty-brown hair got caught in his headset microphone which he always insisted on wearing at his self-help seminars. Most speakers went for wireless microphones, but he preferred the headset. It was his uniform, his crown. The headset commanded power.

Jimmy held his wife's hand and lifted it into the air. The crowd cheered. Some teenage boys whistled loudly.

"Look at my wife, isn't she beautiful?"

As the punters roared their approval, Jimmy Chew beamed proudly. He meant every word. Tall for a Chinese girl with long slender legs, Yue Liang had stood out in a sweaty room at the Marine Parade Community Club. It was one of his earliest motivational talks, mostly housewives and taxi drivers hoping to win the lottery that weekend, but she had come along. She admired his ambition. He admired her legs. They were married within the year. They had decided early that they wouldn't have children. Instead they had promised to look after the five million children of Singapore.

"Yue Liang is right. As a proud, happy family, we are proud to be here to celebrate Toa Payoh's annual fun day and I'll be honoured to speak to you in a little while to help you to help yourself."

The aunties, uncles and middle managers in the crowd fidgeted excitedly. This is what they had given up an afternoon of mahjong for—the free goodie bags and Jimmy Chew's secrets to materialistic success.

"But before I say a few words, would you please put your hands together for my darling wife, Yue Liang, as she performs her latest hit."

Yue Liang pretended not to hear the smattering of groans. She adjusted her short dress and listened as the clicking cameras reciprocated. Jimmy Chew had the headset, but he didn't have the hips.

"OK, then, this is a song that my darling husband and I wrote together after we had visited an orphanage in Indonesia on a recent United Nations trip. We hope it inspires you as much as it does us. It's called *Higher Power*."

Jimmy Chew applauded wildly as he slowly retreated from the stage.

Someone handed a towel to Yue Liang as she tottered down the stage steps in her heels. She had no intention of listening to her husband's spiel again. As she signed autographs and posed for selfies with fans, the singer-songwriter and occasional self-help guru sensed someone standing at her shoulder. Low waited patiently for her to finish. He was in no hurry. He enjoyed watching people before speaking to them.

"You look too old to be waiting for me and too young to be waiting for my husband," Yue Liang said suddenly,

49

glancing up from her own glossy photographs briefly to smile at Low. The inspector was struck by her flawless complexion. There were no lines on her beautiful face. Up close, she was stunning.

Low cleared his throat. "*Wah lau*, there's no fooling you."

"If it's about bookings, you can speak to our manager about that, or if you can't find him, then my husband might find time to chat with you, but we really don't usually speak ..."

"I'm not looking to book you. I just want to speak with you."

"As you can see, I'm very busy, you know."

"Look, the thing is, I don't think this is the place for you to be ..."

Impatient autograph hunters started to brush Low aside as it became clear he wasn't seeking a signature and was getting in the way. As he sought to push through, his phone rang.

"Excuse me, just wait there, Miss Yue Liang."

She ignored him and continued to scribble on photos of herself in short, tight dresses.

Low found a quiet corner near the Burger King tables and pressed the phone hard against his ear. "Yeah, it's OK. I can hear you now."

"We've got the lab reports back from Chong," Tan bellowed down the phone. "It's his fingers around the woman's neck, confirmed, Richard Davie's fingers. He definitely killed her. The bosses are very unhappy, want to close this one quickly, getting a lot of publicity in Australia. The *ang moh*'s family saying if we don't settle quickly, they will come over with private investigators."

"Bastards," Low muttered. His eyes followed Yue Liang as she worked the crowd.

50

"Yeah, whatever *lah*, balls to them. We will check on the Australia side. This Richard Davie had no history of violence, never attacked anybody before, no criminal record, not even a parking ticket, so his family are damn pissed off. They think it's another Chinaman conspiracy. So help me out, *ah*. Find out why this idiot killed that poor woman and then we can get a nice bonus, *basket*."

Low smiled and hung up the phone.

He caught up with Yue Liang as she shuffled along with her trailing fans towards the air-conditioned bus interchange. "I really need to talk to you, Miss Yue Liang."

"And I really need a banana smoothie."

Her fans and lackeys laughed on cue. The inspector ran out of patience. He shoved a couple of fans aside and matched Singapore's most inspirational singer stride for stride as she waved to commuters lining up for their feeder buses.

"I want to know about the job you paid Richard Davie for. Do you want to tell me here or over a banana fucking smoothie?"

Low gestured for Yue Liang to follow him. For the first time all day, she did as she was told.

Chapter 6

JIMMY Chew was talking fast. The words carried more weight when he spoke quickly. He mixed English and Mandarin, used Malay for political correctness and Hokkien for the best punch-lines. He always delivered the best lines in Hokkien. They brought his audience together. The influx of foreigners from China and India had diluted his appeal in recent years, but Hokkien and National Service united Singaporeans just as they united his audience.

Jimmy spread his arms widely, the Christ-like pose again. They shared it. He had looked on with an almost paternal pride earlier when Yue Liang had emulated his physical tricks. Her stagecraft almost rivalled his. The arms open wide suggested inclusiveness, hugging the crowd and bringing them closer to the money-making magician on stage, but they also hinted at resurrection. Singaporeans, particularly the heartlanders, were always hoping to be saved, to be redeemed, to win the lottery at the weekend.

Jimmy loved visiting housing estates like Toa Payoh. They were always more susceptible to his ideas, more gullible. They absorbed his self-help patter; sponges who rarely questioned his reasoning. And they usually bought the most signed copies of his books. The ones who had the least always spent the most at Jimmy Chew's roadshows. The rich expected freebies. The poor coughed up. They needed him more. And Jimmy Chew loved to be needed.

He surveyed the crowd, watching his volunteers at the sides of the stage mimicking his Christ-like pose. The sheep just couldn't help themselves when the shepherd was in command. He captivated like no other. He was handsome, well-dressed and channelled their spiritual weakness to what truly mattered. Money. He made wealth acquisition feel not only obtainable, but inevitable. In the beginning, there was just his word and his word was greed. He made greed socially acceptable. For the poor, he assuaged their pessimism. For the rich, he alleviated their guilt. If the word was greed, then greed could only ever really be good. And his Toa Payoh audience were so desperate to be good. They were hanging on his every word. No one strayed. Neither the Minister—nor his wife—could control an audience in this fashion. Jimmy Chew smiled. It was time to go in for the kill.

"As you know, I grew up with nothing," he said. "My mother was a cleaner, my father was a hawker seller. We lived in a two-room flat in Queenstown. But I made my first million by the time I was 21, made my second million by the time I was 25. Then the currency crisis bankrupted me. I was dead."

He paused to sip water. He wasn't thirsty, but his stagecraft was impeccable.

"But did I take the easy option and take that regular, safe, dull desk job?"

The crowd murmured a few half-hearted "no's".

"I said, did I take the easy option and take a nine-to-five office job?"

The crowd shouted back at him.

"No, I fought back. I returned to the stock market

hungrier than ever before. I went back into the lion's den, unarmed, but viciously hungry. I didn't believe in the global economy. I didn't believe in the Singapore Stock Exchange. I didn't believe in the city experts. Who did I believe in?"

"You!" The crowd were excited now.

"That's right. Me. I only believed in me. No one gave me help when I was down, so I didn't want to trust them now. You must believe in you. No one else will. Self-help is your salvation. Self-help is your security. Self-help is in your soul. You just have to find it and unlock it. And I have the key."

Jimmy Chew picked up a glossy paperback from a make-shift display table, covered in a red cloth with his titles piled high.

"My latest book *My Key to Unlocking Your Wealth* provides the answers. It doesn't have this week's lottery numbers, it doesn't have the latest stock tips, but what it does have is the secret to your success. Ten chapters, ten easy steps for you to take to unlock your potential, so you can take control of your own financial destiny. Don't walk a mile in anyone's shoes, walk a mile in Jimmy Chew's shoes. Are you ready to take a walk with me?"

The crowd cheered.

"Are you ready to take a walk with me?"

The crowd roared.

"Are you ready to walk in Jimmy Chew's shoes?"

The crowd chorused their approval, but this time it wasn't quite as loud. Aunties and uncles were already shuffling towards the bookstand. Jimmy Chew had said enough. He bowed to the crowd, counting them on the way down. He expected to sell at least 200 books in Toa Payoh.

Yue Liang sipped her banana smoothie. She waved to passersby and smiled as they snapped photographs of her. Some teenage girls approached the table and asked for her autograph. She obliged, and then posed for the obligatory photos.

"Make sure they end up on your Facebook and Instagram," she cried after them. "My mother will check, you know."

The girls giggled. They always did. Yue Liang used the same line every time. According to her publicist, about 60 to 70 per cent of all the random photos taken with Yue Liang ended up on social media sites. Her publicist wanted the figure to hit at least 80 per cent before she headed to the States.

"Sorry about that."

Yue Liang looked up at Low from her glass as she sucked hard on the straw. She wasn't sorry. She was reasserting herself. She rarely ceded control in social situations, and was still miffed with the skinny policeman for ordering her away from her fans and entourage.

But the inspector had no time for games. Being bipolar had its advantages, the most obvious being the ability to spot a needy phoney who craved fame and attention to overcompensate for her own insecurities. Yue Liang was nothing more than a needy pain in the arse.

"No more autographs," he snarled.

"I'm sorry?"

She had heard him, but was stalling to regain her composure. His low, flat, aggressive tone had alarmed her.

"No more autographs, no more photographs, no more smiling for fans and no more wasting my time. If you piss me off again, I will formally interview you down at the station and watch you squirm as your arse-lickers try to keep this out of the papers, got that clear?"

Yue Liang put the smoothie down slowly and subconsciously tugged at her dress under the table, pulling the cocktail number closer to her knees. She felt violated.

"Wow, you really are like the good cop, bad cop thing you always see in the movies."

"Who said I was a good cop? Now, why did you go and see Richard Davie?"

Yue Liang fiddled with her straw, stirring the dregs at the bottom. A middle-aged Chinese man in a white vest and scruffy shorts smiled at her as he shuffled slowly through the bus interchange. She reciprocated with a playful nod. Low leaned across the table.

"I'm ... not ... fucking ... joking."

Yue Liang sighed. "Yah, OK, OK, enough already with the bad language, OK ... look, this can't be public, OK? I mean, you can't tell the media, right? I'm going to America soon and this can't come out in the media so soon."

"First, I don't make promises. Second, it depends on what you have to tell me. And third, an *ang moh* is dead and the last case he was working on was yours, so I don't think you're in any position to make demands of me."

"Wow, OK. Are you married? Can't be right?"

"I'm married to the job and all those other fucking clichés, now answer the question."

"You have some serious anger management issues."

"Right, that's it." Low stood up and knocked his chair backwards. Yue Liang held up her hands like a vulnerable child about to be smacked by an irate parent. She had already sensed the reaction. The eyes of the entire cafe were darting between her and the belligerent, skinny Chinese guy standing over her, bullying her.

"OK, OK, enough with the drama. *Wah*, you very *wayang* for a detective, you know? Should be in a Chinese drama. Please, sit down, people are staring at me, and not in a good way."

"Why did you go to Richard Davie?"

Yue Liang flicked her straw petulantly. Tiny drops of banana smoothie sprinkled across the table. "We've got no money," she whispered.

"What? Who?"

"Us ... me and him. Jimmy Chew and his cheap shoes. We've got almost no money left, none. We can barely pay the mortgage on our house in Bukit Timah. Cannot make it already."

"So? You want me to play a violin for you? What's that got to do with Richard Davie?"

"He cannot stop gambling OK. He's out there, bluffing them about spending wisely and investing sensibly and he's spent almost everything. There's not even enough for my US trip, after we've had all that publicity. I said I was being produced by Daft Punk in an LA studio and he's going to make me look like an idiot. We cannot even afford the studio time. Forget the first-class fare, I might even have to fly economy class on SIA. You know I did a commercial for them last time. Remember that song I did in Mandarin? *Fly High*? Number one in Taiwan, they used it on Singapore Airlines and now they won't even give me discount for the business class."

"You didn't need a company like Sports Watch to monitor Jimmy at a casino. Any cheap private investigator in Geylang can do that."

"It wasn't just the casino, it was the betting websites. He was gambling on these sites all over Asia and not telling me. I tried to buy a dress at ION and they rejected my credit card. That idiot had gone way over the limit. Now we've got big gambling debts we cannot pay. So I asked Richard to help me."

"Richard? How did you even know Richard?"

"He came to one of Jimmy's talks. Jimmy always likes it when the *ang mohs* come, the bankers, the fund managers, especially the loud *ang mohs*; they've got a bigger network, bigger staff. Most of them don't buy his rubbish. It takes one to know one, right? But when he does catch one, they can sell more books for him and get him for talks."

"How did you find the money to pay Richard?"

"Oh, he wouldn't take any money from me," Yue Liang replied casually. "He was very kind and generous to me."

Jimmy Chew scribbled his name happily. By his rough calculations, he had signed at least 100 of his self-published books at $20 each, and the queue still stretched back to the silver jewellery shop. Property prices fluctuated, cooling measures burst bubbles, stocks rose and fell, but the motivational self-help industry was a bulletproof market. He couldn't lose.

"And who is this one for?"

"Can you sign it for Charles Chan, please."

Jimmy lifted his eyes up from the table. A nervous, perspiring Chinese man in a crumpled white shirt stood over him. "Are you serious? You want this for Charles Chan?"

"Er, yes, please."

"Is that you? Your name is Charlie Chan?"

"Well, it's actually Charles. I prefer Charles."

"Don't worry, I get it all the time," Jimmy Chew said cheerily, handing back the book. "With me, I'm always being asked, 'How do you find the time to write books, give seminars and design new shoes?' I bet you must get the policeman thing all the time right? What do you do for a living?"

"I'm a policeman."

The other book buyers in the crowd laughed.

"Hey, I like this guy. Do you want to take a photo?"

"No, it's, er, OK, thanks. Loved your speech though."

"Thanks Charles. Keep up the good work. Who's next?"

*

Professor Chong returned the samples to the test tube holder. He removed his gloves and threw them at a dustbin. One of the gloves missed. Chong kicked it across the tiled floor. He was irritated. The hanging at the gay club in Boat Quay was still his primary case, but now the Marina Bay Sands mess had fallen into his lap. He had little interest in either. Drunk, stoned expats going crazy with prostitutes was hardly a dignified justification of his pay packet. And the dead gay man at Boat Quay was a tiresome case, both professionally and personally. The tabloids had leapt on the obvious auto-erotic asphyxiation angle. All gays were into kinky sex. All gays were perverts. Lock up your children in safe, sanitised Singapore. No one reported or investigated the number of deaths that resulted from sadomasochistic sex acts involving heterosexuals. Chong had the figures, but he had learned long ago in secondary school that facts were never allowed to get in the way of a good homophobic story.

And apart from anything else, Chong had been to the gay club in Boat Quay. Not recently—he was pretty much a non-practising homosexual these days—but he had been a reasonably regular visitor in the darker times when gays were not celebrated at trendy Speakers Corner events and toasted by famous artistes. Homosexuality remained illegal in Singapore, but it was now merely frowned upon. When Chong endured the personal hell of National Service, he was spat on.

So he had some sympathy for the patrons and owners of the Boat Quay club. He no longer went there. He was too high-profile and too celibate. But he still knew those who did. They would be stigmatised by his forensic findings. The knife was always twisted in the public domain, but on this occasion his hand was glued to the handle.

He had asked not to be given the case, claiming the

macabre nature of the hanging was unsettling. His bosses never bought it. He had examined worse crime scenes. Besides, they knew the real reason why he didn't want to return to the gay club. And that's why he had no choice.

The last thing Chong needed right now was another complication in another case he didn't want. He picked up the phone.

"Yes, all the blood samples are back," he said. "Yes, the results have all been checked and corroborated. I'll call Inspector Tan. Yes, I'll call him now. This was supposed to be a straightforward case. That's the only reason I took it . . . well, it's not a bloody straightforward case now, is it?"

Low and Yue Liang wandered through Toa Payoh Town Park, the only green spot left in the overcrowded housing estate. The bus interchange across the road had too many distractions; too many giggling schoolgirls and ogling uncles. The green sanctuary was perfect. There were no shops, so there were few people.

They passed some Malay kids peering through the long grass, trying to feed dried anchovies to the turtles in the pond. Low gestured towards a bench shaded beneath willowing trees. Yue Liang sat down and pointed at a stone bridge over the pond.

"You know people used to take their wedding photos here," she said wistfully.

"They still do."

"Do they?"

"Not everyone has their wedding sponsored by Resorts World Sentosa."

Yue Liang smiled at the memory. "That was still a good day though. Great party at the Hard Rock afterwards. Jimmy almost looked handsome that day. I picked his suit,

60

got his hair styled, everything. Now he won't make any public appearance without a tailored shirt and his hair fixed. Before he met me, he was speaking at community centres and libraries, now he fills exhibition centres all over Asia. All because of me."

"But you still need his money, right?"

"I never said that."

"Yes you did. You asked Richard Davie to monitor his betting habits, to track how much he was spending. It was his money. He earned it with the self-help shit. He could spend it however he liked."

"It was our money. He shouldn't have spent it without telling me."

"Please *lah*. You see any CD shops in Toa Payoh? You see any CD shops anywhere? You think those kids over there are buying your albums? They just want photos for their Facebook page. You know the last CD I bought? A Michael Bublé album for a girlfriend I was trying to impress. And she lost the album, downloaded it instead and I still didn't get a chance to shag her."

"You are very vulgar for a police officer."

"And you're full of shit. This is not an equal partnership here, financially, is it? You said it yourself, he packs out conferences at MBS and you sell half a dozen signed CDs for some aunties who still ask if you got cassette tapes. You need his money to make your albums and you're pissed off that you haven't got enough to make them yourself. You bullshit people in your songs, telling them to look for a higher power, when all you look for is your husband's wallet. See? Full of shit."

Yue Liang stood up suddenly and started to walk away. "I don't have to take this from you. This is harassment. You think I got this far from being bullied by men like you is it? I could call the Minister's office right now and tell him about you."

"Tell me what Richard Davie found or I'll call the Minister myself, then I'll get one of my *kakis* to call the media, and we'll tell them that you had a dead murderer investigate your beloved husband for his illegal gambling debts."

Yue Liang stopped. She smiled at the boys feeding turtles. Their innocence was charming. She then glared at Low. "You would do that? You could do that?"

"I will do that. I keep the place clean and green so you can sing your happy songs on National Day. It's a shit job, but it happens to be one that I'm pretty fucking good at. What did Richard Davie tell you?"

Yue Liang sighed with irritation. Her shoulders sagged. The fight had gone. "Something about The Indonesian."

"The what?"

"He said that Jimmy owed money—*owes* money—to some big gambling syndicate owned by this guy. That's all Richard found out. That's all I know. Thanks to that idiot across the road, I've got to worry about some big shot called The Indonesian."

Chapter 7

LOW knew he was taking a calculated risk. Ah Lian had been pensioned off after the Tiger case. Too many faces were aware of his true identity. Tiger's tentacles stretched too far. Ah Lian's cover had been blown. Low was disappointed at the time. Ah Lian had become a second skin. Publicly, he told his bosses the character allowed him to infiltrate the syndicates from the inside out. Privately, he accepted that Ah Lian gave him a platform, a release, an opportunity to vent, to scream, to lash out. Low found the relationship more therapeutic than the lithium tablets Dr Lai was forever trying to shovel down his throat.

The *teh* tasted good. So did the chicken wings. Low always found cheap hawker food to be one of the perks of undercover work. He scanned the coffee shop. There were no familiar faces. It was late and the place was almost empty, apart from a couple of sleepy taxi drivers. Bedok South was chosen carefully as the venue. Too many CPIB raids in the east had made the bookies jittery. The coffee shop's days as a meeting spot were dying. But its history and connections to previous syndicates still made Bedok South a credible location. Dragon Boy would buy it. But Tiger's old faces had all moved on.

Low checked his watch. Tan wanted him at Chong's lab as soon as possible, but he had asked for an hour. He was determined to meet Dragon Boy first. The Indonesian had offended his professional pride. He had no idea who The Indonesian was.

"Hey, *chee bye, lah*."

Dragon Boy waved at Low as he weaved his way around the tables. He was scrawnier than Low and wore black jeans and a tight white singlet that displayed the dragon tattoos on his upper arms. They breathed fire towards his puny neck. His skin was poor, his hair was overly gelled and his teeth were already yellowing, despite still being in his late 20s. He carried a mobile phone in each hand.

"Eh, *basket*, how are you man?"

Both men hugged. The warmth was sincere. Low had a soft spot for Dragon Boy.

"Eh, fuck you, *lah*, where you been, man?"

"Busy *lah*, then? Motherfucker, you saw what happened with Tiger last time, right?" Low replied, savouring Ah Lian's ability to take control. The old loan shark's impulses and instincts immediately returned.

"That's why, *basket*. They pick you up also, right? When I heard they pick you up with Tiger, I said that's it. Ah Lian finished."

"*Yah lah. Chee bye.* But not enough evidence. They try and *tekan* me about Tiger, but confirm cannot make it one."

Dragon Boy laughed. He pulled both his legs up onto the red plastic chair and wrapped his arms around his shins.

"You are one lucky fucker. Better buy 4D. Then how?"

"Then how what? Leave *lah*! First, go Australia, Mel-bum, see how down there, then go Malaysia, China, see how, do some work. Then try Finland, Hungary, maybe Italy, all the *kelong* bastards can make it out there man, but then Tiger case finish, so come back already."

"*Wah lan eh*, so lucky *ah* ... eh, uncle, one *kopi*."

Dragon Boy waved his Marlboro Lights at the Chinese uncle pouring coffee behind the drinks counter.

"Eh, and one more packet ... so how? You still working is it?"

"Of course *lah*, what else? Put on white shirt and sell HDB flats *ah*? Please *lah*."

"That's why. But now very tough right?"

"Everything tough. Everything they shut down one."

The drinks seller dropped the cigarettes on the table. He banged the cup hard enough for some coffee to spill onto the saucer.

"Thirteen dollars," he said in Mandarin, wiping his hands along his apron.

Dragon Boy's eyes flicked up at the overweight Chinese man. "Later *lah* ... *wah lau, basket*, insult me. Think I cannot pay, is it?"

Low laughed as the unimpressed drinks seller trudged back to the counter. The inspector examined the coffee shop again as Dragon Boy sipped his coffee. The skinny gangster winced and spat it across the littered floor.

"*Chee bye, lah* ... eh, uncle. Your *kopi* cold *ah*? Taste like shit. *Kana sai*."

As he rested his elbows on the counter and watched the Chinese drama on TV, the drinks seller ignored the scrawny runt. The small guys always talked the biggest. There was a lot of bark, but hardly any bite, not in Singapore. Both men knew this. The grandstanding was another late-night theatrical bluff. The drinks seller had nothing to fear.

Low leaned closer to Dragon Boy. "So, you work where *ah*?"

"Steady *lah*, Ah Lian. Take your time. Now not so good. You read the papers? Everyone *kena* whack already. You know my *kakis* from last time? You remember Ah Kok and Snake Balls? Arrested already. Cannot make it. The bloody *ang mohs* talk a lot of cock, make noise, this one, that one, Interpol, Italy, Hungary, now got that new one *ah*, Europol, and even Finland. They say they got *kelong* in Finland! Where is Finland? Who stay in Finland? Fucking Santa Claus, is it? Who give a fuck about Finland?"

Low laughed loudly. He had always sincerely enjoyed Dragon Boy's company. The kid had a funny bone. That was reassuring at least. The joker usually survived inside Changi.

"*Yah lah*, that's why. Now everyone trying to fuck us," Low said in agreement.

"So much better last time. No one give a shit, right. No one so *kaypoh*. Everything *kelong*—the '*Gahmen*', the casino, the gambling, the chickens—everything. No one care, we all close one eye. Now the *ang mohs* tell Singapore to whack syndicate and the '*Gahmen*' shit its pants, man. Now the world talk about Singapore, everybody *kaypoh*, '*Gahmen*' cannot close one eye. *Kan ni na.*"

Dragon Boy was primed. Low glimpsed over his tattooed shoulders. Even the taxi drivers had left.

"But there's this new one, right? He making money right?"

"Who? Which one?"

"That one *lah*, The Indonesian."

Dragon Boy's eyes darted towards the floor. He hid his face behind the coffee cup, but he hadn't been fast enough. Low had picked up on the shiftiness. He was positive he saw fear. Dragon Boy had once stood in a Geylang coffee shop filled with *ah longs*, pimps and old-school shophouse gangsters and told Tiger to go fuck himself. He never flinched.

Tiger bought him a beer and promoted him. But there was something different in the eyes this time, something that the coffee cup couldn't cover. There was uncertainty.

Dragon Boy kicked a phlegm-filled tissue beneath the table. "How you know about him?"

"Come on *lah*. Of course I know. You work for him *ah*?"

"No *lah*, no one work for him. In Singapore, no need."

"Don't talk cock."

"I'm serious. Fuck *lah*, everyone want to work for him. You see his websites? Make millions boss, *basket*, got money coming from everywhere—China, Macau, Australia, Africa, everywhere man. The websites make the money, man. Need us for what? We're dinosaurs already, fucking Jurassic Park."

"The old stuff, *what*. Collect the money, runners, *ah longs*, still must have right?"

"This guy don't do that here, he too smart one. He knows everybody hate foreigners in Singapore so he never shit in someone else's house. No need. Everything he play outside, no need for small, small stuff."

"No *ah longs*?"

"What? Stick pig's head on apartment door? For what? He make millions outside. His websites are offshore one. He got them in China ... some say he got in Vietnam. He make outside, come here and wash the money.

"You know why these outside fuckers come here right? Fuck our women and clean their money. I meet these fuckers last time, big gamblers. Last time go Joo Chiat, Geylang; Indians go Balestier. Now Marina Bay. Everything Marina Bay. Some want Malay women, now got African and Russian some more. They got Russian woman now; this Bosnia, Serbia, also got. They say they are models ... models working at Marina Bay. Fuck you, they are chickens, OK? I see them at the Pussy Club."

"The Pussy Club?"

"*Yah lah.* That one *lah*, Marina Bay, on the water one. Pussy Club. They say *towkay*'s club, please *lah*. I know the madam, known her long time already. I knew her last time, when she was nothing. Now she got money, think she got respect. Bullshit. First she get them to hold their champagne, then get them to hold their cock. Call them bottle girls. Bottle girls. Fuck you, they're *xiao mei mei* OK. One night, got three Arabs inside and one girl. Three Arabs from this, what *ah,* Dubai. And one girl. She make $50,000, one night, OK? Where got this kind of money in Singapore? Forget it, *lah.* It's a pussy club for the rich, all control by foreigners one, *kan ni na.*

"But Tiger last time also have. KTV, gambling, girls, you know. We had everything."

"*Wah lau,* finish already. Different world man. Singaporeans got nothing left, bro. Foreigners take everything, take our cars, our houses, our women, even take our *ah longs.* All China one. You go Geylang now, all China one. China girls. China pimps ... except this new one *ah,* The Indonesian ... this one don't waste his time with small-small thing. This one's a *towkay.* I tell you this one *ah,* make Tiger look like a fucking pussycat."

"Wow."

"That's why."

Dragon Boy tapped his packet of cigarettes on the table repeatedly before tearing off the cellophane. He balled it up and threw it across the coffee shop. He lit a cigarette and blew smoke rings in the direction of the no-smoking sign. The drinks seller continued to ignore him. In the early hours, his only business came from taxi drivers, drunken construction workers and plastic gangsters. He took their money, wiped away their globs of saliva and waited for the early-morning, backpack-carrying school kids to waddle in for their hot Milos.

Low lowered his voice.

"So this Indonesian stay in Singapore, is it?"

"Don't know. Always travel one. Never stay in Singapore for long, only come to take our money, *basket*."

"How you know when he's in Singapore?"

"MBS."

Low just sat and stared at his old street *kaki*.

"What?" he said finally.

"The casino, *lah*. Marina Bay Sands. Fucker always gets private baccarat table, the high floor one."

Low said nothing as he sent a text message under the table.

Masked and gowned, Tan and Low followed Professor Chong into his lab. Making no attempt to conceal his exasperation, Singapore's leading pathologist yanked at the drawer with "R. Davie" scribbled across the front. He pulled back the sheet to the corpse's thighs and picked up a clipboard.

"In my defence, I was dragged in straight from the musical. I'd had a few glasses of red wine—I wasn't bloody on duty—and had only a brief time to examine the body. Then I was told, in no uncertain terms, that this was a routine case that needed settling quickly to allay concerns and appease our Antipodeans Down Under. These have not been professional conditions to work under from the beginning and ..."

"OK, Chong, enough already," Tan interjected. "We got other things to do as well, you know. You're not a one-man band. What's the problem?"

Chong exhaled sharply. "He didn't kill himself."

"What? What are you talking about? What have you found?"

The detectives cringed as Chong cupped the dead man's testicles in his gloved hand.

"Believe it or not, his vanity helped me out. The shaved scrotum accentuated the swelling around his left groin. Can you see that there? I did say it was a possibility, there was the swelling, but I couldn't see a pinprick. That's why. Look at that."

The pathologist's gloved finger pointed to the left side of the dead man's shaved scrotum. "You see that. A mole, a bloody big mole. The needle went right through his mole. He wouldn't do that. Who would stick a needle through a mole? Maybe it was a coincidence, but it made the pin prick harder to spot and also concealed the initial bruising, which spread soon after."

"What does that mean?"

"He had the beginnings of femoral artery necrosis due to an intra-arterial injection. This might have indeed killed the poor chap, had the overdose not taken care of him first."

Low examined the corpse's left thigh. "A female what? I must have missed that one in biology, doc."

"It's Professor actually. I don't call you PC Low, do I?"

Low grinned. "Sorry, Ah Lian tends to linger a bit."

"Who?"

"It doesn't matter. Sorry, what happened with this guy?"

Chong's finger pointed to a pinprick inside the unsightly mole at the top of the corpse's leg. "You see that there? Had I been aware that this guy was a regular intravenous drug user, I would have checked, but he wasn't. Had I avoided three glasses of wine, I might still have spotted it. Had this chap not had a mole the size of a muddy puddle, I would've spotted it. That's the point. There's been a clumsy attempt to hide the injection. He's been injected with heroin and it's nudged his femoral artery, hence the swelling. Drug addicts do occasionally make this mistake, but it's not common among users. This guy wasn't a heroin user. Even the traces of cocaine were small. He used it to party, but nothing more than that. Oh, and we found traces of heroin only in his body, but not hers. The heroin may or may not have been intended to kill him, maybe it was to subdue him, but it was enough to leave him dopey."

"So the guy could then throw all those pills down his neck?"

"Or a girl," Low muttered. "Could it have been the prostitute?"

Chong reached for his clipboard. "Ah, yes. Ms Wong Yu Lin."

Low glanced across at his colleague.

"Yeah, just got her prints back," Tan said. "Soliciting in Joo Chiat last time, early 1990s, nothing for a long time already, we'll check. So how? Could it have been her?"

Chong shook his head. "No, definitely not. She was dead at least 30 minutes to one hour before he was, and the impact of the heroin would've left him practically comatose almost immediately. Honestly, I think the injection was used to subdue a big guy quickly and quietly without leaving obvious evidence of excessive force. And you're probably looking at more than one person."

"Why?"

"Look at him. He's a big boy. Well, not down there, he wasn't. But he was a big, burly Australian. Assuming he didn't volunteer for an injection near his balls, he had to be subdued, held down quickly, needle in, and then the pills before he was too dopey. It would all be done very fast, in a matter of minutes, if not seconds."

Low rubbed his forehead with his gloved hand. "There was no heroin paraphernalia in the hotel room right? No needles, spoons, nothing, right?"

Tan shook his head.

"Shit."

The three guys stared at the exposed corpse and his shaved testicles.

Both inspectors watched the numbers go down on the lift's electronic door panel. They stood side by side. The repercussions were unthinkable. Double murders were almost unheard of on the sunny island. Marina Bay Sands was the physical embodiment of Singapore's progress and limitless aspirations. A shimmery bay devoted to wealth creation had emerged from the South China Sea. Marina Bay sat on reclaimed land. The killings could turn the modern foundations into quicksand.

Tan yawned as the lift doors parted. It was late. His dinner would be cold in the microwave and his even colder wife would be asleep in bed, again. They walked quickly towards the car park.

"Well, I know what the Minister will say," he began. "That's why my bosses won't tell him, not yet."

"Yeah, Marina Bay Sands. No chance. We're gonna have to go back now, do the whole thing again?"

"Yeah, the maids, the cleaners, that annoying French manager, security guards, I'll get fresh statements from the lot. We got nothing so far."

"CCTV?"

"Still going through. We checked all the rooms on the corridor. Nothing came up, retirees one side, cannot get their leg over each other, never mind a balcony. Either side gamblers, other rooms businessmen here for conference, in hotel bar, casino, nightclub, all got alibis, all got statements. Even rooms above and below nothing, still checking. But it is the 40th floor, as Charlie Chan keeps reminding me."

"You want him back with you?" Low muttered as he stopped by his car.

"No *lah*, you keep the bugger! He's doing a great job for you."

"*Basket*. So The Indonesian how?"

"I don't know. That's your department. If you don't know him, then I don't know him. You think he's involved?"

"Don't know, but he's the only lead. Jimmy Chew owed money to this guy and Richard Davie found out. It's all I got. Plus he hangs out at the casino. That's the only place I might know where to find him."

"So you're going back to MBS as well."

"No choice."

"*Aiyoh* . . . well be discreet *ah*."

With a bottle of champagne in each hand, Low leaned uneasily over the edge of the marble bar top of Ku De Ta—Marina Bay Sands' rooftop bar and Singapore's most exclusive nightspot—and belched loudly. Ku De Ta stood 57 storeys in the air, sandwiched between the SkyPark and the world's highest, swankiest rooftop swimming pool. Ku De Ta's clientele enjoyed looking down their noses at the rest of South-east Asia. The expats, the bankers, the investors, the sons and daughters of China's political elite and India's most prominent beneficiaries of their caste system came to Ku De Ta to toast their obscene opulence with champagne flutes.

And Ah Lian had managed to offend just about all of them.

Ah Lian was a psychological paradox. He hid the bipolar. He projected the bipolar. He provided a protective shield to suppress the lows. He offered a creative outlet to release the highs. He was both bulletproof vest and ticking time bomb. At times, Low had little control over either. He could only watch as Ah Lian swigged from one of the bottles and waved the other at the DJ's booth.

"*Oi*, DJ, turn it up *lah* ... this one damn solid. Come on, everybody ... *I wonder how, I wonder why, yesterday you told me about the blue, blue sky* ... bastards, sing *lah* ... *and all that I can see is just a yellow lemon tree.*"

A burly, no-necked doorman muscled his way through Singapore's most illustrious jet-setters and tugged at Low's trouser leg. "Get down before I pull you down," he hissed. "Don't be an idiot, OK."

"Balls to you, I'm singing ... *You told me about the blue, blue sky* ... eh, fuck you."

Low was tumbling towards the ground. He had the presence of mind to push the champagne bottles away from him. As the doorman lifted him to his feet, he jabbed the inspector in the solar plexus. The punch was sly, but effective in the darkness. Low was too winded to speak initially, but he admired the professionalism.

The doorman frogmarched him towards the exit and whispered his ear. "You're lucky you're in here, OK? They don't want fuss here, no violence, no police. If this is outside, I kick the shit out of you."

"Hey, I'm not going. I'm here to see Shaun, he's your boss, the manager."

The mention of his employer's name surprised the doorman. Discretion was essential at Ku De Ta. He wasn't buying the bluff.

"Eh, don't take me outside *lah*. I want to see Shaun," Low shouted. "Eh, where is Shaun Mesenas? Shaun Mesenas, it's Ah Lian, it's me *lah*. I went to NS with your brother. Remember? Shaun, where are you, *basket*?"

"I'm here, Ah Lian."

The doorman turned to see his boss, immaculately attired

in a Sacoor Brothers suit, usher a sweaty, skinny *ah beng* into his private office. His boss nodded apologetically at him and led the bumbling drunk inside. The doorman already knew not to ask questions. The tips were fabulous—one girl took him to the disabled toilet on his dinner break just so she didn't have to be seen queuing the next time she came with friends. His old KTV *kakis* would happily take his security gig. Marina Bay Sands wasn't just the preferred destination for punters. The doorman was the gatekeeper to a night in nirvana for the cashed-up kids. They always paid their way. So he wouldn't be whispering a word to anyone. Discretion was essential at Ku De Ta.

Shaun Mesenas locked the door. The DJ's throbbing beats could still be faintly heard. He made his way past Low and sat on a large swivel chair behind a mahogany desk. Low noticed the framed photograph of Shaun and an angelic Eurasian model standing beside a red Porsche. Australia's Great Ocean Road was the picturesque, clichéd, backdrop. It was the essential driving holiday for Singaporeans eager to escape snarling traffic and ERP gantries. The rented car, the clothes, her jewellery—inherited wealth oozed from every pixel.

Suddenly quiet and sober, Low pointed at the photo. "Who's she?"

"My new fiancée, we're getting married next year, probably in Australia, at a Victorian winery, near where we took that photo," Shaun said quickly. "Why are you here, Ah Lian?"

"You know my name."

"You promised you would never come here after the trial."

"And I didn't, about the trial. This isn't about the trial. It's about the murder downstairs."

"What murder?"

Low rested his hands on the polished desk and leaned forward. "Not now eh? I've had a long day and too much champagne on an empty stomach . . . oh, will you cover that or shall I ask for a police receipt?"

Mesenas didn't answer.

"Good, tasted like warm cat's piss anyway. Look, I want to call it a night so I'll be quick. Who's this Indonesian?"

Mesenas appeared to crumple without speaking. He withered before the CPIB officer. The genetic self-confidence that only came from inherited affluence evaporated. The only son of a Eurasian property developer and a retired Chinese TV actress, raised by domestic helpers and packed off to boarding school before his balls dropped, Mesenas had everything. And as Low long ago discovered in his line of work, those who had everything always craved more. Trust-fund babies were forever chasing the buzz. Occasionally, they found it. Mostly, they found Low. He found Mesenas on his hands and knees, leaning over a toilet seat inside a locked cubicle; his flaming nostrils buried in a rich kid's rebellion. He owned the nightclub manager after that.

"So you obviously know him then?"

"I don't know him, no."

Low frowned. "Shaun, I'm not in the mood, OK, not now. Do you want me to formally interview you? Do you want me to lead you through your rich *kakis* out there? Do you want Dragon Boy to find out? I just saw Dragon Boy. He's still as fucked up as ever, always jittery, always angry, you know. What do you think he would do if . . ."

"Yes, yes, all right. Fucking hell. How many times I gotta do this?"

"How many times I gotta do this? Wow, you been back in Singapore for how long? Still got that American accent. Amazing. Do you think you'll ever lose that accent? Or is

76

that annoying mid-Atlantic twang the same at international and boarding schools everywhere? I bet it's the internationally accepted accent of the rich, right, like MasterCard."

"I can change accents when I have to. Just like you can."

"Yeah, yeah, of course. I bet when you're out there, on the dance floor, with those bottle girls, you'll get all down with the hood, right? Talking about your home boys, trying to fuck a hostess, trying to impress some rich daddy's princess; and then you go play the filial son at home, toss the *Lo Hei* at Chinese New Year, smile for Mummy and Daddy's photos, speak with that nice American accent so some of their nice family friends can set you up in here, where you can play *Goodfellas* with your boarding school mates. And then what? And then what happens, Nightclub Man? You cry like a fucking baby when you're alone with me. Who's The Indonesian? I'm not asking again."

"I don't know his name."

Low got up to leave. Mesenas gestured quickly for him to sit down again.

"No, wait, I really don't know his name. I would never ask. Discretion is everything here, you know that. As long as bills are settled, we're quite happy for guests to sign everything back to the room."

"Guests?"

"Yeah, of course. He lives here. Didn't you know?"

"What do you mean lives here? This is a hotel."

"They keep a suite for him at MBS permanently. It's his office when he's in town on business."

"What kind of suite?"

"It's one of the Straits Suites, 50 floors plus, can cost more than 10k a night, man."

"Why would MBS give him a suite?"

Mesenas almost smiled in spite of himself. Considering

he worked undercover for CPIB, the inspector's naivety was shocking. "Because he spends millions in the casino. Why else? The cost of fuelling a private jet to fly him in from Jakarta is still less than what he'll spend on a hand of baccarat."

"So he's cleaning his money in the casino?"

"Of course."

"He's never been checked out?"

"Hey, we're the cleanest city in Asia, right? This is what we do here. Don't you listen to the speeches? We love billionaires in Singapore. We want as many billionaires living here as possible. We've already got Eduardo Saverin. His penthouse is across the bay. I've given the guy a private table. Me. I've served Eduardo Saverin. Mr Facebook drinks in my club. But we're not done. We've barely started on the billionaires. Marina Bay is a magnet. We want them all. And now we've got The Indonesian."

"Fucking hell."

"What? You thought we built this place to give the tourists nice photos from the SkyPark?"

Chapter 8

CHAN watched the Marina Bay Sands casino staff clean up the vomit. His stomach turned when he noticed tiny drops of blood. Their efficiency and meticulous attention to detail both fascinated and appalled him. The gambler had only just thrown up on the slot machines and passed out. A cleaner made a call and an MBS team appeared instantly. They worked with militaristic precision. The red–and–gold carpet was vacuumed and perfumed as a trio of workers took turns to spray various detergents and fresheners on the offending stains. Two other men, presumably from Mainland China, busied themselves with the slot machines, wiping the screens and removing trickles of vomit from the rims of the buttons. The machine couldn't take any cash while it was covered in vomit. The gambler had already been carried out through an emergency exit by a second MBS team. To all intents and purposes, the incident had never happened and the unfortunate man had never existed. Chan nudged his temporary boss.

"Did you see that? They had him up and out in seconds man, damn solid *ah*."

"Don't use Singlish in here, OK. You're a policeman, not

a waiter," Low said, scanning the casino floor, ignoring the clean-up operation behind him.

"Sorry, sir. Did you see his vomit though? It had blood inside. How can?"

The senior officer found the naive questioning annoying. "Look, he was exhausted. He took stuff to stay awake, drink, drugs, probably both, happens all the time. Can you concentrate on what we're doing here?"

"Where did he get that from? Should we arrest him?"

Low could feel his patience evaporating. "For being a drunk arsehole? He got the stimulants from outside somewhere. They need to keep these people awake to take their money. Sleeping gamblers don't gamble. How you think they stay awake all night. Red Bull? You're not in uniform anymore. You're here as a detective. So be a bloody detective and leave the thumb-sucking back with the uniform. Stop worrying about the vomit and focus on your job. For fuck's sake."

The inspector tried counting again. It never worked. That shrink was full of shit. Still, he had to try something. Chan had those eyes, the eyes that old girlfriends always had; the eyes that always left him single. They were a mixture of confusion and fear, darting from side to side in a futile effort to explain the unexpected, volatile outburst. His offhand, casual belligerence offended everyone. Low knew that. But if he could not explain or anticipate his outbursts, his unwitting victims had no chance.

Chan busied himself with his notebook. He re-read his scribbles. Low pushed the notepad into the younger man's stomach. "Are you doing all this to deliberately annoy me? Why don't you just wear a fucking sign? We're not here to interview anyone, just observe. See what this guy looks like, OK? Now go and play one of the slot machines."

"What for?"

"Fuck, so you look like a gambler and not Charlie fucking Chan."

"It's Charles."

"Fuck off."

Chan wandered past a bank of slot machines. Myopic Chinese retirees pressed their noses against the glass screen as the reels whirred around. The officer nodded a greeting at an elderly Chinese woman and sat on the only empty stool beside her.

"Cannot," she hissed.

"I'm sorry?"

"Cannot sit there. Bad luck."

"Oh, sorry, OK. I go somewhere else."

Low was sending a text message when Chan returned. He was having difficulty looking his boss in the face. "The auntie said I cannot play."

"What auntie? What are you talking about?"

"That one over there," replied Chan, pointing out the frail old woman. "She said I cannot sit there because the chair is bad luck."

"Is this a joke? Is there a hidden camera somewhere? You're a sergeant in the Singapore fucking Police Force."

"But she asked me not to sit there."

"So arrest her or shoot her, but sit down, shut up and get away from me."

Low's phone vibrated in his hand. As he read the message, his face brightened. "It's from Mesenas, my nightclub guy ... he's here."

The casino was busy with its usual Asian businessmen, Singaporean heartlanders and curious western backpackers grateful for the free entry and free flow of soft drinks. Without being asked, the gamblers instinctively moved aside for the small group of guests being guided through the crowd. Led by a short Chinese man, the six other men were immaculately attired. Their white shirts were crisp, the trousers pressed and their shoes gleamed. Their hair was all rigidly parted the same way, and stuck fast with handfuls of Brylcreem. They shared an obvious military bearing. Their handsome, middle-aged guide stopped by an empty gaming table. A jittery croupier waited.

"Our friends have reserved this table for you," the smiling Chinese man said. "I usually play in a private room upstairs, but as you requested a smoking table on the ground floor, we've set aside this one for you. These two guys here are our best pit bosses. They will make sure you're not bothered. As you can see, it's baccarat. But I must warn you, this guy is good."

He pointed at the croupier who tidied his chips nervously. The hefty, muscular men squeezed themselves around the table. The one in the middle, sitting ramrod straight, stacked the biggest pile of chips in front of him. He addressed the handsome Chinese man who waited around at his side and pointed at a small TV screen beside the chips. "What's the limit on this table?"

He raised his hands theatrically. "Please, no one's going to insult you in here tonight."

He nodded at the croupier. Another man, the eldest among the six, with an oily complexion and pockmarked cheeks, raised a chunky hand at the end of the table. "And the other thing," he whispered.

The Chinese guide glided along the red-and-gold carpet and placed a kindly hand on the sweaty old man's shoulder. "Don't worry. They'll be waiting for you in the suite when you're ready, with the champagne."

The croupier adjusted his garish, gold shirt and tugged at

his waistcoat. He knew his place at Marina Bay Sands. The ability to be invisible was more valued than the ability to deal cards. The old man pulled the guide towards his ear. "Two right? I asked for two, tall ones?"

His chaperone raised his arms expansively. "Only two?"

Everyone at the baccarat table laughed. The old man counted his chips, refusing to make eye contact with anyone else. "And anything right? No questions."

"You are our guests."

"OK, we play now," the one in the middle suddenly interjected. He was the leader of the group. "Deal the cards and let's have some drinks ... hey, before you go, what do we call you?"

As he gestured towards a petite Chinese girl pushing a beer trolley, the guide laughed self-consciously. "Oh, everyone just calls me The Indonesian. That's easier to remember."

The two plain-clothes officers sat beside each other, feeding notes into a pair of slot machines. Sitting at the end of the row, the inspector had a reasonable vantage point to watch the baccarat table through the insufferable cigarette smoke. The casino's decor, clientele and quality control had deteriorated rapidly since the grand opening. As expected, Marina Bay Sands had succumbed to the lowest common denominator quickly. Cash came before class in Asia. Low knew these people. Ah Lian had introduced him years ago. Money was all that mattered on both sides of the gaming table. This casino had aspirations to follow Monte Carlo, but Malaysia was always going to be closer. For all its grand plans and proclamations, Marina Bay Sands was a neighbourhood Singapore Pools outlet with better carpeting. Nothing more. Engulfed in a nicotine haze, Low started coughing and suddenly thought about his alias. Ah Lian would've approved of the casino's rapid evolution. The place was a shithole.

The inspector could see The Indonesian subserviently handing out drinks. He could guess who the other men were from The Indonesian's obsequious behaviour. A text message from Mesenas had confirmed his suspicions. Beside him, Chan enthusiastically pushed some buttons. "Hey, I just won 10 dollars."

"Shut up. You're supposed to be watching the table, not the machine."

"You said I had to make it look natural."

"To look like a real gambler, not to be Daniel Day Lewis. I want to see where he takes the Burmese afterwards."

"That's who they are?"

"They're the junta."

"The Myanmar junta?"

"No, the Glee club junta."

"I thought they were finished now."

"Some are retired. Some sit on boards. They got to spend their free time somewhere."

"Shouldn't we, you know, call someone?"

"Who?"

"I don't know, the office, the Home Ministry, someone higher up. It's the Myanmar junta over there."

Low discreetly grabbed his partner's hand and squeezed it tightly. "Why don't you use the MBS public address system, idiot?"

"I'm sorry, I'm sorry. I just can't believe, I mean, why? Why would they be here? What are they doing here?"

"What do you think? Gambling."

"Should we do something?"

Low almost felt sorry for the government scholar. Almost. "What shall we do? Fuck up relations between Singapore and Myanmar. Arrest some retired generals for gambling? That's what these people do. You see that Chinese guy there, the tall one in the middle of the Burmese table. According to my source here, he was dealing with heroin. Closed one eye and opened one hand. He's from the Kokang region. Ask Tan or anyone in Narcotics. It's on the border of China, mostly Chinese, opium-rich. Everyone knows about these fuckers—Interpol, the DEA, everyone. They set up shell companies in Singapore to dump cash. And then they come here, race their Ferraris along River Valley Road, molest some bottle girls, play baccarat and scrub their money. And it's been going on for years. Years. And we all close one eye. Why? Because if they don't dump it here, they'll dump it in Malaysia or Vietnam. And they don't want to do that anymore than we do. They've got to clean it and we've got the best fucking washing machines. So ... what would you like us to do?"

"But, I mean, that's not right, is it? I mean, you know, this ... this is Singapore."

"Are you gonna sing the national anthem?"

"But come on, I mean, it's just so ... wrong."

"It's international business. Can we concentrate on The Indonesian now?"

"Well, I don't know. I suppose so. But can't we do something at least? Maybe we can tip off the media."

"And tell them what? That some retired generals and former associates of the Myanmar Government are enjoying a quiet evening at Marina Bay Sands with their *kakis*? I'm sure they've got bigger stories to chase, like a leaky roof at a shopping centre or something."

For the first time, Chan looked at his superior officer, really staring at his cold, almost lifeless, eyes. "You're so fucking cynical."

"No, I'm a typical *kiasu* Singaporean. I only pick battles I know I can win."

*

Low sat in Pierre Durand's plush, Marina Bay Sands office and stared at the obligatory photo of loving wife and kids on the desk. Every workaholic's desk had one. The framed happy snaps always reminded the long-serving CPIB man of the nauseating hypocrisy he faced in his world. They also reminded him of what he didn't have. The Marina Bay Sands manager bounded into the room and sat opposite the untidy policeman, smiling insincerely. The Frenchman irritated Low on so many levels. His unflappable demeanour, his impeccable dress sense, his romantic accent, his condescending, cultured tone and his fawning, grovelling sleaziness when it came to guests with fat wallets; everything grated. Most of all, it was the Frenchiness. The Frenchiness bothered Low. He didn't know why. He didn't have a reason. He wasn't looking for one.

Durand straightened his tie. "So sorry, I'm late. The evenings are always a very busy time for me."

"It's OK. I've got all the time in the world. I'm only trying to solve a murder committed in your hotel. I'm happy to be kept waiting for half an hour in your fancy office while you lick the arses of your guests."

"Detective Inspector, I don't like . . ."

"I don't give a shit what you don't like, especially when we both know you've got half the old Burmese military in your Straits Suite right now, paying $10,000 a night to screw some sweet Singaporean girls. The room and the services, I assume, are being provided by your good self."

Durand shifted uneasily in his seat. His voice had deserted him. He straightened the family photo on his desk.

Low grinned. "Does that make you feel better, to look at that photo. I bet you never signed up for this, right? I bet when you swapped the supermodels, the Formula 1 drivers

86

and the movie stars of Monaco for boring Singapore, you never thought you'd be playing a pimp for Asia's old dictators. What do you do on your day off? Take Kim Jong-Un for a picnic at the SkyPark? Why don't you organise a North Korean basketball tournament of old NBA players on the ice rink no one uses in the shopping mall? You could get a photo of you, Kim Jong-Un and Dennis Rodman. Stick it right there next to the family shot."

"Do you talk to everyone like this in your job?"

"Not really, just arseholes."

"Does it make you feel better?"

"It does actually. I suppose it's the hypocrisy. You see, most criminals, street criminals at least, are stupid. They have street smarts, yes, but no real education. They have no world view, no awareness of their repercussions. They're just poor. They see something they want. They steal it. They don't really think about the consequences. They're pretty uncomplicated people. What you see is what you get. There's a certain sense of honesty about them. They are what they are.

"But you ... smug pricks like you hide behind bottles of Bollinger inside celebrity chef restaurants. You put your kids there in that photo through the finest schools knowing that the money has come from dictators up the road, drug smugglers, money launderers and, as we sit here right now, off the backs of young girls. Girls probably not much older than your pretty daughters in that photo, Singaporean girls, foreign girls who came here for a better life, young girls who are now lying under disgusting old men. Right now, in your hotel. So yes, it makes me feel a little bit better. I'd feel a whole lot better if I could smash that picture frame over your head. But I can't. So, for now, I'll settle for everything you know about The Indonesian. Don't leave out anything or I might say you were uncooperative and smack you anyway."

Chan thought about his pregnant wife at home in their new four-room flat in Punggol. He remembered her joy when they were handed the keys for the first time. He pictured what the baby's room might look like when he finally got around to painting the walls pink. He wondered if his widowed mother would be happy to live with them in *"ulu"* Punggol after spending most of her life in Toa Payoh. She would miss the wet market in Lorong 7. He calculated how much money would be left in his account each month once the mortgage had been taken out after his wife had stopped working. He smiled as he thought about his daughter waddling along the floating platform at Sengkang Riverside Park on lazy Sunday afternoons. He focused on his beautiful Singaporean family. He tried so hard to think about his unborn baby. He did everything he could to stay with his little girl, but the images were shattered by the rhythmic cries of the girls behind the door of suite 5189, the 51st floor, the Straits Suite. They were coded cries for help.

He heard the sound of men, brutal men, army men, barking orders, issuing instructions—how to stand, how to lay, how to turn, how to bend, how to hold, how to squeeze, how to moan, how to yield, how to submit. He wanted to bang on the door, but he was explicitly ordered not to intervene. He just had to listen; an unwilling Peeping Tom monitoring the misery of the helpless, the defenceless, the invisible. He heard a fragile female voice call out "stop". She was shouted down by mocking male laughter, her pleas unable to compete with the Mandarin ballads professing undying love in the suite's KTV lounge. Old men giggled like schoolboys. They found her fear funny. Her anxiety aroused them. Pain had been their profession. They got off on other people's terror.

Chan tried one more time to concentrate on his family in their new four-room flat in Punggol, but he had lost them. His simple, gentle Singaporean life was a million miles away from Marina Bay. He was lonely. But he was glad he was alone in the corridor on the 51st floor. He knew that Low would make fun of his tears.

Low threw the beer down his neck and started on another. The cleaner from Beijing shuffled across and removed the empty can, eager for something to do. The scruffy officer was the only customer in Fatt Choi Express. The steamboat was decent, but food ate into gambling time. Punters only slumped on restaurant tables when they had nothing left to give.

Low struggled to straighten his crumpled shirt as he surveyed the casino floor through the restaurant window. They crouched, hovered and dashed between gaming tables like clockwork mice, unsure of what they were doing or where they were going but kept moving nonetheless. As he swirled the melting ice in his glass, he chuckled. Marina Bay Sands had succeeded where Singapore had largely failed. The casino was a true social leveller. Taxi drivers rubbed shoulders with multi-millionaires on the ground floor, where smoking was permitted. Outside they were strangers. Inside they were equals, united by their gambling and nicotine addictions. They were the same. They would both be skint in the morning.

He spotted Chan squeezing his way through the crowd and raised a beer can. As the younger policeman opened the restaurant door, he rubbed his eyes. He smiled at his boss, but the smile didn't reach his eyes. Low envied his junior partner's emotional honesty. He used to feel like that.

"Everything OK?"

"Yeah, fine boss. They've all gone to sleep, I think, drunk and fucked."

"Come and have a drink. What you want?"

"OK, OK, a quick one *ah*. Just a beer."

"One Tiger here, please," Low shouted brightly to one of the cooks before turning back to the red-eyed idealist. "So how?"

"How do you do it, I mean how do you ..." His voice trailed away. He filled the gap by opening the beer can dropped on the table by the cook, pouring slowly into a cold, ice-filled glass.

"How do I what? Put up with all the shit?"

"No, the shit is fine. It's the scum, just the scum. I mean it tests us. It ... you know ... it tests our ... what's the word ... our humanity."

Low laughed. "Wah, steady *lah*. So *cheem ah*, your English? *Basket*, that's a university word, a government scholar word, cannot *tahan* such a big word. Too late already."

Chan stared at his beer glass. "Fuck you," he cussed. "I thought you said no Singlish in the casino floor."

"*Wah*, finally, you're getting some balls. There's hope for you yet. We're not on the casino floor, we're sitting in the magnificent Fatt Choi Express, doesn't count. Cheers." Low bashed his glass against Chan's and patted his partner on the shoulder. "It does get better, really."

"No it doesn't. You know it doesn't."

"No it doesn't. But if you can't take a joke, you shouldn't have joined, right?"

Chan drew condensation patterns with his forefinger on the side of his beer glass. "Do you know what they were doing up there in that suite while he's down here?"

"Of course. They were shagging lots of pretty, slim

90

young girls, mostly from China, maybe some from Vietnam, Eastern Europe, maybe even one or two from Singapore. If anyone asks, they say they are models, or bottle girls. That's the one they like now at stylo-milo places like this one. Bottle girls. They get paid to pour champagne for these bastards. Some heck care *lah*. Working girls in their old countries last time, working girls in their new country. Either way, they're now being paid better than you and me to shag monsters from Myanmar."

"I signed up to stop this shit."

"What do you want to do? Prostitution isn't illegal. Unless they steal some peanuts from the mini-bar or smash the piano, there's nothing we can do."

"They weren't having sex up there. They were ... like animals ... like fucking animals."

Low put his drink down slowly and sighed. "You should go home now. Go home to your wife."

"Why? Because I cannot make it working with the CPIB? No need to patronise me."

"No, no, not all ... because you can. You still care *lah*. You should try and keep that, hang on to it. It's a good thing. You don't want to end up like me."

"Please. You're a legend. You know you're a legend. Everybody knows your cases, how you caught Tiger, undercover for one year plus, brought down a whole syndicate."

"Yeah, I'm a legend," Low repeated sarcastically, turning to face his impressionable colleague. "And look what it made me. Look what I have to give. You tell me there are fat, disgusting generals up there doing terrible things to those girls and all I can think about is that door up there, where The Indonesian went after he pimped out the girls. I don't want to lose him tonight."

Low pointed to the third floor, where the whales liked

to swim. "He's up there, in the Ruby Room. It's the only room he plays in. He can play on the top floor if he wants, but he prefers the Ruby Room. Won big there last time, so he thinks it's lucky. I got all his gambling habits from that French manager, once he'd stopped crying. So he's in there right now. And I know I won't leave until he comes out of that room. It doesn't matter if I have to wait until the next morning. I will sit in this empty, depressing place, drink beer and watch those escalators, waiting for him to come down. I will not move. That's what I've become. That's what makes your legend, ignoring those poor fish drowning in the Straits Suite to try and catch Moby Dick. And I won't stop until I catch him. I don't even want to stop."

"Then I'll stay with you."

"No, you won't. No need. As you say, they're all asleep. If he goes back to their suite, I'm here. Go home. Go and kiss your wife goodnight and rub that pregnant belly."

Chan nodded. He finished his beer and stood up. "How did you know she was pregnant?"

His boss raised his glass to toast himself. "You just said *what*. I'm a legend."

Low was careful to maintain his distance. He knew he was unsteady on his feet. That bastard had left him drinking beer for three hours, but his senses were slowly returning. He followed The Indonesian across Bayfront Avenue. He had taken the extra precaution of hanging around the taxi stand before trotting towards the pedestrian crossing as the lights changed. At 3 a.m., there were only a handful of giggling expats and a few Chinese gamblers waiting at the kerb. The darkness helped, but the lack of any street traffic made the policeman too self-conscious.

He almost lost The Indonesian in the long, expansive

Marina Bay Sands hotel lobby. His target had stopped to chat with a concierge and Low had to loiter conspicuously around a marble vase that towered above him. The lobby was lined with those ridiculously tall, ostentatious vases filled with trees; an artificial forest inside the hotel to match the man-made gardens outside. He browsed the MBS tourism leaflets, all making the same boast on the cover: *Every moment rewarded*. For whom, the inspector wondered. When he looked up, The Indonesian was striding briskly towards the Paiza lift lobby in Tower 1, private access for those staying in the suites above the common punters. Emboldened by the beer, he ran past the three bubble-patterned glass counters without thinking, almost knocking over a pot of purple orchids before pushing the button. The orchids on the pristine lift doors parted once again to reveal The Indonesian alone in the lift. He smiled.

"Good evening," he said, in impeccable English.

"Evening, evening, sorry about that," Low said, genuinely flustered.

"Which floor?"

"Sorry?"

"Which floor?" The Indonesian stood with his finger poised over the panel of floor numbers and his hotel card key still in the slot.

"Oh, sorry, right. Er, 50th floor, please. Thanks."

The doors closed and Low silently cursed. The bloody beer and the sudden realisation that he didn't have a hotel room card key had muddied his thinking. He picked the 50th floor because it was the first floor he chanced upon in the lift. He would get out first.

"You don't have a key?"

Low patted his pockets. "I must confess, I had too many beers at the casino. I've left the key in the casino with my wife. She's on her way back from the roulette table now. She's not happy."

"I can imagine. Ah, well, I trust you."

They smiled at each other and then turned awkwardly to watch the floor numbers race past on the electronic panel overhead. They stood in silence. The Indonesian was to the inspector's left and slightly in front of him. Low was struck by how handsome the guy was. His hair was swept back effortlessly, rather than anally. He had been blessed with high cheekbones that gifted him a warm, trusting smile. He was dressed casually, but smartly; every inch the modern Asian businessman that Singapore coveted. Physically, he was the ideal salesman.

The lift stopped abruptly at the 50th floor. Low's ears popped. The Indonesian kindly pushed the button to hold the doors open.

"Thank you," said the Singaporean, making clear eye contact this time. "And thanks again for using your room key. Good night."

The Indonesian nodded and smiled. "Good night ... Detective Inspector Low."

Chapter 9

FLANKED by a pair of prison officers, Low swept along the corridor. He swallowed hard. He feared no one as Ah Lian. But he felt exposed without his Singlish shield. He was in no mood to have his buttons pushed this morning. Changi Prison always made him aware of his transparency. The irony was not lost on him. The inmates saw through him in a way the outside world never could. They saw him for what he really was. He knew it wasn't Ah Lian who protected him. Detective Inspector Stanley Low was his best disguise. His police badge shielded him from an uncomfortable truth.

He opened the door and walked straight to the table, sitting down immediately. He addressed the prison officers. "You can wait outside by the door," he said. "I'll be fine."

"Are you sure?" said Tiger.

Low finally looked at his former boss. Tiger still had the swagger, but not the size. The old loan shark had shrunk in the endless spin cycle of Changi Prison. Naturally stocky, the skin under his tattooed arms now sagged. His fists were chunky and his knuckles puffy. His hair remained boot-polish black, but his face had turned coarse. The deep rings further blackened his soulless eyes. He was pushing 60 when Low first went undercover, but Singapore's proudest gangster finally looked his age. Changi neutered them all in the end.

Low drank from a bottle of water on the table before answering.

"How you been?" he said finally.

Tiger stretched out his legs under the table and rested his hands behind his head. He was going to enjoy the mild interrogation. He had nothing else better to do. "You look older than last time. Too much stress, is it?"

"They told me outside that you not causing any problems anymore. Settled down already. That's good."

"I hear you still not married? C'mon *ah*, mus' be like me, mus' have children. Have one for you and one for Singapore. You remember that one? No *lah*, too young, you still a kid. But you mus' do that, have one for you, one for Singapore. Otherwise how? Too many foreigners. Cannot. Enough already. Even my daughter mus' go overseas. You know she's in the UK now? Neurosurgeon. Working and studying, same time, damn smart that one. She's going to be an expert ... expert for this."

Tiger tapped his forehead and went on, "I say to her, you train to understand about your father, is it? You want to know about my brain, is it? She laughed and said she wants to work with children. I said, *yah lah*, work on me, before I *blur*. But she's very smart. She gone very far already with her studies."

"Well, you paid for it. All her university education paid for by a gambling syndicate, not bad right?"

"I hear they give you a new partner, very *blur* one," Tiger said suddenly, both men verbally fly-swatting each other. "Can't be as much fun as me right?"

"We were not partners. I was an undercover CPIB officer. You were a loan shark, a pimp, a bookie, a match-fixer, a gangster."

"But I took my daughter for steamboat every Sunday, correct? Never miss," Tiger interrupted, savouring the memory. "Marina Bay, *wah*, their steamboat the best last time. Best in Singapore. And now it's gone. You know I used to take my little girl for steamboat and then fly kite last time, Marina Bay. Every weekend, steamboat, video arcade and fly kite. Marina Bay used to be for families, Singaporean families. Now they put that big ugly hotel there. Build those silly, fake gardens, take away the steamboat. You tell me, how is that for Singaporean families?"

Low leaned across the table. "Tiger, you owned the video arcade and the bowling alley at Marina South. You made your runners hang out at the bowling alley. And you used the steamboat restaurant to clean your money."

"Eh, still the best steamboat in Singapore."

"It was," Low admitted. They smiled at each other, acknowledging a mutual admiration for their work ethic. They were both the best at what they did and they knew it.

"Still go for steamboat?"

"Not really, no time."

"*Bak kut teh*? Must go for *bak kut teh,* right?"

"Sometimes."

"Still go KTV at Balestier?"

"I never went KTV."

"Still miss working for me?"

"Fuck you, *lah.*"

The response betrayed Low. It was too quick, too rehearsed and too obvious. They both missed working together.

After the prison officers re-joined Tiger, Low closed the door and stepped into the corridor. As he held the phone, he peered at Tiger through the glass panel. The imprisoned gangster grinned back at the policeman who once caught him.

"This better be bloody important," Low growled down the phone.

"You told me to keep you updated," replied Chan, his wounded voice echoing down the line.

"Yes, yes, all right, get on with it. I'm in the middle of an interview here."

"I followed the suspect into The Shop-pes."

"The Shop-pes?"

"It's the Marina Bay Sands shopping centre called the shops. It's spelled s-h-o-p-p-e-s. I think it's old English and the correct pronunciation is shop-pes. But I should probably just call it the shopping centre, right?"

"Are you finished?"

"Yeah, well, he went into a tourist shop, not the one with postcards and plastic Merlions. That one *ah*, the one in here for the *towkays* and businessmen for conference centres. They sell gold-plated Merlions, Eiffel Towers and Empire State Buildings, you know. I think it's so they can exchange gifts at meetings and delegations with people from other countries, you know. Some of it quite nice, you know."

"Are you on commission at this place?"

"He bought an Indonesian temple or something, it was gold. And then he went back to his hotel suite. Guess how much it was? It was 40K. Forty thousand for a gold temple on a plaque. Unbelievable. That was more than the deposit on my flat."

"And then what happened?"

"Nothing, he went back to his suite like I said."

"So he bought a souvenir?"

"Yes, boss."

"Charlie?"

"Yes, boss?"

"Go away."

*

Low returned to his seat in the prison's interview room and put his phone on the table. It buzzed and vibrated almost immediately. Tiger nodded towards the phone. "*Wah*, busy *ah*?"

Low slid a photograph of Richard Davie across the table. "Do you know who that is?"

"Yeah, of course. It's the dead *ang moh* in all the news, *wha'*. You think my daughter will do this, working on dead people, studying their brains. Not nice, right?"

"She's studying neurosurgery you said, not forensics. She wants to keep them alive, not deal with them when they're dead. Did you know him?"

Tiger leered at the photo then pushed it away dismissively. "Please *lah*, I never work with *ang mohs*, especially after last time. You remember, right? They got very big mouths, always want to talk, talk one, talk to news, talk to TV, talk to police, now they talk cock on Facebook. Singaporeans always better. Been trained to be quiet, from kindergarten, trained to nod heads, say yes, don't ask questions, like sheep, sheep better. Just tick boxes. Tick boxes, don't talk. I only work with people who like money and tick boxes. That's why you're a lousy Singaporean. You're like an *ang moh*. You don't tick boxes. You ask too many questions. You *ah*, cannot make it."

"I caught you."

"You got lucky *wha'*. You didn't catch me. I got caught. People fuck up on my side. Never work with people who ask questions. And never work with people who are too *blur*. Little bit *blur*, can, just nice, don't ask question. *Blur* like *sotong*, cannot, always cause problem one. Where's the other photo?"

"What photo?"

"The other one *lah*. TV say two people dead, *wha'*."

"Her name has not been made public yet. We don't know who that person is yet, no firm ID, no one missing, there's no family looking for anyone. We're still looking for a match."

Tiger laughed. "You know *lah*, but too sensitive right. Local, is it?"

"Just think about this photo."

"Show me the other photo? The crime scene one, come *lah*."

Low took another swig from the water bottle, ignoring the request. "Did you know what Richard Davie did? What he really did?"

"Everybody knew. These *ang moh* bastards do what we do with their *cheem* computers and '*Gahmen*' call them heroes. They thank them. They thank the foreigners. And then they pay them some more."

"No, they track betting patterns and illegal syndicates to spot any irregularities so people like me can build a case. You tracked betting patterns and built syndicates to make money."

"I was still the best."

"You were the best, in your own time. Now you're a dinosaur. You're an analogue man in a digital world."

Tiger chuckled and crossed his arms, his tattoos poking out from beneath his T-shirt sleeves. "*Wah*, very deep *ah* that one, very *cheem ah*. I don't even know what you just said. Insulting me, is it? You think you insult me, you say I'm lousy, I get angry and talk about the new guys is it?"

Low sat up suddenly. He looked concerned. "Hey, look, if I offended you then I can only say ... I don't give a shit. I didn't come here to massage your ego, or talk about the good old days, or pretend that I miss you, or show you photos of dead *ang mohs*. I came here to make your life better."

"How?"

"Well, I'm going to ask the prison officers to close one eye

100

to the illegal phone you keep in your cell; the one you've had since you were on remand and used to call me on; the one you used to call me to ask about your daughter; the one you used to ask me to make sure your daughter got out of Singapore safely; the one that I know your daughter still calls you on late at night. That one. That will make your life better, right? But if you don't help me, I will take the phone away, you will be punished and I will make sure you are denied all public payphone privileges. Try explaining that one to your daughter. Oh, wait, you won't be able to because you won't have a fucking phone. Tell me about Richard Davie. Now."

Tiger unfolded his arms and rubbed his palms along his thighs. "You won't take my phone away."

"It's already been taken away. The phone's already gone. That's the only way you can look at it. You can only try and get it back from this point."

"*Wah*, Ah Lian, you really grow up. You got big balls now, *ah*? I'm so proud."

"No more fucking around. Richard Davie."

Tiger looked directly at Detective Inspector Stanley Low. The man he had known for a year as Ah Lian. The man he had trusted. The man who had shot down Singapore's last tiger.

"You know that singer, the one always singing about making money," Tiger said.

"Yeah, Yue Liang. What about her?"

"Richard Davie was screwing her. He was screwing her right up until the week he died."

Low looked through the window at Tiger. The *ah long* was joking with the prison guards, gesticulating theatrically as he told another story, probably one making fun of the idiotic Ah

Lian. The inspector turned his back on the room. "Why are you calling me now?"

It was Leonard Viljoen on the phone. He hadn't been acting CEO of Sports Watch for five minutes and was treating Low's number like a personal hotline. He infuriated the inspector more than he could say.

"You told me to call immediately if I came across anything important," Viljoen replied.

"Well, what is it?"

"It's Jimmy Chew. We've traced a large gambling outlay from a poker website out of Macau to one of his Singaporean credit cards. It's a reasonable amount, around $60,000."

"Yeah, so? You told me this before. We all know he's a heavy gambler. His wife came to you guys in the first place. Are you gonna tell me I need an umbrella when it pisses down?"

"This is a new bet, his latest bet. He lost the money two days before Richard died."

Low returned to his chair and faced Tiger. "Now, where was I?"

"Looking like shit. You look 10 years older than when I saw you last time outside."

"You'll be at least 10 years older when I next see you outside."

Tiger scratched his tattooed arm. It was a lion draped in a Singaporean flag. For a former house breaker, loan shark and racketeer, Tiger had always been fiercely nationalistic.

"C'mon, Ah Lian, no need for such cheap shots, *wha*'. You're the smart one. You mus' be the smartest Chinaman I know."

"Why?"

"Because you caught me."

"You caught yourself."

"How?"

"Got too greedy. Everybody does it. You're not special."

"No, can't be. Greedy never mind. Someone gets caught, mus' be a trap." Tiger pointed at his favourite protégé. "You caught me."

"You think Jimmy Chew trapped this *ang moh*?"

Tiger rubbed his face and looked away. He nodded towards the prison officers standing guard in the corridor. They were chatting idly, paying no attention to the interview room.

"People always ask why I was the '*Kelong* King of Singapore' for so long. How I make so many fixes, got so many gambling syndicates, got so many loan sharks, bookies. But you know why, right? You know why. It's not me, it's them. Look at them outside, supposed to be prison guards. *Blur* like *sotong*. You could beat me in here. I could beat you, try to escape some more. You are unarmed. I could overpower you, correct? Look at us. I am bigger than you. You are a skinny Chinaman. But look at them ... talking cock, talking nonsense; girls, drinking, gambling, TV, Man U, talking shit, not doing their job. That's why that terrorist escape. That's how he got away, Mas Selamat, *chee bye lah*. Because Singapore pays shit, Singapore gets shit, like these two outside. See? Peanuts and monkeys. They say globalisation good for Singapore. Nonsense it's good for Singapore. It's good for me. You outsource everything, you get cheap shit. I make money on cheap shit. Outside, I buy these people. Inside, I buy these people. Singapore pay them shit. I pay them better. Singapore loses. I win. Why Singapore never learn *ah*?"

Low picked up his phone from the table. "All right, Tiger. I played your game last time, but now no need. I'll get them to search your cell. Your phone is gone. And you won't use the payphone anymore."

"*Wah*, steady *lah*, cannot joke anymore is it, Ah Lian? Last time you were the joker, funniest *ah long* I ever had."

"That wasn't me."

Tiger scrutinised Low's tired face and nodded knowingly, as if finding what he was looking for. "It was you, Ah Lian. It was definitely you. This one not you. This one I don't know. This one cannot *tahan*. This one tired, fed up *lah* . . . that one *ah*, the funny one, the joker . . . that was you. And you miss him. You want him back. That's why you see me."

Low pushed his chair back and stood up. "I know you can buy another phone from one of your monkeys, but I will see what other things I can take away."

"Wait, wait, OK. Calm down. *Wah lau*, you so serious one now . . . *relak lah* . . . come, sit down, sit down . . . OK, OK, no need to get so excited. OK, do I think Jimmy Chew *tekan* the *ang moh* because he was screwing his wife last time? And the *ang moh* knows about his gambling debt some more . . . no. Cannot. Jimmy Chew talk cock. He play big man on stage, the *towkay* one, but he's not me. He's not you. He cannot play gangster. He's not a killer. He might talk and talk until so boring someone dies, but a killer? Forget it *lah*."

"But this *ang moh* dying solves all his problems, right?"

"How? Jimmy Chew still got debts. Owe money, pay money, correct? You know, *wha'*. Last time, someone owe me money, die-die must pay. I die-die one, still must pay. Even I sit here, they still must pay. Owe money, pay money. That one fixed. Never change."

"But if Richard Davie was also screwing his wife?"

"Please *lah*, everyone gets screwed. Jimmy Chew never owe money to the *ang moh*. If he owe money outside, must still pay outside. This Richard *ang moh* dead? So what? Nothing changes."

"So he must still pay this Indonesian?"

Tiger sat back in his chair. He looked down at his Singapore lion tattoo and smiled. "*Wah*, not bad *ah*. How you know about The Indonesian already?"

In the corridor outside the interview room, Low considered throwing the phone against the fluorescent tube above his head. "What do you want now?"

"I'm with The Indonesian," Chan whispered down the line. "I'm standing in the same room with the guy."

His boss found the excitement misplaced and unhelpful. "Well, what are you doing with him? I told you to back off didn't I? He already knows who I am. I told you to leave him alone and stick with Jimmy Chew."

"I did, boss, I did. That's what I'm saying. They're here now. Both of them, all three of them, Jimmy Chew, Yue Liang and The Indonesian, right in front of me. I'm looking at them right now. They're all in the same room."

Chapter 10

JIMMY Chew balanced the marble base of the Indonesian gold temple on the palm of his hand. He adjusted his headset microphone with his other hand. He inhaled and waited. He ran his fingers through his expensive spiky hairstyle. He checked the smooth white shirt, three buttons undone, beneath the black jacket, no tie. He didn't do ties. He wasn't old-school high waistbands and buckets of Brylcreem. He carefully sidestepped conservative, religious affiliations, but didn't publicly reject them either. The pretty-boy pastors limited their market. Their presentations were undeniably flamboyant—effeminate even—but their audience was too narrow. Jimmy knew the value of a pink dollar and cultivated a discreet following with the help of a gay stylist. He didn't discriminate. Cash came in all shapes, sizes and genders. He was a modern metrosexual motivator with a pop star wife. They were Singapore's golden couple, the perfect combination; rock stars selling wealth through speech and song. They were just what Singapore's elite needed right now. They made the rich feel good about themselves. Self-reliance was the natural state of Asians. Welfare was for the weak. Greed was good because it created good for others. Jimmy Chew helped others to help themselves at a never-ending buffet of financial growth. And no one loved a buffet as much as Singaporeans.

He held the Indonesian trinket high so the spotlight bounced off the gleaming gold. "Now come on, ladies and gentlemen, we can do better. We have many millionaires in this room. I know because my books made most of you millionaires."

The audience laughed politely at their $10,000 tables. South-east Asia's wealthiest men and women had agreed to attend the charity dinner to raise funds for an Indonesian orphanage that no one had heard of, much less cared about. But there were was always business to be done at the Sands Expo and Convention Centre—or better yet, the casino— and a chance of getting a photo with the wife in the latest issue of *Peak* magazine. Plus, Yue Liang had been booked to sing her latest hit, *Higher Power*. The downside was the audience had to suffer her idiotic husband with the headset telling them how to make money. They knew how to make money. They bred money. It wasn't the humidity keeping them in Singapore. They certainly didn't make their fortune after queuing up for one of Jimmy Chew's childish self-help books at a local shopping centre.

"Come on, good people. We're currently at $70,000," he shouted over the chinking wine glasses. "This is for the kids in Indonesia. We're doing it for the orphanage. Have a look again at this piece. It's a beautiful depiction of an Indonesian temple, nine carat gold on a marble base. I know there are many Indonesian businessmen, diplomats and even a few ambassadors in the room. This is the perfect gift for a visiting VIP or even one for those feeling a little homesick about the old country. Remember, it's not about the cost. It's about out-bidding your rival. As I said in my last book, *Six Steps to Being Super Rich*—signed copies of which will be auctioned later—if you and your friend are cornered by a lion in the jungle, you don't have to outrun the lion, you just have to outrun your friend."

The audience murmured, but Jimmy Chew sensed that the older Chinese *towkays* at the top tables were eager to move on to the next item up for auction—dinner with his wife. He gestured towards a table of middle-aged men. Stern, serious and unsmiling, they all sat up straight and never spoke. "It looks like our beautiful Indonesian gold temple is heading to Myanmar. A gift for Myanmar's favourite lady, Aung San Suu Kyi perhaps?"

Making no attempt to hide his anger, a thickset man at the head of the table started to rise. The guy beside placed a firm hand on his shoulder and he returned to his seat.

"OK, then, the temple is heading to our Burmese friends from the North ... going once, going twice ..."

"Eighty-eight thousand, eight hundred and eighty-eight dollars."

Everyone turned towards the back of the South-east Asia's largest ballroom. One man stood at the back with his hand held high. Spontaneous applause echoed across the banquet tables. Jimmy Chew bowed theatrically. "Going once, going ... ah, what the heck, gone to the wonderfully generous gentleman at the back of the room."

The Indonesian raised his glass towards the excitable auctioneer.

Chan left the ballroom and jogged towards the men's toilet. An elderly Chinese man, perhaps in his eighties, shakily handed the young detective a towel. He smiled and handed the uncle $10. "Can just step outside, uncle, one minute, can? Must make a private call, *ah*?"

He flashed his police identification. The old man

shrugged and shuffled into the corridor. Chan crouched beneath the toilet cubicles, checking he was alone as he called his boss.

"Ah, hey, it's Chan, sir. I'm still at the Sands. It's a charity auction, organised by the ASEAN business leaders community, whatever that is, and they're selling all kinds of shit for crazy money, boss. There must be more than a thousand people in there, mostly foreigners, but some Singaporeans, I think. Our Indonesian *kaki* has just bought back the same gold statue thing that I saw him buy before in the shopping centre. Is he mad or what?"

"He's money laundering," Low mumbled.

"He's what?"

"He's money laundering. He's cleaning his money by . . . where are you? Are you still inside the charity dinner?"

"No, boss, I'm inside the toilet. It's OK. I checked. There's nobody here. I told the toilet cleaner guy to go outside for five minutes."

"The one who gives out the towels and soap? You told the cleaner inside a VIP toilet to leave a VIP event? So it's empty? What if one of the guests walks in? These bastards expect to have their hands washed for them. What will the cleaner say if anyone asks where he's been? Who else has the authority to tell him to go away? Why don't you just put your policeman sign back on?"

"Sorry, boss."

"Get back in the dinner, see how close these three idiots are and speak to me later. But get the bloody cleaner back first."

Low stared at the framed black-and-white print that hung behind Leonard Viljoen's office. Was Muhammad Ali pleading with Sonny Liston to get to his feet or instructing the overweight, washed-up chump to stay on the canvas? Did the image capture a man's exasperation or his empathy? Low wasn't entirely sure any more. He had always sided with Muhammad Ali. He knew that much. Now he sympathised with the older, wiser, exhausted boxer lying on the canvas, a broken soul who saw no merit in going another round to satisfy something as quaint as pride. He had long ago accepted why Sonny Liston went down so easily. Now he wearily understood why he didn't bother to get back up. Ali was ready to meet the world. Liston already knew what the world was like. There wasn't anything left worth fighting for. Low recognised the weariness. He even admired the honesty. But he had to be like Ali today. He needed to sting.

Viljoen caught the police officer admiring his beloved artwork as he breezed into his office. "It's a great image, isn't it," he said, adjusting the frame.

"It wasn't crooked," Low snapped.

"Ah, well, force of habit. It definitely isn't now," Viljoen said, standing back to admire the iconic print once more. "How can I help you?"

"You know how you can help me, Mr Viljoen?"

"Lennie, please, call me Lennie."

"Don't start with the 'call me Lennie' shit again. Tell me about Jimmy Chew's most recent gambling."

Viljoen fumbled with some papers on his desk before finding the spreadsheet he wanted. "Ah, here it is."

Low scanned the desk and examined the spreadsheet. It was almost the size of A3. "You leave this lying around for anyone to see?"

"The cleaner is the only one who comes in here. And he's from Myanmar, doesn't speak a word of English, I made sure of that. He's a wizard with a vacuum cleaner, and so much cheaper than the Filipinos that we had before. Mind you, when it comes to personal hygiene, I probably prefer the Filipinos. I mean ..."

"So this piece of paper?" Low interrupted. He wasn't in the mood.

"Yes, right. Thanks to the information supplied to Richard from Yue Liang, we could trace her husband's gambling quite easily."

Viljoen picked up a pen and pointed to a line graph on the spreadsheet. "As you can see here, he really is the most gullible of punters. Over time, we noticed that there were sudden spikes in his gambling, particularly poker. So Richard spoke to Yue Liang and swapped notes. You know, compared his diary, that sort of thing. His heavy gambling always came after a big corporate event or book launch, i.e. when he got paid."

"Well, you can expect another one in the coming days then. He's at one right now."

"Is he? What is it?"

Low tapped on the spreadsheet. "Carry on, Mr Viljoen."

"Yeah, right, well, over the course of the year, his betting outlay is around $1.5 million." Viljoen cast a glance at the detective, looking for a reaction. There wasn't any. "But he's won quite a bit of that back of course. It seems he's not actually that bad a poker player. But he's still down around $400,000. This latest loss puts him close to half a million, which is here."

Low followed Viljoen's pen. "And this bet was placed two days before Richard died. You are positive?"

"Well, two days before his body was discovered. I don't know when Richard died, exactly of course. But the credit card transaction is easy to trace. One of the beauties of online gaming, we're not chasing cash payments and scribbles on scraps of paper anymore. We know what he spent, when he spent it and where he spent it."

"And the website is registered in Macau."

"Of course; it's illegal to place a bet online in Singapore, full stop, unless it's with Singapore Pools. Why do you think Singapore Pools is setting up their own online gaming website? There's too much money being leaked online. Just by having an account with a gaming website, he's broken the law God knows how many times already. He could be arrested just for this, you know."

Low glowered at the South African. "Don't tell me how to do my job, Mr Viljoen. Who is running this website?"

Viljoen looked out of his window. There was a yachting regatta at Marina Bay. The sunlight twinkled on the water as the boats glided along. Viljoen found himself smiling. He adored the view. He had come a long way from Cape Town. "I, er, I mean, that's not something I can say for certain. We try not to speculate here."

"I'm telling you to speculate here. You know the modus operandi for most of the Asian syndicates. You know their VPNs, where they base their websites, how they take bets, their volume, their turnover. Is this one Singaporean, Chinese, Malaysian, Eastern European? What?"

"It's, er, probably the one you left off there. It seems to fit the pattern of this Indonesian character?"

"Do you have a name?"

Viljoen suddenly appeared nervous. He fidgeted in his chair and adjusted the framed family photo on the desk; the wholesome image of the devoted husband and father. "No, no, just a rumour. That's why I don't like to speculate. We analyse online gambling data, patterns. We don't really analyse individuals. We leave that to you guys."

"How do you know he's Indonesian then? And who's

112

Indonesian? The head of a syndicate, the website adminis-trator, Jimmy Chew's personal assistant, who are you talking about?"

Viljoen continued to fiddle with the family photo. He turned it away from him, scratching away at the cardboard stand behind. "He's . . . well at least I think he's . . . the, er, guy behind the website . . . the one who Jimmy Chew pays . . . at least, that's what I heard, I think."

Low's eyes widened. He examined the family photo and then Viljoen's face. The South African struggled to maintain eye contact. Low returned to the photo—the perfect photo, the perfect wife, the perfect kid, the perfect bloody lawn in front of a perfect black-and-white colonial bungalow. It was perfect. Everything was just so perfect. "You've had sex with her haven't you?"

Viljoen flushed. He tried to watch the yachting regatta, hoping his profile would hide his blushing cheeks. The boats continued to bob along the bay, moving away from him. Cape Town felt a long way away.

"Who? What do you mean?"

"You shagged his wife didn't you? Yue Liang. You had sex with her."

"What? That's ridiculous. How could you even . . ."

"You said it yourself last time, when you were doing that cocky expat thing. You said something about how you wouldn't mind hanging out of that."

"But I'm married. Look at the photo."

"I'm looking at it, same as you. You haven't stopped look-ing at it, drooling like a puppy. If you made the doting Dad routine any more obvious, you'd get a pack of cards out and play happy families. When did you shag her?"

"But I didn't . . ."

Low edged towards Viljoen. He visualised the chemicals

fizzing in his brain. He always did when the anger bubbled. He saw and heard a fizzing sensation, like an Alka-Seltzer being dropped into a glass of water. It was a strange way of identifying and personalising the aggression that came gift-wrapped with the bipolar, but it was better than all that counting shit Dr Lai made him do. If he saw the anger, he could control it, make it work for him. After the fizz came either a creative burst or the uncontrollable urge to punch someone. The mania made it impossible to guess which side would win. His eyes alone were enough to make Viljoen instinctively push his executive chair backwards.

"You shagged her," Low hissed. "That's how you know about The Indonesian. There's no way a fuckwit like you could have worked out who The Indonesian was before me. Richard was smart. I didn't like him much, but he knew his job. But even he couldn't give me the man. He could give me the figures, the gambles, the bets, the payouts, but he couldn't give me a name. Names don't pop up in data or on gambling websites. They're not fucking Facebook pages. And they don't pop up on these spreadsheets. Unless I'm missing something here, the only person I know that believes Jimmy Chew owes money to this Indonesian is Yue Liang. He must have cried to her about it one night. But that's it. So either Jimmy told you. Or she told you. And I don't see you being into buggery, even if you are South African. So I'm going with the wife. When did she tell you?"

Viljoen tried to suppress the pain rising at the back of his throat. He ran a finger along the framed photo. Low grabbed the frame and slammed it hard, face down, onto the mahogany desk.

"There. Does it make you feel better if you can't see them? When did she tell you about The Indonesian?"

Viljoen jumped. The bluster had gone. Fear consumed

him. The detective jabbed his finger against the back of the photo frame.

"You want me to call them? Do you want me to do that?" Low barked, his rage taking control. "Open your fucking mouth or I'll pick up the phone. When did Yue Liang tell you about The Indonesian?"

"The same day she told you," Viljoen croaked, barely able to get the words out.

Low sat back in his chair. He smiled at the parasite before him. "She went to you after she met me?"

Viljoen cleared his throat. "No, I, er ... I called her ... Richard had her number ... and after I found out about Jimmy's latest gambling losses, I thought I would try to help."

"No, you didn't. You thought you'd try and get into her panties. You thought about opening her legs while her previous *ang moh* sponsor was lying in the mortuary."

"No, no, no. I thought maybe she would find the information useful. So I met her, at her place in Bukit Timah, while he was out giving some seminar and told her. And that's when she told me about The Indonesian guy, and told me how powerful he was and how scared she was."

"What was she wearing?"

Viljoen eyed the scruffy Singaporean nervously. "What?"

"What was she wearing?"

"I can't really remember."

"Yes you can. Of course you can. You've dreamt of this moment, fantasised over it, wanked over it. Just you, home alone with her. I know I would. She's a walking wet dream. Everyone knows that. Even she knows that. And Richard definitely knew you knew that. That's why he kept talking about it, right? You know what you fuckers are like over here. If you've got a Porsche waiting for you in the garage, you want to tell everyone about it. You want to take photos of it.

You want it up on Facebook. You want to show all the old school friends back in South Africa how well you've done, especially the bullies who made your life a misery. You were nothing over there, nothing, a quiet little mouse, but here you're a Singaporean lion, a white god and you want the world to know. You're not being bullied any more, you're doing the bullying. You're doing the bragging. You can't help yourself.

"And Richard couldn't help himself, kept talking about her in the office, right, wetting himself over the water cooler. Showing off about it, bullshitting the whole time that he was shagging the hottest celebrity in Singapore, the one with the ass in the hip-hop videos, the one with the best tits in Singapore. Richard couldn't help himself. He was squeezing that ass. He was grabbing those tits. He was doing what every man in Asia wanted to do and he had to let someone know, someone he could trust, someone who would really appreciate his conquest, someone who would be jealous. So he told you. And the jealousy gave you a hard-on like your wife hasn't given you in years. So you thought, I want that. I can have that. If Richard had it, I can have it. I'll give her what Richard gave her. And then she can give me what she gave Richard. And I'll know what it's like. I won't have to dream about it anymore. I'll have it forever. Every time I shag my wife, I can think of her; her celebrity, her fame, her ass, her tits ... now, what was she fucking wearing?"

"I really don't think ..."

"Right, fine. I'll ask your perfect wife and your perfect child."

"What?"

"I'll visit your home and see if they have any idea what Yue Liang was wearing when you visited her when she was

116

home alone that night, that night when you told your wife you were working late."

"You'd do that?"

"I'm doing it, bastard. Tell me what she was wearing."

"A silk negligee," Viljoen muttered.

"Yes, yes, of course she was. She did want you after all, almost as much as she wanted Richard, maybe more if she was wearing the silk negligee."

"It wasn't like that."

"That's exactly how it was. The silk negligee is perfect for that ass and those tits. It's your fantasy fulfilled, right?"

"She turned me down, at first."

"So you forced yourself on her? Even better. *Wah* the Chinese papers will love that. *Ang moh* rapes sexy Singapore singer. Steady *lah*. You foreigners take our money, make fun of our poor people, riot in Little India and now you rape our women. You people are animals. Imagine the outrage. Even if it's not true, they'll still love it. Newspaper sales are declining. They're desperate. I've got an old crime reporter who looks after me with match-fixing stuff. He'll do. And I'll get some officers from another department to come down shortly. That's me done. Thanks for your time, dipshit."

"No, no, she turned me down, really, said she didn't know me and it was too soon."

Low stood up and stuck his face into Viljoen's. "Yes, yes, you degenerate bastard, so you forced yourself on her. The silk negligee was there, the tits were there, right in front of you. Normally, they're on the cover of a magazine, but they were right in front of you. You could see them, close enough to touch them. You'd earned them. You'd given her some good info and you'd driven all the way over, why waste it? Richard had her. You should have her. I mean look at him, he wasn't even as good-looking as you. I bet you played the

117

numbers game, didn't you? Every time he told you what a shag she was, you played the numbers game and thought, She's out of your league. He didn't even come close. But you and her were compatible. You were both in the same league. They weren't. You deserved her. She was yours. A dream shag after a long day. And now you're done. You're a fucking front page waiting to be printed."

"No, no, I didn't do that, I really didn't." Viljoen struggled to hold back the tears. "I didn't do that. I really didn't do that. Please don't tell my wife. My boy, he can't ... he just can't ..."

"Not my problem, rapist. He's just lost his Dad. He's going back to South Africa. And you're going to jail. I hope you don't have a sensitive arse. They love white arseholes in Changi. It's a rare treat for the *ah bengs*."

Viljoen started to sob as Low picked up his phone. "I didn't do that. I would never do that. She's beautiful. She's beautiful. I wanted it to be beautiful, I wanted her to want to ... I would never ... so I asked her again, just one more time. I leaned over on this sofa, a long leather sofa and I said she should want to ... said she should really want to ... because, you know, she wouldn't want me to ...to ..."

Tears rolled down Viljoen's cheeks. "She wouldn't want me to help the police and the media with their enquiries regarding Richard."

Low slumped back into the chair. For a moment, he didn't know what to say.

"You blackmailed her?"

"No, no, I helped her. I just wanted to help her. That's all. I was helping her. She needed my help. She had to think about her career and I ... I just wanted to ... you won't tell my wife, right? You can't tell me wife. This would kill her if she found out."

Low could barely raise his voice above a whisper. "You blackmailed her? Just after your friend was killed? You blackmailed her just so you could screw her. What kind of animal are you?"

As he continued to cry, Viljoen tried to assert himself. He wiped the snot and tears on the cuffs of his expensive white shirt. "I was just helping her. She was standing there, beautiful, lost. She was so vulnerable. I had to help her ... I had to. Anyone would. But you won't tell my wife right? You can't tell my wife. I've told you what you wanted to know. You can't tell my wife. My son ... please, you can't tell them."

Low stood up and grabbed the photo frame. He gently put it back into position on the desk, the photo facing away from Viljoen. "It's such a shame. They really do look like a nice family," he said.

The smiling Singaporean looked down at the weeping South African, then added, "Of course I'm going to tell your wife."

Chapter 11

YUE Liang scrunched up a cotton wool ball and wiped the foundation from her cheeks. She was wearing more Studio Mac than she used to. Her reflection in the mirror needed fudging. She was puffy. The crow's feet around the eyes were spreading. Botox was the obvious answer, but the murder made that impossible. The Singapore media mostly respected its artistes and there was no paparazzi culture to contend with. But these anti-government websites and wannabe journalists hounded her online. They said she couldn't sing. They said she had been entirely manufactured by her husband, that they were a pop bubblegum money-making machine, that she had a face like a horse and belonged at the Singapore Turf Club. The vitriol was spiteful and uncensored. Her beloved fans in the Government tried to play catch-up, but they couldn't close down the websites fast enough. She was persecuted so much online, the mainstream media had begrudgingly joined in. It was very lame and tentative, gently poking fun at the clothes she wore to the music studio each day, the puerile nature of her motivational lyrics and her grandiose claims of performing for a higher purpose for all Singaporeans. But further attacks were imminent. She knew that. The pot shots were mostly petty and cowardly, but the Richard Davie thing would finish her. Sleeping with his disgusting South African colleague had bought some time, but the whispers would reach the mainstream media eventually. And if the online crusaders found out, she was as good as dead.

She ignored Jimmy Chew as he blundered into her dressing room. She continued to remove her make-up. She refused to make eye contact through the mirror. None of this would have happened if her moronic husband had managed to keep his credit cards in his wallets.

Jimmy kissed her on the right cheek. She grimaced and brushed him off. As always, he was oblivious to rejection. "Great show, right? Plenty for the auction and plenty for me," he jabbered. "Got 11 name cards all interested in booking me for a seminar; if only half of them are genuine that's some serious money."

Yue Liang rubbed moisturising cream onto her cheeks. "That'll be good news for the illegal poker websites."

Jimmy put his hand on her shoulder. "I told you. I've stopped that. I'm focusing on my business and your career now."

Still unable to look at him, Yue Liang forcibly removed his hand. "If you're going to lie, don't do it while you're touching me. I'm not one of them outside. Don't bullshit me. Save it for your seminars."

Jimmy Chew stepped back. He seemed to wither, visibly hurt by the criticism. "I do everything for you, you know that. Everything. My whole career is for you and your career."

"You'll start singing in a minute. Have you booked my studio time yet?"

"What?"

"My studio time in LA. Daft Punk. They've said they'll consider producing my next album, but we've got to pay them. Everyone wants them now. So we've got to pay. Just working with them is a No. 1 on iTunes."

"Yeah, I know, of course it is."

"We want a massive rollout, global digital release, just like Beyoncé."

"Yeah, yeah, I know. We will."

Yue Liang put down the tub of moisturiser and scrutinised her husband. He looked even more pathetic in reflection. "You owe me this. The gambling, the shitty roadshows and seminars for *towkays*, you promised me you'd have enough money."

"I will. I do. I do, really. I'll get it together. These six or seven seminars should be more than enough."

"And first class? The bloggers will hammer me if they see me flying economy. Even the Chinese TV artistes go business class. Fix up something with SIA."

"Yeah, yeah, of course, first class, duh, what else? Of course first class."

"And the hotel?"

"I haven't done that yet. Let me settle the studio with Punk Daft first. Then I'll settle the hotel."

Yue Liang slammed her blusher brush on the table. "It's Daft Punk, you moron. Daft Punk. Are you sure you can do this?"

"Yes, of course, Daft Punk. I know that. I'm not a moron. I just spoke to a thousand multi-millionaires out there, held them in the palm of my hands for two hours. I do know what I'm doing."

As she swept the blusher brush across her flawless cheeks, Yue Liang laughed dismissively. "Please. I can raise more money for us with one push-up bra than you can talking shit for two hours."

*

Tan wanted to go home. He was tired and ready to return to his lovely wife's Peranakan cooking. No one made better *laksa*, and he was starving. He looked down at his bulging stomach, his constricted shirt tails desperate to burst free from his waistline. He used to be a slim man; a handsome man. His wife always said he looked like the actor Lim Kay Tong from *Growing Up*. Now she said he looked like Moses Lim from *Under One Roof*. He knew he wasn't that big, but he was ready to go home. And he was ready to retire. Stanley Low and Charles Chan still had the hunger—Chan had the enthusiasm, Low the tenacity—but the weary inspector had visited too many crime scenes. He found the blood stains tougher to scrub away.

He rested his head on his elbow and took a weary, sideways view of the monitor screen. He had stared at the door of room 4088 for hours. He could point out every scratch, mark and blemish on that bloody door. He counted every corridor light, every smudge on the window at the end of the corridor. He watched the other hotel guests staying on the same floor pass beneath the CCTV camera, stepping on the plush, swirly leaf-patterned brown carpet, dashing to and from the lift. In MBS robes, swimming costumes, suited and booted, frilly frocks and bleach-stained Bermudas, drunk, sober, beguiling, bedraggled, they all came and went to the rooftop pool, the restaurants, the mall, the theatre and the casino. He watched the world go by in a dingy police audio-visual room. On a small screen, he saw life being lived on video replay while he merely existed. Wealth, legitimate or otherwise, waltzed down the Marina Bay Sands corridors at regular intervals. Tan still wasn't sure he had enough savings in his Central Provident Fund to retire after 27 years in the Singapore Police Force, the Central Narcotics Bureau and its Special Task Force. That pissed him off. He loved his country, but he didn't recognise his country on the hotel's security cameras. The money, the confidence, the clientele; they were all foreign. As the inspector stared at the screen, he felt like a stranger in his own police station.

Eventually, he pushed some numbers on the desk phone beside him. "Hey, Charlie *ah*? ... Eh, don't start that now *ah*? Don't like it, change your name. You still at the charity thing? ... Ah, good, can come here and take over from me ... *Basket*, I been watching for hours. Can put in for overtime, I had enough already ... I watch this video the whole day they died. The whole day. I watch this corridor, the corridor above, the corridor below, nobody suspicious really goes into the room, not the whole day, no one, just the room service guy who left the *makan* outside, the cleaner who found them, and us. It doesn't make any sense."

Yue Liang brushed her hair vigorously in the mirror as Jimmy Chew changed shirts in the cramped dressing room.

"I'll need to get my hair restyled before the next video."

Jimmy stood over his wife, bare-chested. He was wiry, but already had the makings of a pot-belly. "You don't need your hair done. I love it like that."

"Different video, different look, you know that. We've done the geisha, the schoolgirl, the tiger mom, the businesswoman; this one needs to be different."

"You want this one to go viral in the US, right? How about the SPG? The *ang mohs* still love the Sarong Party Girl?" Jimmy laughed as he grabbed a fresh shirt from the hanger.

Yue Liang stopped brushing her hair. "Moron. No one knows what an SPG is outside of Singapore."

"Not an SPG exactly, you know, just like a hot Asian

chick, like Madame Butterfly. You know, you could get a tan, wear a long skirt, a cute vest and a tight bra, that's the *ang moh*'s dream, right?"

Yue Liang stiffened in the chair at the words "*ang moh*". "You just get the studio booked."

"I told you. It won't be a problem. All I've got to do is . . ."

There was an abrupt knock on the dressing room door. The couple stared at each other. Jimmy gestured for his wife to stay seated. "This is a private dressing room, who is it?"

"Ah, just a fan looking for an autograph," a voice behind the door replied.

Jimmy thought he was being strangled. He recognised the voice. Beads of sweat trickled down his back. "Ah, we don't usually open the door for autographs."

"Well, actually, it's more than just an autograph. I heard about Miss Yue Liang's pop career and I'm very interested. Perhaps I could help."

Yue Liang wiped her face quickly with a tissue. "It's OK, it's OK. Of course you can come in."

She pointed at her dithering husband and then the door. "Open it," she hissed.

"But we don't normally . . ."

"Just open it."

Yue Liang adjusted her breasts, improving the cleavage in the mirror. She smiled broadly as the attractive, well-dressed Chinese man entered. He shook both their hands warmly. Jimmy recoiled as their palms touched. Yue Liang gazed at his lightly-tanned skin and chiselled jaw line. "You're the one who bought that Indonesian temple. The gold one. It was so much money," she gushed.

"Ah, it was for a very good cause back in my country."

"You're Indonesian?"

"I am. But I seem to spend most of my time in Singapore these days, Miss Yue Liang."

"Ah, Yue Liang is fine. Everybody calls me Yue Liang."

"And everybody calls me The Indonesian. The nickname's a bit literal, but hey, that's Singapore, right?"

Yue Liang laughed too loudly. Her mask slipped. Her ignorance appeared false. Her husband busied himself with his shirt buttons. The Indonesian studied both of them carefully. Jimmy was a bundle of nerves. The wife was flirting. They were both desperate.

"Your song was beautiful by the way. *Higher Power*... such an uplifting song."

"Thank you, that's really kind."

The Indonesian gestured towards a chair beside Yue Liang. "May I?"

"Oh, of course. Come, come," she replied, patting the seat. Jimmy hovered behind them awkwardly.

"Thank you. I heard you say out there, and your husband said it several times that you're hoping to go to the US for your next album."

"Well, that's the ambition. With digital music now, the market is much bigger. Songs must cater to the world. Singapore and the Mandarin market in Taiwan just isn't enough anymore. Besides, my Chinese is terrible so I'm pretty much stuck with the English-speaking market."

"Well, that's your world, of course. It's not really mine. But I love your voice. I think you look great and I'd be happy to help produce your new album."

"You're a producer?"

The Indonesian laughed loudly and shifted in his seat. "No, I'm not. I know The Beatles and Bahasa ballads, that's it. But I might be able to support someone who knows what he's doing."

126

Yue Liang jiggled in her chair. She made little effort to contain her excitement. "You could do that for me ... for us ... why?"

"Singapore's been really good to me." The Indonesian inched his chair closer to Yue Liang. Their knees almost touched. He inched towards Singapore's most popular singer. His nose came close to her hair. "Can I say, you really have the most beautiful hair. May I?"

He held his hand out expectantly. He wanted the hairbrush. Yue Liang turned slightly towards her husband. Jimmy tucked his shirt into his waistband and pretended to ignore them both. Yue Liang flicked her hair back, smiled nervously and handed the brush to The Indonesian.

"Thank you," he whispered.

Without talking, he brushed the singer's long, silky hair. He moved slowly and gently. She closed her eyes and sighed. The Indonesian returned to the top of her scalp and dragged the brush a little more forcefully. Yue Liang groaned.

"That's nice. That's really nice," she murmured. She didn't open her eyes.

"Thank you," he responded, patting her knee. His hand caught her inner thigh, caressing it smoothly. Yue Liang winced slightly. She considered opening her eyes, but thought better of it.

As he lifted his hand and ran his fingers through her hair, The Indonesian turned and grinned at Yue Liang's husband. Jimmy tucked in his shirt sheepishly. He didn't look up.

The housemaid had to be lying. That was the only conclusion Chan could draw. His conspiracy theories were always being dismissed as the naive cries of youthful exuberance, but he was certain he was right this time. He yawned and pulled his notebook from under a clutter of papers left by Tan on the desk. He found her details: Madonna, Filipino, 35, worked at Marina Bay Sands since the integrated resort had opened in 2010, clean record, popular with staff and customers, two children back in Manila being raised by her younger sister, husband AWOL, parents dead; she was the textbook foreigner in Singapore. But still she had to be lying. She visited room 4088 three times. She cleaned the room before Richard Davie's arrival. She found his body the following morning. But she also went in to turn the bed down in the early evening.

The sergeant glimpsed the monitor. The frozen CCTV image captured her swiping the door lock with her card key at 5.45 p.m. She was the only person to enter the room after the room service guy earlier in the afternoon, and he was asked to leave the food outside. His story checked out. Tan knew all of this. He had viewed the footage. But he didn't know about Madonna. He hadn't interviewed her. Chan had. The junior officer rifled through the folders on his desk and retrieved Madonna's statement. The statement he had taken and she had signed. There it was. She cleaned the room. She found the body. She called her manager. She never mentioned the visit in between. It was brief. The CCTV footage had her in and out of the room in less than two minutes, but it was enough. And it was a lie.

Chan wiped his eyes and reached for his phone. "Boss, it's me ... *Yah lah*, sorry so late, didn't mean to disturb, but no choice. We gotta get the Filipino back in ... *Yah lah*, the room cleaner. She lied to me last time. You saw her go into the room three times, right? Right? She told me only twice ... Yep, I'm looking at her statement now, she said twice. How can she forget? She's bullshitting. This could be it."

Madonna looked dazed. She could not stop crying. She was terrified of the two Chinese police officers sitting on the other side of her table. She was adamant that she had done nothing illegal, but accepted that her innocence counted for nothing. They served Singapore. She was not Singaporean. Her word against their word was no word at all with the Ministry of Manpower. Foreigners were a dirty word in Singapore since the Government published its latest population targets. Singaporeans were squeezed and lashing out at the easiest, weakest targets. Filipinos already outnumbered native Eurasians. If they eventually outnumbered indigenous Malays, the public backlash might be brutal. As was expected of subservient Filipinos in Singapore, she smiled politely and quietly went about her business of washing the bed sheets filled with semen, blood and vomit at the country's most luxurious hotel resort. She kept her head down and her mouth shut; out of sight, out of mind. Singaporeans preferred it that way. But two Singaporeans were now ordering her to keep her head up and start talking. The tension was palpable, her fear self-evident. As Madonna wiped away her incriminating tears, she didn't see a cold instrument of law enforcement. She saw an unwanted exit visa.

"I've done nothing wrong, really," she sobbed. "I just want to go home and sleep. I'm so tired."

Tan almost nodded in agreement. He stole a glimpse at his watch. It was almost half past three. His wife had earlier scolded him for waking her up as he got dressed. He was back on the sofa again. After too many late nights and missed dinners, he had been struck out. He nudged the younger policeman under the table. This was taking too long. Chan laid out six CCTV images across the table. "Can you see that, Madonna? Look at this one. That's you going into room 4088 at 11.32 a.m. on the first day to clean it. That's you leaving the room the room at 12.11 p.m. Very good. The manager tells us that each room must be cleaned in 45 minutes. You are very efficient."

The young detective pushed two of the photos towards the Filipino. "Now, see these two. That's you going into the room, after knocking several times, at 12.05 p.m. the following day. And then, there's you coming out again, screaming and running down the corridor, still 12.05 p.m. You told me about those visits, right, Madonna? But you didn't tell me about this one, right?"

Chan lifted the other two photos and waved them in front of Madonna's face. "You went in again at 5.45 p.m. and were out again by 5.46 p.m. That's the day they were killed, Madonna. That night they were killed. And you saw them, right? You saw them at 5.45 p.m. You see the clock there? The camera never lies, but you did. Why did you lie, Madonna?"

Madonna blew hard into a tissue. "I didn't lie. I didn't. I just forget. I see so many rooms in one day. I cannot remember so many rooms. I turn down all the beds, must get to every room on all my floors. I don't have time to wait. Look. The camera is there. We all know that. We are always being watched. I must go in, go out, I cannot wait or disturb the guests."

Tan folded his arms on the table and scowled at the distraught woman. "Come on, Madonna. You are not looking at the photos. Or you are stupid. Look at the photo. Madonna. Look at the photo, now please, Madonna. You see your cleaning trolley? You see on the side? Can see or not? That is a clipboard. That is your clipboard. Every time you clean a room, change sheets, whatever, you must record on the paper there, right or not? You must tick the box, put in the time and then give to your supervisor. We checked with your supervisor. You wrote down room 4088, and put the right time, 5.45 p.m. You have to put down the right time, you know right? You not *blur* one. You know the boss can check all your routines on the CCTV in the corridor, just like us, so you cannot bluff one.

"Look at the photos, Madonna. *Look at them.* You went inside their room. You were inside for almost two minutes. The next person to go in the room, the person who found a dead body, was you, Madonna. We've checked and rechecked every minute of this CCTV footage. The only way into that room is through that door. It's not a suite. It doesn't have two doors, just one, that one. No one goes in before you. No one goes in after you. No one. The room service guy left the trays outside. So it's only you. No one else. And we have two dead bodies. Do you want to remember now, Madonna? Do you want to get your memory back or not? Or you want to be our prime suspect? I don't think you killed these people, I sure don't. But you're not helping us. The last person to see them alive is you. The first person to see them dead is you. You either go back home to bed or you go to a jail cell. Got no other choice."

Madonna rocked backwards and forwards. "But I been told I cannot say, I must not say ... he said I cannot say."

Tan leaned closer. "Who said? Who said you cannot say anything? Tell me."

"Him, of course. I cannot lose my job."

"Who are you talking about? Please. Don't waste my time."

"My boss. It's the same for everyone. No one can say what we see inside. We see so many things, but we can never say, even to you. It's our hotel policy."

"Who says, Madonna?"

"Our manager. The hotel manager."

"Who? Pierre Durand?"

"He says we can call him Mr Pierre."

"That's nice. What else did he say?"

"He will fire me."

"He won't fire you. But I can keep you here if you don't answer my questions. What did Mr Pierre say to you?"

"He says our guests pay a lot of money for their privacy, so if we see anything—anything at all—in the hotel room, even if by accident, even if we did not mean to see, we cannot say to anyone, not to our friends, not to anyone, not even the police. Mr Pierre tells us all the same thing. Privacy costs a lot of money at Marina Bay Sands. So we must give it to them."

Madonna continued to weep quietly. Tan held her hand gently on the table. She was a kind soul. "You must tell us what you saw. You cannot get into trouble if you tell us, OK? Double confirm, you will not lose your job. I guarantee that. We will deal with Mr Pierre later. Just tell us what you saw, OK?"

Madonna's gaze shifted uneasily between both officers.

"It's OK, really," Chan assured.

The plump Filipino sat back and faced the white wall behind the policemen. Her eyes widened. "I knocked several times. You saw on the video, right? I knocked three times first. There was no 'Do Not Disturb' sign. But I waited. You can see on the video, right? I waited. I knocked three times. 'Hello, housekeeping, bed turning down service,' I said clearly, loudly, but I didn't shout. We're not allowed to shout. I opened the door, only a little bit, but only after I knocked three times. I opened the door and looked inside. It was a mess. It was still so early, not night time, but the room was a mess. There were empty plates, rice on the floor, bottles on the floor, knickers, and bras, and, you know, other things to use for sex. I saw the white powder on the bedside table. I knew it was cocaine. But I did not say anything. The other maids say it keeps the guests awake. So they can gamble more. They stay awake, but they go crazy, cannot think, lose more

132

money. One time, I go into a room and this businessman ... you won't tell my boss, right? You cannot tell Mr Pierre."

"Just tell us what you saw in this room, Madonna," Tan said softly, tapping the photographs.

"I step inside the room and close the door quietly. I stand just inside to take a look."

"Was the balcony open?"

"No, it was closed. The net curtains were also closed. The room was quite dark, but I could see it was a mess. Sometimes I clean up a little bit, take away the dirty plates. I can do that. So I take a look. The bedroom is empty. And then I hear them. I hear them first. And then I see them, the white man and the Chinese woman, through a gap in the bathroom door. It's not fully closed. She was older than him. They are not wearing any clothes and, you know, I see that they are having sex. Sometimes we see this. We are a hotel. People go to a nice hotel to have a good time. That's why we knock so many times, but sometimes they still cannot hear us. So we just leave quickly. No one ever complains because everyone is embarrassed. But this one was ... different. It looks different. He is behind her, pushing her against the sink. They are standing in front of the mirror. He is pushing against her really hard. I can see they have more cocaine there. I see it on the sink all around them."

Madonna hung her head, humiliated by the memory. "I step backwards slowly and grab the door handle. I was scared. There was too much drugs and it was so ... fierce. It wasn't normal. They didn't look happy. As I start to turn the handle, he stops. He just stops. I think he hears me. So I freeze. I don't know what to do. I wait for him to turn around. I am so scared. The room is silent. I cannot open the door. They will hear me. I cannot move. But then he leans over the sink and goes for the cocaine. He puts two fingers in it, rolls them around until they are white. Then he lifts up his two fingers and rubs them between her ... you know ... her breasts ... and then he pushes his fingers into her mouth. He tells her to suck his fingers. And then he starts again, much harder, so fierce. And then ..."

Madonna lifted her hands into the air suddenly, bringing them together slowly. "He puts his hands around her like this ... around her neck ... and then says 'Relax'. That's all he says ... relax ... and he's pushing her so hard. She's making this funny sound like a ... like a ... it's not a real sound. She's pretending she's happy, but she's quite loud. And then ... oh Lord, please forgive me ... and then, she sees me. I think she sees me, through the mirror. Through the door. She looks into the mirror and sees me, right at the back of the room, over his shoulder. I cover my mouth. I think I'm going to scream. But my voice is gone. My arms and legs don't know what to do. I cannot move. I feel sick. We just look at each other. I wait for her to scream, or point, or shout, or do anything. But she just looks at me. And then, she puts her head down into the sink as he squeezes tighter ... squeezes and pushes. She gets louder. The sink makes her voice louder like a ... like an echo. She's so loud. She is so noisy. And then I realise. She is, I think ... she is trying to help me. I think she is helping me to leave. She makes noise so I can leave. So I open the door and get out. As I close the door, I just see her fingers grab onto the sink. I can see her fingers squeezing the side of the sink. Her hands holding on ... and I leave her there ... I leave her with him."

Chapter 12

DR Lai was wearing her pant suit again. Low always liked his psychiatrist's pant suit. Power plays intrigued him. He flicked at the leaves of the tall, rubber plant beside his uncomfortable leather chair. The room was decorated with the usual postmodern art, bought off the rack at IKEA, probably together with the plant. IKEA was popular for a reason. The place epitomised Singapore. It was a fast track to respectability; an artificial representation of materialistic wealth and comfort. The CPIB inspector never shopped at IKEA, but then he rarely shopped. All those people crammed into one location and fighting for space increased the chances of a manic episode, and he needed little encouragement at the moment.

He leaned forward. "I like what you're wearing today," he said, fully aware that he was flirting.

Lai crossed her legs, balancing her notepad on her knees. "I know you do. You said that the last time I wore it."

"Ah, so why do you keep wearing it for me, then?"

"I don't wear it for you. I see up to eight patients a day, five days a week. The hours are long and my wardrobe is small. Why did you miss the last appointment?"

"I didn't miss the appointment. I postponed it until today. That's not the same thing."

"You didn't turn up. You missed the appointment. Treatment can be improved with a level-headed consistency, regular hours, regular days and no erratic swings in schedules and day-to-day engagements."

"For Christ's sake, I'm an officer with the CPIB. Much of my work has been undercover. The *kaypoh* bastards that referred me here in the first place are the same people who can call me any time of the day or night to follow a lead, you know that."

"You didn't call my receptionist to change the appointment."

"No, I didn't. I was busy at the time interviewing a material witness in an ongoing double murder case. I'm so fucking sorry."

Lai brushed off the sarcasm. "Do you think you're being unnecessarily belligerent?"

"I don't know. Do you think you're being an unnecessary pain in the arse? You told me not to miss appointments and I understand that. I'm sure your BMW out in the car park doesn't pay for itself. So I'm here. I'm making up for the missed appointment and I'm here."

"And?"

"And what?"

"How do you think you've been this week? Any episodes? Any outbursts?"

"In the last hour? No. In the last week? I don't know. I lost count by Monday."

"What happened?"

"Nothing. I don't like Mondays. Is that where you shout, 'Tell me why'?"

"I can't make you take your condition seriously. I cannot force you to take medication. That's your prerogative. I cannot force you to do anything unless I consider you a threat to yourself or others. But you have bipolar II disorder. It's an ongoing disorder that requires ongoing treatment to manage the symptoms. The condition will not go away with the next big case you crack. It doesn't work that way. You will ride the high when you solve a case, I'm sure. It could conceivably trigger a period of hypomania, but ..."

"There is no 'but'. Why is there a 'but'? I find out why two people were killed in a hotel room and everyone will be happy."

Lai sat back. "But only for a little while. And it could go the other way, it's impossible to predict. The aggression is tougher to handle. Your previous episodes demonstrated that your mania highs are usually followed by a sustained period of anger and then depression. So the higher the euphoria comes if and when you solve this particular case ..."

"I *will* solve this case."

"... The euphoria that will undoubtedly arrive when you solve this case will possibly be followed with an overwhelming sense of anti-climax and worthlessness, perhaps even self-loathing, just like before."

Low fidgeted in his chair. "Ah, what do you want me to say? What the fuck do you want me to do? You want me to drop the case? Is that it? You want me to step down from the case, walk away from a double murder so I don't feel a little bit down in the dumps for a few days. Where do you think we are? Kindergarten? We're not Americans, we're Asians. No, fuck that. We are Chinese. We don't go crying to teacher. You know that. We're raised by tiger moms, not pussy dads crying that their parents didn't hug them enough. We breed tough. We die tough. We don't get all weepy about our feelings here because no one gives a shit. No one has the time, not even me."

"Then why are you here?"

137

"They sent me here after the Tiger case."

"I know why you were sent here, but I don't know why you're still here. You don't have to keep coming here. No one is compelling you to come here. I assume there must be a part of you that wants to get better. Why do you think you keep coming back?"

Low grinned across the glass table. "I can't surf the net for porn all the time, can I?"

Chan handed his boss a cold slice of pizza. He dropped pepperoni on the keyboard. Tan wiped away the grease with tissue paper, balled up the tissue and threw it at his sergeant. The monitor in front of them displayed the paused image of Madonna leaving room 4088 at 5.46 p.m. The picture was blurred, but her expression was unmistakable. She was horrified.

Tan tapped the computer screen. "So how? What do you think, Charlie?"

The younger man considered correcting his name, but quickly changed his mind. Time was getting on and the case was stalling. The boss had good reason to be grouchy. He took a deep breath. "I don't think she did it."

Tan turned to face his junior detective as a gloop of mozzarella cheese swung from his chin. "*Wah*, steady *lah*, Sherlock. You work that out for yourself is it? So clever *ah*. Sure get promotion now ... of course she never did it. She was only in the room for a minute. Where got time to hold down the strong *ang moh*, give him an injection, then give him tablets, then throw the girl in the suitcase. You think she's that Nicolas Cage, is it? *Gone in 60 Seconds*? *Wah lau*."

Chan looked hurt. "But she did hide this from us the first time. She never told me about going to the room three times. Why didn't she tell me?"

"Because she caught them having sex. Because she'll *kena* big-time from her French boss. She goes and tells 'Mr Pierre' that she went into the room and saw the cocaine, the kinky sex, then how? You think what? The Frenchman supports a Filipino cleaner over an *ang moh* big shot staying in an MBS suite? You see how unpopular Filipinos are right now? Don't joke. She'd be fired, poor thing."

"So you want me to speak to the manager, Pierre Durand?"

"What for? Talk to you for what? No need. Besides, if we need to *tekan* the fella, I'll ask Stanley."

Chan fiddled with the cold pizza slices in the box. He was clearly offended by the curt dismissal. "I can interview the manager, you know."

Tan looked up at him. "What? I know you can. *Wah*, so sensitive *ah*? But your best strength, also your biggest weakness. You're too nice, too correct, too much a government scholar. That's OK. I need that. You're very good with the government people, the families. You're handsome, polite, people trust you. All that I need. But that French manager is your typical CEO, full of bullshit. He'll bluff you one, because he's a bastard. So you need to be a bastard."

"I can be a bastard, especially after I heard what those fuckers were doing to the girls in the Straits Suite."

"Yeah, I know you can. So can I ... when it's necessary. We have to be," Tan chuckled as he bit into his pepperoni. "But no one can be a bastard like Ah Lian."

Lai watched the policeman fidget in his chair. He was attractive in an unconventional, almost un-Chinese kind of way. He was unkempt, certainly, punkish even; Singapore's answer to Sid Vicious. When he occasionally swaggered into her office in his white vest, he was more *Die Harder in Asia*;

Bruce Willis with twice the belligerence and half the charm. But his remarkable intelligence and quick wit aroused her curiosity.

Stanley Low was the worst kind of psychiatric patient because he was too self-aware of his own illness. He knew the benefits of bipolar; the incredible surge of energy, the manic desire to achieve. He was even aware of the advantages of his milder bipolar II, where there was still a sense of elevated creativity and ambition, but the mood swings didn't quite scale the heights of recklessness and megalomania of some of her other patients. Low had Napoleon's work ethic, but he never thought he *was* Napoleon. His intellect was occasionally boosted by a double shot of inspiration and industry. And hers wasn't. She recognised and diagnosed the bipolar condition, but could never fully understand it. Her highs came from further academic study and too much wine around Arab Street at weekends. Her highs were artificial. She willed them to happen from within. She made them happen. Low's highs were unstoppable; a freight train always threatening to hurtle off the tracks. She didn't want his illness. But from an academic perspective at least, she envied his untameable explosions of ingenuity. If nothing else, those firework displays in the brain must have been pretty damn colourful. But her professional and personal experience left her in no doubt. She wouldn't swap places with a bipolar patient for all the hedonistic highs in nirvana. She wouldn't want the lows, but mostly she wouldn't want to be like the inspector flicking her favourite rubber plant. Stanley Low was her brightest patient. He was also such an insufferable asshole.

Lai suddenly realised she had been doodling on her notepad for too long. She straightened her shoulders and put her pen down. "So, would you say you are at least trying to curb your aggression?"

He shrugged like a petulant child. "Not really. I need it to do my job."

"So anyone working for the Singapore Police Force can't do their job properly unless they have bipolar II and anger management issues?"

"I don't work for the Singapore Police Force. I work for the Corrupt Practices Investigation Bureau."

"OK. You know what I mean."

"They certainly won't do it as well as me."

"You solve every case you are assigned?"

"I have so far. And I'll solve this one too."

"But you're not a one-man police force. I assume your colleagues solve cases too?"

"Ah, you mean the normal ones. Yeah, OK. Look at the two guys I'm working with now. One is overweight, his blood pressure is sky high and he looks at least 10 years older than his age. He's a decent, old-school detective. He calls himself an old-school detective. He's dependable, solid, did some great things in narcotics with the Special Task Force; one of their pioneers back in the late 90s, some big busts. But his patriotism sometimes blinds his judgement. His marriage is alive, just, but ready to flatline at any moment. And the other one is a young kid who has just finished puberty and still cries at crime scenes. He's a government scholar, which means he'll instinctively say 'yes' to all his paymasters without questioning. Reasoning and initiative are skills best left to his superiors. He still believes that we're a sunny island in the sea all singing the same song. All the men in power dress in their purest whites, businessmen are good corporate citizens and police officers are so fucking noble, we might as well be riding horses and wearing a gold badge."

"Is a degree of idealism and a belief in right and wrong a bad thing?"

"Yeah, it is, in my job."

"But I'm sure you see the hypocrisy. If your world is rotten from the inside out, why are you so compelled to defend it? If everyone is morally and ethically moribund, why protect them? Why not leave them to fall into this abyss of their own making?"

"*Wah lau*, moribund? Abyss? Are we making poems now? We'll be doing storytelling sessions next. Actually, no, wait, I've got a story. You want to hear a story?"

"Is it relevant?"

"You like stories."

"Maybe we should keep the focus on you."

"Listen to this story. You'll like this story."

"There might not be enough time left . . ."

"When I first joined CPIB, I had this source, a contact, a construction worker from Bangladesh. He would give me tip-offs about a local gambling ring, nothing big, just a small illegal betting house in Bedok. But I was eager and desperate to make arrests, so I paid him a couple of bucks for *makan* and he gave me a few scraps here and there. Mostly he was working on the construction sites, scaffolding, back when it was all timber scaffolding, remember that last time? That's how he got me the scraps. A lot of the local Chinese and Indian supervisors were big gamblers, heavy gamblers, all bet outside. He found out which shophouses they used, the gambling dens, which bookies runners they used; small stuff. But I used him.

"One night I meet him in the coffee shop and he's got a black eye. He tells me the supervisor hit him for making a fuss. He tells me his *kaki*, his best friend from the same Bangladeshi village, falls through the timber scaffolding and breaks his legs, no compensation, no money for medical, nothing. My guy complains, says he's going to the Ministry

142

of Manpower, so the supervisor whacks him to keep him quiet. He comes to me crying, saying they are threatening to break his bones so he cannot work. They tell him to close his mouth or they break his legs, just like his *kaki*. So he's scared and asks me to help. I need him happy and working, so I go to the construction site as Ah Lian. I introduce my famous gangster to Singapore. And guess what? I'm a natural; it's unbelievable. I'm just a bloody natural. I'm like Daniel Day Lewis in a white singlet. I make up some bullshit story to the supervisor. I say, 'Fuck you *lah chee bye.* Cannot upset these workers OK? They all very good customers for my boss, if cannot bet, got big problem, OK? You fuck them, we fuck you.' So it stops. For a while. And my guy is very happy. But I can only do it once. I can only bluff these people once. I cannot risk blowing my cover and if I send in the Ministry of Manpower to investigate, the contractor could lose the contract, the workers could get sent back, anything can happen. But I'll lose my source. The man is feeding me my crumbs. I can't lose him.

"Of course, after three months, he starts complaining again. The supervisors are bullying his friends, not paying them, not giving them *makan*, giving them shitty housing, too many accidents on the site, it's not safe, cutting too many corners. I tell him I will fix them after I've settled my gambling case in Bedok. Be patient. Next time, he comes back with a cut face, tells me he fell off the scaffolding. I tell him to wait first. He comes back and tells me he's got another friend in the hospital, broken arm this time. I tell him to forget about it. He comes back and tells me they kept his wages because he's not working hard enough. I tell him just to focus on my illegal bookies, keep giving me the information and everything will be all right. He comes back and tells me he's going to the newspapers with payment slips that he says have been forged. He says he's going to show the newspapers his shitty living conditions and get them to interview the other fed-up workers. I tell him not to do anything until I've settled my case ... *my* case.

"The next time I go to the coffee shop, he doesn't turn up. Bastard. I was furious. About a week later, I see him again, in the newspaper, under a fucking blanket. They found him in an alley. He went to the supervisors after work one night and tried to give them one last chance. He told them he was going to the newspapers. He was so naive, so gentle, so fucking stupid. He actually told the supervisors he was going to tell the whole story if they didn't improve working conditions on the construction site. He gave these guys one more chance to do the right thing. He asked them to be fair and kind. So they beat him to death with scaffolding poles."

Lai sat and stared at the inspector. His eyes seemed to probe her, penetrate her. Eventually she breathed out and said, "How did you feel about that?"

"Honestly?"

"Yes."

"My first reaction was, 'Shit, I've lost my source'."

"How do you feel about it now?"

"The same as I did then. If you accept that the world is full of selfish bastards, then you are never disappointed. All I can do is catch as many as I can."

"Do you really believe that?"

Low pushed himself forward in his seat. "I followed that case through, right to the end, OK. The supervisors who killed him were of course the same fucked-up gamblers, the ones gambling with my illegal bookies. We got them in. We gave them the old-school CPIB treatment, held them for days, no lawyer, no phone calls, no sleep. We gave them ... you know ... actually, you don't want to know what we did to them. That's not your Singapore. It's my Singapore. We gave them the CPIB treatment until we got what we wanted. What *I* wanted. They confessed in the end. They always do. They told us everything. My Bangladeshi guy had asked them for an extra 20 bucks a month in his pay packet. That's it. Twenty bucks. So they crushed his skull with metal poles. That's the world I live in. I don't have your luxury of optimism. I'll do whatever it takes."

"What do you think about the poor man who died?"

Low shrugged. "He escaped."

Tan belched loudly as he lifted the pizza box. The desk was lost beneath piles of files, papers, empty coffee cups and cold, cheese-covered slices of pepperoni. "Is there any pizza left?"

Chan raised his crust in the air. "No, this is the last slice."

"Idiot. I'm still hungry. Pizza not enough for lunch. Is there any more food around?"

"I think there's some *keropok* next door. The cadets outside had some *goreng pisang* downstairs. You want me to get for you?"

"Please *lah*, I'm not going to steal supper from police cadets."

Tan downed the dregs of old coffee and shuddered. "We've hit the wall with this hotel room. Leave the Indonesian link to Low. You go with the dead girl Wong."

"I tried already. She had no family. She lived alone in a three-room flat in Balestier. She was just a KTV girl."

"Hey, balls to you, OK. Her name was Wong Yu Lin. She was 45 years old. She was a Singaporean, killed by a foreigner in my bloody country. I don't give a shit about her job, OK?"

"Sorry boss." Chan had forgotten the inspector's unshakeable patriotism. His boss' generation took such pride in their

HDB flats, mostly-reliable buses and trains, decent schools and hospitals and regular employment, as if that was enough to be grateful for in life. The much-travelled scholar struggled with the naivety.

"I know uniform are doing Geylang and Joo Chiat. She was arrested there before, but that was a long time ago already. Check out the other places. Go Orchard Towers. Use your initiative. If you say Wong is from Balestier, try Balestier."

"There's not much red-light stuff around there now, boss. Most of them moved out already. Can make more money in town, Orchard, Marina Bay, CBD. Hey, the Kallang side is booming with all the development around the new sports stadium and MRT in Jalan Besar, got construction workers looking for cheap girls."

"OK, fine. Try Kallang, Little India, Desker Road. But Balestier first, still got some KTV lounges down there and the *bak kut teh* damn *shiok*."

The young officer smiled. "You just want me to bring you back more food."

"You ate all the pizza. Make sure you bring back extra soup, plenty of pepper and garlic. Go *lah*."

As he shooed the kid out of the audio-visual room, Tan rubbed his hands together childishly. He adored pork rib soup, and Balestier's was still the best. He treated local food like a rabbit's foot. He couldn't make arrests without it. He couldn't understand the modern fixation with western muck like pizza. *Bak kut teh* was one of the few things that still made him proud to be Singaporean. Not much else did.

A phone started ringing. Tan sighed before rummaging through the mountain of mess on the desk. He located the phone beneath pizza-stained photos of Richard Davie and Wong Yu Lin's corpses. "Hey, hello ... Yes, it is Detective

Inspector James Tan ... What? When? Cannot be. You serious? ... Oh shit."

Lai held the door open for her unrepentant patient. This stubborn policeman pricked her professional conscience. He would never accept the appropriate treatment, so his condition could never be properly stabilised. They both knew this. And yet he kept booking sessions and she continued to take his money. She often wondered who was being violated in this arrangement. "So same time next week then?"

"Yeah, of course, as long as there aren't any major national crimes in the meantime," Low said as he strolled towards the door. "I wouldn't want to miss any appointments and incur your wrath again."

Lai smiled. He was impudent in a darkly funny, grotesque kind of way; a poster boy for bad bipolar patients. He was intelligent and occasionally witty, but forever tied to his belief that only he could save the world. He thought he was Superman with a police badge. She knew he was a mentally ill patient in urgent need of mood-stabilising medication. It was a shame really.

She tried one more time as he passed her in the doorway. "Do you ever feel guilt? When you knowingly abuse people when the mania takes over? Do you wish you could pull back?"

Low stopped and turned back. "Never. That's how I minimise those lows that you fuss over. I just focus on the highs, make them work for me. It's always about the bigger picture."

"And what's that?"

"Catching the fuckers."

Low wandered through the car park and switched on his phone. There were several missed calls, all from the same

147

number. Almost immediately, the phone vibrated in his hand. It was the same number. "Hello, who's been calling me so many times?"

"It's me, Tan. Where have you been?"

"Hey, James, this isn't your number."

"No, I'm still in audio-visual."

"Ah, really, what have you found?"

"Nothing, look, shut up. You know your gambling data guy, the South African."

Low rolled his eyes. "Yeah, Lennie Viljoen. He's an idiot. What does he want now?"

"He's dead."

Chapter 13

THE air-conditioning made little difference. Sweat trickled through Low's damp hair in the late afternoon sunshine. He parked beside a Ferrari and flashed his police ID at a fussy car park attendant who was about to move him on. Battered old Toyotas coming to the end of their 10-year cycles didn't fare well between the Ferraris at the Fullerton Hotel car park. One of Singapore's oldest and grandest colonial buildings was rightly proud of its heritage and exotic splendour. The hotel might sit in the shadow of the gambling leviathan on the opposite side of the bay, but the Fullerton was around long before Marina Bay Sands. The integrated resort was the new kid on the block, but the old dame had been turning heads for decades and still did. Her sex appeal had never diminished; if anything it had increased as the sterile skyscrapers mushroomed around her. The Fullerton was a MILF surrounded by younger, glassy-eyed beasts all jostling for Marina Bay's attention. As he pulled his cap down low, Low stood beneath the imposing granite pillars of the Fullerton's colonnade and sighed. He felt so small.

The gawkers had already gathered. Low pushed his way through the crowd behind the bus stop. On both sides of Fullerton Road, tourists and locals jostled for a better

149

position. Even the Merlion was being ignored. After a buffet lunch in Chinatown, the coach parties couldn't believe their luck. The lion-mermaid thing wasn't going anywhere, nor was the Singapore Flyer or Marina Bay Sands, but the police would remove all the body parts soon. The tourists snapped quickly. They were already uploading their photos on Facebook as Low ducked under the police tape around the hotel's garden.

Uniformed officers pushed the rubberneckers back into the main road, forcing car drivers to honk their horns furiously. They no longer had a clear view of the crime scene on the Fullerton's manicured gardens. The long, sheltered bus stop and the hotel's screening bushes afforded the police some privacy. A video screen at the bus stop ran ads for upcoming musicals at Marina Bay Sands on a loop. Low carefully sidestepped the shrubbery as he heard the familiar, authoritative voice of Professor Chong from inside the police tent. "Head suffered massive trauma upon impact ... skull entirely smashed ... legs shattered ... left arm severed at shoulder, suggesting the impact was on the left side ... extent of injuries to arms, legs, shoulders and back would seem to corroborate eyewitness accounts that the victim jumped from the top floor ... ah, Detective Inspector, over here."

Low peeked into the makeshift tent favoured by the Singapore police to keep out onlookers and flies, and to keep in the smell. Dusk was still a few hours away. The heat was insufferable. Chong stopped the voice recorder on his phone and waited for the inspector to crouch down alongside him. Low raised his forearm to his nose and bent down beside the chubby pathologist. Singapore's humidity had no sympathy for the dead.

Low recoiled slightly as he kneeled beside the disfigured

150

remains of Leonard Viljoen. "Fucking hell," he exclaimed. "His face is gone."

"What did you expect? You see kids when they fall off scooters and scrape their faces. But that's nothing more than a cheese grater along the cheeks. He's jumped from the rooftop balcony. The scrapes along one leg there, they look like scratches rather than impact wounds. His leg might have clipped that slanted slate roof up there and bounced him heaven knows where. He appears to have hit the pavement face first. The cheekbones are shattered, his nose and his left eye were pretty much torn off and ripped out on impact and his brain is, well, you can see, it's everywhere. The brain turns into mashed potato. In fact, we couldn't contain it all inside the tent. At least 20 per cent is still scattered around the garden, in the bushes, maybe even around the bus stop and the pavement. We've covered as much as we can with the sheets. The poor man is everywhere."

Chong examined Viljoen's head again. The left side of the dead man's face resembled a scooped-out coconut husk. "Suicides in Singapore are invariably the worst. We don't have easy access to guns or drugs, but we all have access to high-rise buildings. So we jump. It's easy, accessible and so incontestably efficient. Even in death, we're so damn *kiasu*. The trouble is, of course, suicide leaves such a ghastly mess, especially when it's in the middle of the day like this, such a dreadful fucking mess."

Low watched the perspiring pathologist. He had never heard the old man swear before. He cleared his throat. "But it's definitely suicide?"

"Oh, I would think so, based on what James has already told me and the witness statements, and the way he fell."

"The way he fell?"

Chong rested his hands on his knees and faced the shabby

officer. "Consider the height of the Fullerton Hotel compared to HDB apartments and condos. It's not particularly high, barely 40 metres tall. There is still some control of the body. When people are pushed from such heights, shorter heights, there is often a conscious, or even subconscious, attempt to break the fall, to protect and cover the head and torso, to even try and land feet first. From these heights, there is a kind of psychological desperation, a stubborn belief that 20, 30, 40 metres gives us half a chance if we somehow land properly. It makes no difference of course. Their femurs are smashed into a hundred pieces, but there is a discernible difference in how they land. Bodies from five or six storeys are rarely the same as those who fall from 40 storeys. Look at this man, your man. Look at the mess. He went down head first. He practically dived down, deliberately and quietly."

"Quietly?"

"Ah, that's the other tell-tale difference between accidents and suicides. According to eyewitnesses, he never screamed."

The inspector stepped outside to answer his phone. Onlookers instinctively took photos of him as they pressed against the police tape traversing the crime scene's perimeter. He checked his cap again, pulling it over his eyebrows. Crime scenes in such high-visibility areas did him no favours. Of all the places that bloody South African could've killed himself. "Yeah, hello, where are you?"

"Right above you," Tan replied.

Low craned his head. His colleague was standing on the decadent glass balcony that protruded from the Fullerton roof, his bulging stomach leaning over the letter 'T' of the Fullerton sign. "Oh, yeah, I see you."

"Come up now, and don't let anyone else follow."

*

Low nodded a gruff greeting as he passed a gaggle of uniformed officers standing around gossiping. The top floor of
the Fullerton Hotel was certainly plush. The carpet scrunched
beneath his feet and the polished glass tables gleamed in the
Marina Bay sunlight. A suited hotel executive busied herself
with the table, checking her watch constantly and trying
to kill time. If that idiotic suicide victim was still alive, she
might have killed him. On top of the negative, superstitious
aspects of a man jumping from her bar and restaurant balcony,
which would obviously hurt trade in the coming weeks, he
had to go and throw himself off the building in front of the
busy lunchtime crowd. Her hotel bar and restaurant was
now closed to paying, refined guests and open only to non-
paying ruffians doing pitiful impressions of organised police
officers. She couldn't even think about laying out her evening
menus. Her professional training forced her to smile at the
Chinese inspector dressed like a gangster in his baseball cap
and scruffy jeans as he made his way around the empty tables.
His mental illness forced him to ignore her.

The two inspectors met on the balcony. Tan checked over
his shoulder to make sure no one else was within earshot.
"Hey, Stanley. You saw him then?"

Low peered down at the crime scene, uniformed ants
scurrying around their queen pathologist throughout the
Fullerton gardens and inside the police tent. "What's left of
him, yeah. Those cleaners all the way over at One Fullerton
will be jet-spraying his brain off the pavement for days."

"You have to be so graphic *ah*?"

Both men watched the crawling cars snake their way
around the crime scene along Fullerton Road. Traffic
stretched back to Suntec City and the Nicoll Highway.
Sheltered from the sun beneath their umbrellas, tourists huddled on the kerbside. Amateur and professional photographers

swarmed everywhere, clicking from the street, from cars, from the tops of buses, from the old Clifford Pier, Change Alley and the office blocks, even from the *sampans* taking tourists through the artificial bay. Tan sighed. Viljoen's death had promoted the case to the front pages. Online crusaders would swiftly follow suit.

Low frowned. "Why did he have to do it here?"

"Who knows? The symbolism? Marina Bay Sands would've been the last thing he saw," Tan said as he pulled a piece of crumpled paper from his pocket. "That's why he did it."

The letterhead bore Sports Watch's distinctive logo. The handwriting was surprisingly legible and clear. The note read: *"You left me with no choice, Low. Are you happy now? Please, please don't tell my wife. There's no need now. Fuck you."*

Low swallowed hard. The words blurred on the paper. He was losing focus. That familiar sickening feeling rose from his stomach and washed over his body. His confidence evaporated. His thought process vanished. He suddenly felt exposed, naked. His worthlessness was self-apparent. Even Tan would be able to see it. Negativity flooded his brain. He was awash with bitterness and self-loathing. He stopped hating the world. The world now hated him. He was shrinking, imploding from within. He could no longer look his colleague in the eye for fear of being exposed. Weakness was crushing him. His mind was melting, his dignity dissolving. He had to escape before anyone else noticed. But there were no words. Words were his enemy now. Every aggressive utterance would be an act of self-flagellation. He would beat himself before beating others, lashing out indiscriminately, exposing his sick soul and blowing his cover. But he had to say something. He had to find the words. He had to find words. Find them. Find them now.

"So ... what do you ... I mean ... where ... where was this found?"

Tan studied his colleague's face hidden beneath the cap. The eyes darted around like pin balls as the inspector tilted from side to side. Finally, the older man pointed towards a table that Low had missed earlier. A folder, a phone, a wallet and an empty beer bottle had been neatly laid out. The table had been taped off.

"It was there inside that folder," Tan said, pointing. "Everything was premeditated. The suicide note was written on his company paper and no pen was found on him, so it looks like he wrote it in the office and brought it here for you with the folder. The folder seems to contain the gambling records of Jimmy Chew, and the websites and syndicates he was using, nothing you didn't already know, but I'll let you take care of that. But he brought the note and folder in for you, had a beer, walked out to the balcony here and jumped. We haven't checked the phone yet."

"It ... er ... it won't tell you much ... the last call will be to his wife ... probably just a couple of minutes before."

"How do you know?"

"That's all he was thinking about ... that's all he would've seen in his mind before he ... that's why he jumped ... I think it's best if ..."

"Hey, are you OK or not?"

"I'm ... er ... I mean, you know ... the note is a bit of a shock and ... I'm ... it's hard to think."

"Would you have told his wife about Yue Liang? You know, Viljoen's wife. Would you have told her? I know you said you would, but it wouldn't have helped our case either way."

"I don't know ... I mean, I don't know ... maybe ... can I keep the note?"

Tan snatched the note back. "Of course not, *wah lau*. Are you OK or not?"

"No, no ... I mean ... maybe I could use the note to ... I don't know ..."

"Come on man. You know you can't have this note, you know *what*. Only one other officer has seen it, a *kaypoh* uniform guy who got here first and had a look through the stuff on the table. Then I arrived and took it. But it's a suicide note with your name on it. You made a threat ..."

"Yeah, but, I don't know ..."

"You made a threat and he's dead. He was involved in an ongoing murder case. Come on man, you know all the investigations lately, anything involving government body, stat board, police force, anything, must be investigated. We can't buy new police bicycles without being checked. And you're CPIB some more. CPIB got enough problems. Cannot have any more bad publicity, there must be an internal investigation."

Tan put the note in his pocket and smiled gently before continuing, "When the time is right of course."

"So how? I don't know ..."

"Go home, rest *lah*. Leave Chong and the team to finish up here. You shouldn't be here."

Low adjusted his cap and stared at Tan's polished black shoes. "Yeah, yeah, OK, can. Thanks."

Tan watched his friend shuffle away, slowly and pathetically. He didn't recognise this pitiful, broken man. "Hey, Stanley, wait *ah* ... would you have told his wife or not?"

Low stopped but didn't turn round. "Probably."

His friend turned back to the organised chaos beneath the glass balcony. Uniformed officers were extending the crime scene, stretching the police tape past the shrubbery and onto Fullerton Road. Onlookers pointed to the pavement beside the bus stop. A horrified mother hugged her young daughter, covering her eyes. She was hysterical, wrapping her arms tightly around her mother's waist. Tan exhaled loudly. The little girl had found another piece of Leonard Viljoen.

"I walk this street every night," Julie Teo told Chan, "and I never meet any Yu Lin. Don't get many locals like last time. Even if you never show photo, I would still know. You look around already? Where got Singaporeans? Locals almost finish. We just come here for *makan*, KTV maybe. The pretty ones can go Marina Bay or Sentosa, outside casino, maybe Clarke Quay, get *ang moh* customer, but the rest, forget it, *lah*. Cannot compete. You see the girls come here from China, Vietnam, Philippines, so young, so skinny. Pimps don't give money for *makan*, so cannot get fat one. So sad. And now they even got from Cambodia, only 15 years old. Virgins some more. The customers pay extra for virgins you know."

Chan nodded. He detested this part of the job. He'd rather direct traffic in Mountbatten Road than interview young girls with old faces outside a Balestier KTV lounge. They looked after their bodies, but their faces betrayed them. They were still pretty, but the eyes were vacant; pretty and vacant. They were haunted. No amount of foundation or eyeliner could hide that.

"So you think around here, Balestier, Whampoa, Serangoon side don't have Singaporean, er, Singaporean . . ." the blushing detective struggled to find an appropriate euphemism.

"Whores *lah*! I know what we are, can."

Chan's face turned puce. "No *lah*, I didn't mean . . ."

"Hey, you catch assholes, I sleep with them. What to do?"

"You're a good woman, Julie."

"That's what they tell me before. Then they go back to their wife."

The impressionable officer laughed. He had always liked Julie. Their paths had first crossed when he was still in uniform. His driver had wanted to move her away from Joo Chiat's landed properties and private streets after the neighbourhood police post received too many complaints from prominent residents; the ones not employing Julie's services. But Chan refused to escort her away from the rich and shove her into a housing estate for the poor. The hypocrisy bothered him even as a rookie. Singapore became a tale of two cities the day he was discreetly asked by his superior office to dump Joo Chiat prostitutes at a nearby HDB coffee shop in Marine Parade. The rich refused to tolerate sex and sleaze on their doorstep. They paid for it to come to hotel suites at Marina Bay Sands instead.

"Why you end up in Balestier, Julie? There cannot be many customers here these days."

"Still got. The *makan* over there brings taxi drivers, the shops still bring contractors, electricians, some construction workers, you know. As long as still got *bak kut teh*, can still make it. We all come for the *makan*, right?"

"But you can do better somewhere else."

"Better how? More foreigners, more *towkays*? Forget it *lah*. Here, everybody local, like me, I prefer local, just like last time. More respect. If some foreign asshole beats me in Geylang, then how?"

Chan pointed at the famous *bak kut teh* stall on the corner. The owner attended to a long queue as customers balanced bowls of soup on stained trays, searching for empty stools. "You *makan* already?"

"*Yah lah*, no choice, KTV busy soon. You go inside?"

"Yeah, went there first. I check with everybody on this street, no one knows Yu Lin. Cannot be right if her address is just behind the shophouses."

"It's correct *what*. Shit outside our houses for what? Eh, good luck *ah*, must get ready."

"You look good already."

"Please *lah*. Keep your sweet talk for your wife."

Low rolled onto his side and stared at his battered air-conditioning unit. The rattling was driving him crazy. He stretched across to his bedside table, picked up his wallet and threw it at the rusty contraption wedged into his bedroom window. It missed. The wallet hit the tiled floor. Coins rolled under the bed. Low pulled the duvet to his chin and noticed a couple of tiny cockroaches attacking the cold chicken rice beside his wallet. One cockroach climbed over the open polystyrene lid and crawled across the dried clumps of white rice before settling on the loose flesh of a boiled chicken wing. The other cockroach balanced on the edge of the polystyrene lid as it made its way to the corner of the packaging. As Low observed the cockroach's progress, it appeared to slip, missing the chicken rice and landing on the tiled floor on its back. The cockroach wriggled its legs furiously, spinning around in circles. Slowly and quietly, the inspector reached behind his bedside table and unplugged his alarm clock. Gently sitting up, he wrapped the plug cord around the alarm clock before taking the small, round device firmly in his right hand. He threw the alarm clock hard at the cockroach eating the chicken wing. The alarm clock smashed into the polystyrene box. Rice and chicken bones slid across the tiled floor as chilli sauce splattered against the wall beneath the air-con unit. Low slipped beneath the duvet once more and closed his eyes.

He ignored the rattling air-conditioner. The cockroach lying on its back continued to kick its legs.

Chan picked up the bowl and slurped the dregs of his *bak kut teh*. Soup dribbled down his chin and the pork ribs tickled his lips, but he didn't care. He wasn't in Marina Bay now. Balestier people didn't cast judgements.

"Hi ham-some."

With the bowl still in his mouth, two heavily made-up women joined him at the table. Sweat drizzled down his face as the peppery soup worked its way through his pores. On the edges of his chin, the perspiration joined the *bak kut teh*, forming tiny tears of unattractiveness. He wiped the lot onto his shirt, leaving a yellowy streak along his forearm. The young officer was aware of what he looked like right now. He was anything but handsome.

"Hello ladies, everything OK?"

The younger, prettier prostitute caressed his hand on the table. "Yah, you very ham-some."

Chan raised his hand and pushed his thumb against his ring finger. "I'm also very married."

"Yah? All our customers married, *what*."

The detective eyed them both curiously. They were too attractive for Balestier, too upmarket. Their clothes were put together, rather than thrown together, and they looked less beat-up than usual. They were out of place. "Hey, you are both local, right? Why are you here?"

"Same as you . . . *makan*," said the younger woman, happily adjusting her cleavage. "This *bak kut teh* the best, healthy and cheap. After this, no need dinner, only supper when we finish."

Chan nodded towards the quiet Balestier Road as a bus trundled past. "But no business here, right?"

"Hey, you ask a lot of questions."

160

"I'm police."

Both women stared at the young Chinese guy in a smart but unremarkable white shirt. The young, pretty one laughed. "You say you are, so must be is it? You think we *blur* is it? You say you are police and get a free fuck? What? You think we KTV *xiao mei mei* is it? Cannot bluff me one."

Chan smiled and slid his police ID across the table. It stopped beside a greasy pork rib bone. "So I photocopy this is it?"

The women hunched over the table, examined the photo closely before looking up at the smug detective. "Yah, so what? You still looking for a free fuck?"

"No, I'm looking for girls who know this woman."

He handed them a photo of Wong Yu Lin. "You see this woman before?"

"Yeah, of course. It's Rosie. She used to work at that KTV lounge over there last time."

Chan was sure the women would hear his thumping heart. The beats were deafening. He inhaled sharply. He had to remain detached. He had to be hard and aloof, just like his cold bastard of a boss Stanley Low. "Her name was Wong Yu Lin."

"Is it? Don't know. We just call her Rosie."

"OK, so how you know her?"

"We were neighbours last time, in Whampoa. She helped us when we started, told us what to do, who to get, how to see rich guys, how to see assholes, how to see policemen."

They both laughed. Chan didn't. He had to keep them on track. "Yeah, yeah, so she lived around here, right?"

"*Yah lah*, used to be in same block as us last time. Some of the girls live in Whampoa, Balestier. The HDB here very close to CBD, can just take one bus, MRT from Novena, very convenient, and rent cheap. OK *lah*, not cheap, nothing cheap like last time, but can still make it."

"So you worked with her before? You had the same ... the same ..."

The young, pretty one flashed a furious look at the detective. "Eh, we don't have pimp, OK? Look at us. We don't need pimp. We don't work here. We're not Geylang girls, OK? We don't waste this on taxi drivers and construction workers. We go Clarke Quay, Marina Bay, get nice *ang moh* or China *towkay*. We don't fuck shit, OK? She was the same," she said, tapping the photograph of Wong Yu Lin slowly, gently.

Chan noticed the attractive woman's tenderness. She really was quite beautiful. She had alluring eyes, razor-sharp cheeks and silky hair. She deserved better. He wanted to take her away—that was his weakness, as Detective Inspector James Tan was always quick to point out. Besides, she had made her bed, and it would always be somewhere else, with someone else, until she got lucky; until she hit the jackpot and reeled in one of her naive, love-struck punters permanently. And she would. A randy *towkay* or a *blur ang moh* flush with cash and no common sense; she'd force a ring on a rich finger in the end. And then, of course, they paid for her services every day. The meter would never stop running then.

"Hey, I'm sorry. I didn't mean to, you know. I just need to find out about this woman, Wong Yu Lin. So, did you all go to the city together?"

The prostitute grabbed the detective's lime juice and sipped slowly. She wiped her mouth, never taking her eyes off Chan. "No *lah*, we never worked together. She was too old, almost 50 already, but still pretty right?"

Her friend nodded as she continued. "She was ready to retire. In fact, she did retire last time. She left for a long time and then, suddenly, she come back, saying she must find work. She always went into the city, always Marina Bay, hotel, casino, since it opened. She told us. Don't waste time at the wrong time. She always said that, right?"

Her friend nodded, smiling at the memory.

"That was her favourite. Don't waste time at the wrong time."

"What did she mean?" Chan asked.

"Well, don't waste time here, in the heartlands, no need—too many police posts, too many locals always complaining. Singaporeans always complain. Plus now got too much competition from China girls, Vietnam girls. Too much honey, not enough money. Orchard Towers even got Russian girls some more. How to compete with *ang moh* hair? Even if we dye hair, cannot make it against Russian girl, blonde hair. So, we go into city, the new city. First, go casino. Marina Bay. Get them early when they stop for *makan*, still happy, still horny, still got money. When it's late, forget it *lah*. They gamble all night until money finish. That's it. So after Marina Bay, go Clarke Quay, or Scotts Road, a lot of *ang mohs* around that Marriott, the Hyatt. Always catch one at that nightclub next to Hyatt—BRIX—so easy one. Wear the sexy, red G-string, get them drunk, but make them pay first. Still horny, still got money, but most cannot make it. Finish five minutes, fall asleep. Just nice. Come here for supper."

"But Miss Wong mostly went to Marina Bay?"

"No choice, too old already. *Ang mohs* don't want old ones, unless they want the MILFs. See so much porn, everybody want MILF. Sometimes tourists want the Asian MILF, so she go Marina Bay. Still got *towkays*, or worst case, can get old China man, Japanese, then can make it."

"She gets all her customers herself?"

"No *lah*, of course not, some Indonesian help her."

Chan felt a tightening, tingling sensation in his stomach. "An Indonesian guy? Does he live around here?"

"*Yah lah*, he live in Toa Payoh," she sniggered. "Are you mad or what? Of course not. Hey, are you gonna pay me? Take up so much time. I talk so much already. You give me 50 bucks."

Chan laughed incredulously as he pointed to his watch. "We only talk for five minutes."

"Ah then? Must get the bus, but it's too late already. Now must take taxi. We need $50 for the taxi."

"Are you going to Johor in this taxi or what?"

"You want our help or not?"

Chan reached for his wallet. "Yes, yes, OK. Wait first."

"Eh, what are you doing? Not here *lah*, policeman, outside when we finish."

"OK fine, whatever. Where does this Indonesian live?"

The prostitute sat back contentedly, clearly satisfied with the financial arrangement.

Her friend nodded in agreement. "I think can *lah*," she said.

"OK *lah*, but 50 bucks OK? . . . She said he stay at Marina Bay Sands. His clients the best, money damn *shiok*. Rosie only work for him, no need anyone else."

Chan could almost see the promotion and the pay rise on his bank statement. "Did she say who he was getting for her?"

"No need. We don't talk like that. I saw her just last week, or maybe the week before, cannot remember, at the coffee shop. She said that Indonesian had a good one for her, very rich one, at MBS. That was last time I saw her. She OK or not?"

Chan studied her face closely, looking for an angle, a bluff. She appeared to be sincere. "You don't read the papers? The Chinese papers?"

The prostitute flashed her captivating smile again. "What for? Can get lottery results on my phone."

164

Chapter 14

LOW had no idea what the time was. As the sunlight gradually streamed through the window grilles into his bedroom, he guessed it was late morning. He felt the damp patch around his back, but he refused to move or switch the air-conditioning back on. With the duvet pulled back, he looked down at his pathetic body. Skinny, but flabby, a clichéd Chinese policeman gone to seed. He had always hated his body, fucking *ah beng*'s body.

Everyone called him *ah beng* at school. He was almost bilingual, but predominately English educated and still they mocked him; the squatting, skinny gangster. His wiry frame betrayed his obvious intelligence. No matter what he said, no matter what he did, he was the *blur* one; the skinny one with the greasy black hair; the idiot; the *sotong*; the bookie; the durian seller; the *ah beng* squatting on the MRT train. He was an intellectual in a gangster's clothing. He was a fucking waste of space.

He hated everyone for stereotyping him, for judging him. He hated himself for being judged. Just one look and he was pigeonholed. They all thought they knew who he was. But he knew who he was. He could fool them, but never himself. They saw Ah Lian. He saw a detective inspector. There was nothing between them. They were both parasites—one destroyed his environment, one destroyed himself. What was the difference? On any given day, it was a coin toss. They all hated Ah Lian. He loathed DI Stanley Low. He was useless, fucking useless, nothing more than a playground bully forcing others to give him what he wanted. He abused them, mocked them, ridiculed them, crushed them, harassed them, haunted them. Because he could. He didn't do it for a case. He did it for himself. He ripped their insides out, scooped them hollow until there was nothing left to give. Perhaps then they might be as empty as him, as disgusting as him, as pathetic as him. If he convinced them to hate themselves as much as he hated himself, he might sleep better. But Low didn't sleep at all. Self-loathing fed insomnia. The lows kept him awake. The highs kept him awake. He only slept when he was Ah Lian, working undercover. He slept enough for both of them. Low didn't deserve sleep. He didn't deserve anything. Ah Lian kept him going. Low kept him in bed. He couldn't face the world if he couldn't face himself. He couldn't confront himself. He just couldn't, not today. Low turned away from the mirror on his bedside table and closed his eyes. He hated mirrors, almost as much as he hated himself.

It was a struggle for Chan to balance the silver tray filled with four pieces of *prata*—two egg and two *kosong*—a plate of fish curry, another of mutton curry, a lime juice and a *teh tarik*. He pushed past the queue and squeezed between other diners at the bustling coffee shop before reaching Tan's table. With his tongue hanging out, he gently lowered the tray onto the table. His boss gestured towards his mouth. "Come on man, are you a kid or what? Put your tongue away."

"My tongue?"

Tan mocked the junior officer, poking his tongue out and nervously holding an invisible tray. "Ooh, must not spill the tea, must not spill the curry. Sit down. Idiot."

The attention had made Chan nervous. He clattered the tray onto the table and curry splashed across the tea cup.

"*Wah lau*, Charlie, are you butterfingers or what? Sit down *lah*."

"Well, you make me nervous. Make fun of my tongue. I don't know my tongue flaps around when I'm concentrating."

"You must make your wife very happy."

Both men laughed. The younger officer surveyed the busy coffee shop. Families, young couples, foreign workers and businessmen huddled together, sipping fresh fruit juices and dipping *roti prata* knuckle-deep into their curries. "Why you make us come all the way to Jalan Kayu? Can get *prata* anywhere."

"This is the best *prata* shop in Singapore. Been coming here since I was a rookie."

"Yeah, but they got Jalan Kayu *prata* at Tanjong Katong, got another good one opposite Kallang MRT. This one so far from the office."

"This one is the best. This one is a good place to talk without being disturbed. This one also near my house."

Tan bit into his egg *prata*, licking his fingers as the fish curry trickled down his hand. "So how? They were certain they knew her, is it?"

"They picked her out, boss, called her Rosie. They knew where she lived last time, the KTV lounge where she worked. I spoke to the doorman outside the KTV, he also confirm. Plus, a Tiger Beer lady at one of the coffee shops nearby said she used to go in there for supper. It's definitely her."

"Yah, so? We know she lived in Whampoa before."

"Yah, but these girls said she mostly went to Marina Bay

Sands and only worked for The Indonesian, since she came back from retirement."

"Only The Indonesian? No one else? They never saw her with any *ang mohs*, never see her with Richard Davie before?"

"Nope. They never saw her with anyone. She never brought customers home, they said. She always went to them at Marina Bay."

"And the girls definitely said she only worked for this Indonesian? No one else?"

"That's what they said."

"Shit."

The phone rang. Low ignored it. The phone rang louder. He pulled the duvet over his head. The phone rang louder still. He sat up in bed and glared at his mobile as it slowly vibrated its way across his bedside table. The phone continued to ring. He thought about answering it. He also thought about throwing the phone out of the window. Instead he rolled onto the other side of the bed. It made no difference. The ring tone chimed against his eardrums. He picked up the other pillow beside him and threw it towards the phone. The pillow missed, hitting the edge of the bedside table and plopping onto the leftover rice and chicken bones. Tiny cockroaches scampered away from their feast, scurrying into the comforting darkness beneath the bed. Low put his hands over his ears, but it made no difference. The phone rang so loudly he was sure his eardrums were bursting. He pressed his palms firmly against the sides of head, visualising the blood that must have been trickling through his fingers.

Tan licked his fingers and eyed his junior colleague's leftover *prata* on the silver tray. "You finished *ah*?"

Chan tugged at the bloated waistline of his pressed, black trousers. "*Yah lah*, enough already."

"You leave the best *prata* in Singapore. You mad or what?"

"It's the same everywhere, *what*."

Tan frowned as he tore the *prata* into two, taking the larger piece. Singapore food was like his family. He could criticise it, but no one else could. "Don't talk cock, OK? They cook every piece fresh, OK, every piece. You go void deck coffee shop, they cook all in one shot, sit there on the shelf, all the oil goes hard, and then they reheat some more, makes the whole *prata* taste like cardboard. Here it's soft, tender, hot and look . . . look at my hands . . . hardly any oil."

Tan held up his fingers proudly for his naive partner to examine. "See that? Tell me where got *prata* like that anywhere else."

"Tanjong Katong."

Tan waved his suggestion away. "Please *lah*."

"It's the same Jalan Kayu *prata* what. They just take the recipe to a different shophouse."

"Talk cock. Jalan Kayu *prata* must be in Jalan Kayu, that's it. You take Cadbury's chocolate out of the UK and bring to Singapore, you think it still tastes the same? You bring Guinness from Ireland over here and think it tastes the same. Rubbish."

"But the *prata*'s not leaving the country. It's just going a few kilometres up the road."

"Don't be a smart arse. As soon as the *prata* leaves Jalan Kayu, it's not the same Jalan Kayu *prata*, that's it."

"OK, fine. It's not the same. What you think about this *ang moh* guy, Leonard Viljoen?"

The perspiring inspector reached across the table and grabbed the last piece of *prata*. "What you mean what do I think? He's dead."

"I meant, you know, with Stanley."

Tan stopped chewing. "Hey, you just got promoted is it? He is called Detective Inspector Low."

"Sorry, boss, I didn't mean that. It's just that, he hasn't come back to work since the suicide. He won't pick up the phone. He won't answer my calls, your calls, what's happening?"

"He'll be fine."

"But the suicide note and everything, there will have to be an internal investigation, right? I mean, I know you've got the note, but some of the officers saw it, and I even heard some of the guys in the office discussing it. You know we can't keep secrets anymore. Everyone upstairs paranoid about internal corruption, so many cases already. Imagine if social media gets this, or those clowns working for Anonymous, imagine that. The hackers are killing us with their bullshit. But this one is real. If they find out about the suicide note then ..."

"I said he'll be fine." Tan folded his *prata* and focused on mopping up the last of the mutton curry around the edges of the silver tray.

The sun had set hours ago. Low was certain of that. The bedroom had cooled and he could hear the faint echo of a gecko's clicking behind a picture frame. He considered getting up, but found the damp sweat patch strangely comforting. His perspiration protected him, gluing him to the bed. No one judged him in an empty bedroom; only that fucking mirror on the bedside table, and he refused to look at it.

The phone rang again. Low sighed heavily. He couldn't handle another critical voice listing his shortcomings. He didn't need to pick up a phone to hear that. That voice was already in the bedroom. It never left him. His worthlessness was not up for discussion. He extended his arm to switch the phone to silent mode and noticed on the touchscreen that the number had been withheld. For a second, he contemplated answering the call until he caught a quick glimpse of himself in the mirror on the bedside table; that fucking, two-faced mirror. It betrayed him instantly. He tried to look away, but it was too late. His protective, manufactured illusion was shattered. He saw an unshaved, unloved, shrunken, grubby, feeble little man staring back at him. His scream almost drowned out the sound of his phone smashing through the mirror. A glass splinter flew into his face, leaving a jagged cut just below his right eye. Low pressed his hand gently against his cheek and felt the blood trickling through his fingers.

Chan checked again that he was alone. Then he refreshed his office laptop screen again. The Guy Fawkes masks smirked back at him. They called themselves Anonymous, a collective of political hackers, or "hacktivists". The international website championed their anonymity, inviting anyone to come forward to allege corporate, religious or government corruption. They boasted of their cyber-attacks in the US, exposing military personnel, military contractors and police officers. *Police officers.* Chan guided his screen cursor over the words. *Police officers.* The words glowed beneath the cursor like halos, whiter than white, untarnished and unblemished. The detective thought about clicking. He wanted to click. He was desperate for more information on the supposedly crooked cops in the US. He wanted to know if the leaks led to positive action and the relevant law enforcement agencies had been suitably punished. More importantly, he needed to know if the original source had been revealed.

Chan knew of Anonymous' hacking work in Singapore. Everybody did. An entire cyber-surveillance team had been haphazardly thrown together to deal with it. Initially, they worked blindfolded; analogue officers searching for a digital needle in an invisible haystack. The newspapers, town councils and the government stat boards had already been hacked, but the police force remained untouched. No one within CPIB knew of any planned cyber attacks, but then the hackers probably didn't know that a detective inspector had bullied an expat into jumping off the Fullerton Hotel roof.

Chan admired his temporary boss' success rate. The uniformed guys had nicknamed Stanley Low "Harry's" because he had put so many people behind bars. The Tiger syndicate bust alone made him a legend in law enforcement circles. But Chan stubbornly—and proudly—held on to the idealistic principles that Low frequently ridiculed. His wife was pregnant. He didn't want his child raised in a country where police psychologically tortured anyone they didn't like. Low abused from behind the safe shield of a police badge. It wasn't right. Chan had to take a stand. He was going to make his voice heard the modern Singaporean way—anonymously. As he clicked on the link, there was a knock on his door.

He slammed the laptop screen down. "Ah, yes, come in."

A young uniformed officer came in and shyly handed over a pile of DVDs. "Er, sorry to disturb you Detective Chan, but here's the other CCTV footage you asked for."

"Ah, great, thanks ... and it's Sergeant Chan by the way."

The officer's face dropped. He was very young, possibly still a cadet. "Oh, so sorry *ah*, I didn't mean to ..."

"I'm only joking, *wah lau*, toughen up. Now go and get your detective sergeant a tea with extra milk and sugar."

Crouching on all fours, Low picked up the shards of glass in the gloomy bedroom. He felt the splinters cut the skin on his hands and knees. The sharp slices of pain made him feel better.

He swept the broken glass into the palm of his hand with his bleeding fingers and dropped them into what was left of the chicken rice's polystyrene container. As he bent over, blood dripped onto the tiled floor. His cheek was still bleeding.

The phone beeped. Low realised he was smiling at the vibrating contraption beside his knees. He was surprised it was still working. He turned the phone over to read the glowing text message in the dark. It read: "*I THINK YOU'VE KEPT ME WAITING LONG ENOUGH.*"

The phone number was unfamiliar. Low was suddenly alert. He had everyone's number worth having, and no one had his number unless he allowed them to have it. CPIB was not allowed to share phone numbers of its employees under any circumstances. Receptionists were fired for less. He was considering calling the number when he suddenly jumped.

Someone was banging on his front door loudly.

Low reached for the illegal gun that he always kept under the bed.

Chan found himself running down the corridor. Two plain-clothes officers he didn't recognise moved aside as he passed. They uttered something derogatory in Hokkien, but he didn't care. Euphoria carried him along. Finally, he had made a genuine breakthrough in the Marina Bay Sands case. Finally, he had justified his rank. Finally, he would be taken seriously by his sarcastic superiors. Finally, he would be eligible for that promotion and he could achieve his uniquely Singaporean dream of buying his own car. Fuck the ERP charges. His work was worthy of a decent bonus. No one would be making snide Charlie Chan jokes at the end of the financial year. His discovery would make him the prince of the police force. They would remember his bloody name now.

*

Low tried to check that the pistol was loaded in the darkness as he edged his way around the bed. The compact Beretta was small and easy to conceal, but tough to examine without a light. Crouching, he wiped the perspiration from his forehead. His brain had been poached in warm, damp sweat, possibly for days. He needed to be clear. Adrenaline surged through his shattered body and he savoured the hit like a lapsed drug addict. The sudden high kept him alive. He needed Ah Lian now. Low was too unreliable, too brittle, too unpredictable. He was fucked without focus.

The door knocking got louder. Blurry thoughts raced though his mind like spinning bullets in a gun chamber. He couldn't afford to play Russian roulette now. He had to be certain, had to be positive, had to hit the target first time. Few people knew where he lived. That was the first problem. CPIB officers were not allowed to give out their addresses, and they were never provided under any circumstances ... *any* circumstances. Low had always been meticulously thorough when it came to his identity, home and background. When he was undercover, he always rented a second flat, usually a two-bedroom shithole in a dilapidated shophouse around Geylang, Joo Chiat and occasionally Bedok. He always moved around, never outstayed his welcome. And he never went home to his Toa Payoh apartment when he was undercover, no matter how long the case lasted. It was too risky. Tiger once got wind of a bookie's runner working for the CPIB and persuaded him to stop by writing *"owe money, pay money"* across the kid's back with a *parang*. Low later discovered that the bookie's runner did have a cousin working for the CPIB, but it had been a coincidence. The kid barely knew his cousin at CPIB and had no idea where he worked. He hadn't been talking to anyone. So Tiger paid his hospital bills and sent him a get-well card. He wrote "*owe money, pay money*" in the card.

A fist pummelled against the front door as Low peered around his bedroom door and into the hallway. His gun led the way. The banging was far too loud. That gave him hope. Whoever they were, they weren't going to kill him. Still, the Marina Bay Sands case troubled him. It wasn't his case. He wasn't undercover. He didn't know the key players. Sliding along the corridor in his boxer shorts and waving a gun around was an appropriate metaphor. Low was scrambling around in the darkness. He had three dead bodies—two had a tenuous link to an Indonesian money launderer and the other had a clear link to him. He was chasing shadows. The case had made him uncomfortable since he was brought in belatedly. He liked to know the prime suspects. He compiled dossiers and organised case files. He had to know everything about the people he was pursuing or copying. In some respects, he was a textbook Singaporean civil servant. In medical terms, he was a textbook bipolar patient.

Low tiptoed across his sparse living room, his gun trained on the front door. The gun was the other concern. It wasn't his, not legally at least. All firearms had to be signed off and left at work after each shift, but Ah Lian needed a gun so Low secretly kept one for him. Tiger once took him to a betting shophouse where a bookie believed he was owed a greater share. Tiger's pistol whipping changed his mind. Tiger had earlier handed Ah Lian a little Beretta, bought from a reliable supplier in Bangkok. Ah Lian had been given the compact pistol as a precaution. As a precaution, Ah Lian had never given the gun back.

Low stood at the side of the door. He raised the gun to his eye line and pressed it against the doorframe. As a thin strip of the fluorescent light from the HDB corridor slipped beneath the gap at the bottom of the door, the inspector peeked down at the two, slender shadows; the guy's legs. Low and his uninvited guest were standing side by side. He heard the faint scraping of a shoe against the corridor's concrete as the guy took a half-step forward. The door banging almost knocked the gun out of Low's hand. He fixed his aim. His heart pounded as he moved his left hand towards the door handle. He held on tightly and took a deep breath.

The door was almost ripped from its hinges. The policeman was surprised by his own strength. He lifted his arm in the air. "We were looking at the wrong room ... we were looking at the wrong room."

Tan gritted his teeth, pulled off the last chunk of *satay* and threw the wooden stick into a polystyrene box. The inspector chewed on the tender beef. "Eh, I'm trying to eat here. What are you talking about?"

Chan slammed the office door shut and dropped a DVD on his superior's cluttered desk. "It's there, boss. It's right there. We've got a definite link this time. We were looking at the wrong room. We were looking at the wrong bloody room."

Low suddenly heard his psychiatrist's advice. *Count backwards, ready ... three ... two ... one.* He pulled the door handle sharply and swivelled into position in one fluid, rehearsed move. Before either man had a chance to blink, Low's gun rested on the door grille. The barrel was poised between the other man's horrified eyes. His gun hand was steady; his instinctive aim perfect. He couldn't miss. The other man took a step back and raised his hands in submission.

"Yes, very good, detective inspector, very good, now do you think you might put that away and let me in."

Without speaking, Low unlocked his door grille for the Minister of Home Improvement.

Chapter 15

AS he sat down, the Minister of Home Improvement noticed the blood, both under the eye and around the hand. It was drying, but the knuckles were caked in the stuff. The unravelling officer had obviously punched something. "How did you do that?"

"Ah, I dropped something in the bedroom."

"Ah, OK. Yes, these things happen. Hope you're better now."

They both knew they were lying, but they had to pick their battles carefully. The Minister expected both the inspector and his apartment to be a mess. He didn't expect the gun on the coffee table. He nodded towards the black pistol, careful not to touch it. He had been trained to trust no one in Singapore. He represented Singaporeans, but he was careful never to trust them. The populace was always so wearily unpredictable, rarely capable of making the correct decisions. The right people had to make all the decisions; educated people, groomed people, cultured, compatible people with similar interests and intellects. The gene pool was closely controlled, but there was always the risk of it being contaminated; a catastrophic scenario for a tiny island with limited resources. The Minister was on the side of the angels; the whitest and brightest. There was no other side. This mental case with gnarled knuckles and a stolen gun tiptoed along the precipice. He had to be pulled back for his own good, for the sake of his sanity, not to mention his country. He had to see the right way; the Minister's way. There was no other way. The middle ground was built on quicksand. Singapore would not shrink and vanish on the Minister's watch. He gestured towards the blood-stained gun.

"I know you guys at the CPIB have to take your work home with you. But I'm pretty sure that you're not allowed to take that home. I'm fairly sure that's not standard issue. I thought we used the Taurus Model."

Low adjusted his clammy boxer shorts in the armchair. The cheap, wooden frame creaked as he moved. "*Yah lah.* When it's an undercover case, sometimes there are special circumstances. In CPIB, you are never entirely off duty."

"We never stop working, right? Look, I know you're one of the most respected officers in the bureau. They all speak very highly of you. I completely understand why you need that. It does make me a little nervous, a firearm in an HDB flat, as I'm sure you can appreciate. But like you say, you're a special case, which I can fully appreciate."

The Minister sat back on the uncomfortable sofa. There was nothing homely about the apartment. This rather grotesque policeman wasn't home much. He examined this bloodied, brittle man. He skipped a dinner for *this*? Still, he had read the file. Every police officer had a file and Stanley Low's did make for decent reading. The guy's street smarts were valuable, but he rarely acquiesced; a questionable quality among civil servants. The experienced parliamentarian didn't expect much truth to be spoken in the conversation. The detail was always in the deceit. He leaned forward and offered a concerned frown. "But the most important thing is you're OK?"

"I'm fine. Couldn't be better, should be back at work tomorrow."

"Yes, the suicide was a nasty business. And he never did us any favours jumping outside the Fullerton Hotel like that, a real tragedy. At least when it's around here, a housing estate, it's more ... more ... what's the word ... manageable. But the Fullerton, opposite the Merlion, tourists everywhere, those smart phones ... this is a difficult case for everyone."

"I'm sorry."

"Hey, it makes a change from anonymous hackers and corruption cases, right?"

"I suppose," Low mumbled, picking at a small piece of glass still lodged in his bloody hand. "Why are you here? How do you know where I live?"

The Minister smiled. "We're the Government. We work for each other. We support each other."

"*Wah*, that's great to know, gives me a warm glow. I'll remember that the next time I wave my red and white plastic flag on National Day. What's really happening here? Why is a minister turning up at an HDB flat, unannounced, alone, at night? Normally you guys don't go anywhere without a dozen lackeys in baseball caps and bright T-shirts. And you don't go anywhere near an HDB estate unless there's some communal garden to open or a multi-cultural dance to watch."

The Minister chuckled. "That's pretty observant. Those community events can get repetitive, but we must represent our multi-racial constituents as often as possible."

"Why are you here?"

"The Home Ministry is ultimately responsible for all police investigations. We've got a double murder at Marina

Bay Sands. MBS is a symbol of our economic growth, our place as a vibrant hub for international investment and our tourism industry of course. But let's be honest, it's very much a polarising symbol, from a societal point of view. Any negative publicity damages a brand that must be cultivated carefully. So this case is an open wound for us that must be cauterised as soon as possible."

Low acknowledged the cuts on his hand. "That's very good. It also goes without saying. So why are you saying it? Why are you banging on the door of a shitty apartment in the middle of the night to say it?"

"Yes, sorry about the hammering on the door. I really didn't mean to intrude, but I was outside for a while and was rather apprehensive about being seen."

"Why are you here?"

"Yes, well, the suicide. It puts the Ministry in a difficult position, the suicide note and so forth."

Low grinned. "It's amazing, isn't it? We beat our chests and shout in outraged indignation at the thought of national secrets being leaked online by some *blur* hackers, but someone on the inside leaks information to you in an ongoing murder investigation in a matter of days and what? What happens to them? They get an extra month's bonus at Christmas? Some extra casino chips from our friends at MBS? Is that the state of play now? We've got undercover CPIB investigating undercover CPIB?"

"I appreciate your frustration, but surely it's better that this information comes across my desk, rather than a reporter's desk."

"Please *lah*. That story doesn't go in a newspaper unless you say it does. We leak when we want. We sting when we want. You know that. I know that."

"I'll leave the conspiracy theories for the bloggers. I

understand your anxiety, but I don't have much time. We must ensure that this suicide note stays here. That means no rash outbursts, no verbal abuse in public, no alcohol-fuelled rants, no sudden revelations to a psychiatrist."

Low suddenly didn't feel well. His empty stomach rumbled and spun violently. He focused on his bloodied knuckles. He tried to ignore the dizziness. "You know I see a psychiatrist?"

"I believe she was recommended to you by the director. She's one of the best."

"And she reports to you, I assume?"

"Of course not. It would be unethical to disclose any details from her sessions with patients. She would lose her practice. But she does offer general advice on any of her patients who are employed, directly or indirectly, by the Home Ministry."

"Well, that's half the fucking country. We're either all in therapy, or all in denial. Either way, we're in your fucking pocket."

"Look, you still have a great career ahead of you. Your track record is remarkable. Your work in bringing down an illegal betting syndicate—Operation Tiger, I believe it was called—remains a landmark case; a case that Training Command will be using for years as a teaching tool, a case I'll happily continue to mention at CPIB dinners. We get the bureau director's feedback. We know how good you are. We don't need to upset our South African and expatriate friends in the private sector, not now. And the case doesn't need any more distractions."

"If you say so."

"Calm exteriors, that's all we ask for. A little bit of anarchy beneath the surface keeps everyone happy; it's a safety valve, everyone lets off a bit of steam. It takes their minds off all the foreigners, ERP prices and the packed trains and buses. We can rock the boat now and again, but we can't change the motion of the ocean. Are we still a *sampan*? Are we an ocean liner? It really doesn't matter. It's all about the motion of the ocean. We're too small to destabilise the status quo. I hope you can see that. We keep things in-house, lock the doors, batten down the hatches and wait for this thing to blow over."

"I think you might have some mixed metaphors in there."

The Minister smiled. "It's from my debating days, still can't help myself. I always was the flowery one."

"I'm not going to tell anyone that I convinced a guy to throw himself off the top of the fucking Fullerton Hotel, am I?"

"Great, perfect. I just felt I needed to check. So I'll help you with your loose end and then you can help me with mine."

"What's that?"

"Your Indonesian suspect."

Tan admired the enthusiasm, but Chan was making a mess of his desk. "Hey, come on man, you're knocking my folders everywhere. I've got a system, you know. I know where everything goes. Hey, don't put that file there. I still got two sticks of *satay* left."

Chan busied himself with clearing a space in front of the dusty DVD player. He moved aside a couple of stained paper cups and the dregs spilled onto the floor, just missing Tan. "Hey, sorry, boss."

"Yah, you will be if you make any more mess. Enough already. What's going on here?"

"Just watch."

Chan struggled to drop the DVD onto the tray. His hands were shaking. He pointed the remote control at the TV screen as security footage of the Marina Bay Sands hotel corridor appeared. His colleague rolled his eyes and reached for the *satay*. "Please, not the hotel corridor again. I seen it so many times I could paint you a picture. Come, switch it off, and I'll do you a police sketch. I've watched it for hours already, nothing happens."

"It's not the corridor for room 4088. Watch."

On the security footage, Wong Yu Lin appeared, almost a ghostly figure drifting towards the camera. The inspector almost spat out his *satay*. "Shit ... that's ..."

"Just watch." Now the younger man was the calm one.

Wong's long black hair was neatly tied back. She wore tight jean shorts. Her black bra was tight and pushed her cleavage above her red blouse. She stopped to check her make-up, practically in front of the camera. She flipped open a compact mirror and examined her complexion. Unhappy with the shine, she grabbed a tissue and wiped her forehead and cheeks. The hotel's air-conditioning made little difference. She dabbed at the powder cake and brushed her cheeks carefully, almost lovingly. She smiled sadly at the tiny mirror.

For some reason, the haunting smile made Tan check the clock on the security footage. Wong Yu Lin would be dead within a few hours.

Satisfied with her appearance, she headed for a hotel suite and stopped outside. Tan jabbed a chubby finger at the screen. "*Basket*, that's ... that's ..."

"Yep, keep watching."

Wong knocked on the door and waited. She peered up at the camera in the hotel corridor. The dead woman made direct eye contact with both policemen. The two men fidgeted uneasily. Her frailty unnerved them. The door opened.

The Indonesian smiled warmly, kissed the prostitute

184

firmly on both cheeks and then closed the door quickly behind them.

Tan poked the screen repeatedly with his *satay* stick. "This is confirmed?"

"The same day, the same afternoon, just a couple of hours before she checked in with Richard Davie."

"So she shagged them both in the same day?"

"No. Watch."

"I'm watching. I'm bloody watching."

Chan fast-forwarded the disc and hit play as the door opened again. "Now, watch this."

"*Wah lau*, if you ask me to watch again, I'll stab you with this *satay* stick. I'm watching."

On the monitor screen, The Indonesian opened the door widely to suite 5189—the Straits Suite; his suite—and gently ushered Wong back onto the corridor. She closed her handbag. Chan hit the pause button. Adrenaline had kicked in again. "You see that there? You see it? This is only four-and-a-half minutes after she went in, four-and-a-half minutes, so not enough time to have sex, but enough time for that ... look. She's clearly putting something in her handbag, something she didn't seem to have when she went in."

"Do you know what it is yet?"

"No, not yet, I'm trying to blow up the image, but it's too grainy at the moment, very hard to see."

"Bugger, it could be anything, lipstick, money, condoms, anything."

Chan's face dropped. His shoulders slumped. "But I've got her going into The Indonesian's suite just hours before Davie was poisoned and she was killed. This is Tower 1, the same tower as room 4088, only 11 floors apart."

"*Yah lah*, have to take different lifts though. Suites have a different lift right, for the high floors? Cannot use staircase, all private one. Cannot access the rooms from the suites. This means nothing, *what*."

"Come on boss, she was closing her handbag. He could've given her something—the drugs, the needle, anything. Are you being serious? We're following a guy who Richard Davie was investigating and he's the last person to see Wong alive? I mean, I don't know, if this isn't a good enough lead . . . same day, same tower, same suspect . . . I mean . . ."

The inspector jabbed the stammering detective in the arm. "You really are *blur*. I'm joking, *lah*, *basket*. This is great work, man, damn solid, really. I'll make sure the right people find out about this. Today, Charlie Chan, you make me proud to be Singaporean. Right, let's get Low up to speed and then we get moving."

Tan stood up suddenly and slapped his sergeant on the back. Chan winced. "Get moving?"

"Yes, get moving, come on. We're gonna bring this bugger in for questioning."

The portly policeman gestured towards the TV screen as he grabbed his car keys. Chan beamed like a proud schoolboy just promoted to class prefect, and followed Tan out of his office. He slammed the door shut and their euphoric voices trailed away. In the corner of the otherwise darkened office, the TV glowed. The hotel security footage had been left on pause. The Indonesian stared at Wong Yu Lin. His smile was frozen.

The Minister of Home Improvement eyed the broken policeman with a curious mix of detachment and disgust. Men like Stanley Low were a necessary evil in Singapore. They were necessary to deal with the evil. The Minister wasn't religious, but he was Old Testament in his views on law and order. It was a simple matter of trust. People couldn't be trusted. He learned that early on in his scholarship as he was fast-tracked to the front bench. People had to be told repeatedly what was best for them, and even then they couldn't be relied upon to tick the right box. They couldn't be trusted to vote, buy a house, pick a school, choose the right degree or take the correct career path. They couldn't be left unsupervised anywhere really. It wasn't a reflection on Singapore. It was simple genetic Darwinism. Some are smart. Many more are dumb. There will always be right and wrong; sheep and shepherds. Every country had them. Passports didn't matter, but political correctness did.

The Americans were only half right. They said it was the economy, stupid. Singapore knew better. It was the stupid, stupid. They held a country back. Welfare states and a feeble adherence to egalitarianism sustained the stupid and weakened their economies. Political correctness killed them. Privately, foreign leaders begrudgingly envied Singapore's emphasis on eugenics—nurturing the strong and pacifying the weak. Publicly, they were chained to the failing socialist principles of a different century. The Minister always made the same joke in such private circles. He hadn't banished stupid people entirely. They had just been quietly ushered towards the larger, greener homes of Johor and Perth. Had he been allowed to build even smaller shoeboxes, he might have squeezed them all out. But he couldn't. Even the educated elite expressed dissatisfaction at the shrinking size of Singaporean homes. (As landlords, they struggled to rent them out.) So, the remaining sheep had to be herded into manageable quantities around shopping centres, sex and gambling. Sometimes they got restless. Occasionally they got rowdy. That's why the Minister needed a sheepdog like Stanley Low. But the problem was always the same with men like Stanley Low. If they barked for too long without the sheep paying attention, they started to bite. The Minister's job was to whistle them back into the pen.

"Look, as I said before, the CPIB can rock the boat. That's your job. You should shake things up. People expect that from time to time. It's exciting even, makes for good gossip in the coffee shop. But when it involves another country, when you start talking about Indonesia and Myanmar, then we go back to disturbing the motion in the ocean, and we're too small, too exposed to deal with regional tsunamis. It only takes a small thing—like the naming of a couple of Indonesian ships for instance—and we're back to square one. Remember, we're a tiny island constantly surrounded."

Low flexed his injured hand. "Who's talking about Myanmar?"

"I'm sorry?"

"Who's talking about Myanmar?"

"We know about the Marina Bay Sands surveillance."

"So?"

"We're just wondering if it helps your case."

"Whose case?"

"Your case."

"So it is my case?"

"Of course."

"Then why are you telling me which leads to follow?"

"I'm not suggesting how you do your job."

"That's exactly what you're doing."

"I'm just explaining that relations with our neighbours will always be delicate."

"OK, fair enough, but what's the big deal? These guys are not driving around in Porsches and insulting Singapore's poor people on Facebook. They're low key. We've been low key."

"We don't want to move into unchartered territory here."

"Please *lah*. This isn't the first time these jokers have come

188

here to get laid, get on the blackjack table or get the latest plastic surgery. They've been coming here for years."

"This might be a little different."

"How?"

"This is a murder investigation."

"So what are you saying? Don't follow the leads? Check the passports of all prime suspects first before interviewing them?"

"I'm not saying that at all."

"That's exactly what you're saying. You people wear your anti-corruption statistics like a badge of honour and then something like this comes along . . ."

"And we expect a thorough and transparent investigation, with all lines of enquiry open, interviewing suspects only when there is enough evidence to do so. Of course, I'm not here telling you how to do your job . . ."

"Then why are you here? You're not here to win my vote."

The Minister of Home Improvement smiled at Low. "You really do have an impressive resume, you know. It's been a great career."

"Yeah, yeah, yeah, heard it all before. The only difference now is I don't have a career to think about, because I don't really give a shit. I don't have a family to care about because I'm not married. So what's left? My savings? My HDB flat? You can have it. I don't like housework anyway."

The Minister checked his watch. "I really do have to get going. Please, continue to follow your leads, but if you're going to interview anyone, maybe check in with our team first. There has to be substantial evidence to build a strong case."

"Who are we talking about here? KTV girls at Orchard Towers? Illegal bookies? Website hackers? Or Indonesian money launderers hiding in a Marina Bay Sands hotel suite?"

The Minister started to get up. "With a case of this magnitude, you're always going to need the proper clearance from the appropriate authority."

"Why do I suddenly feel like a bad guy here?"

The Minister smiled. "Get some rest, get back to work and let's wrap this one up as soon as possible. These online hackers are driving us crazy, making a real mess of our websites. We could really use your expertise and contacts."

Low stood up and smiled ruefully. He nodded at the Minister. "Ah, right. So the wheels are already in motion. I'll be switching cases."

"No, no, not in the short term, but I think it was Jeremy Bentham who said the greatest need for the greatest number. Majority always wins, right? These hackers affect all Singaporeans. The majority must be protected."

"Should we not also protect Wong Yu Lin?"

"Who?"

"The 45-year-old dead Singaporean who was strangled and her naked body shoved into a suitcase."

The Minister of Home Improvement put a firm hand on Low's shoulder. "Of course. She deserves justice. I'm sure you'll find who did it Stanley, if there's enough time. But everyone's innocent until proven guilty."

"But some will always be more innocent than others."

The Minister offered his hand. Low reluctantly reciprocated with his bloodied hand. He squeezed hard, savouring the slight squelch. The Minister smiled and then brushed the blood off his palm. It really was nothing. He checked his watch a second time. Even at this time, he was late for another appointment. He closed the door grille behind him and admired the panoramic view from the corridor. The lights of other HDB estates around Toa Payoh twinkled in the darkness. In the distance, the shadows of MacRitchie's forest canopy framed the gloominess. A bus passed below, whirring as it went by. The streets were otherwise peaceful. As Low watched him through the door grille, the politician nodded appreciatively. "You see that? Calm exteriors. That's all anyone really wants, you know."

Chapter 16

TIGER laughed loudly as Low sat across from him in the Changi Prison interview room. He slapped the table dramatically. "*Wah*, steady *lah*, Jackie Chan. Been fighting again is it? You look like shit."

The inspector expected as much. He did look like shit. He was dressed in an un-ironed T-shirt and jeans and hadn't shaved for days. He was pretty sure he had showered before leaving the apartment, but his right hand remained dotted with dried blood stains and tiny cuts. There was also the gash beneath his right eye, which he hadn't bothered to treat. An unattractive scab was slowly forming. "So, what do you want, Tiger?"

Tiger raised his tattooed hand and pointed a finger at his old protégé. "No *lah*, what do *you* want?"

"Tiger, this time, I got no patience, OK. You sent me a text message."

"I send you SMS almost every day. Mostly, you ignore. I forward you jokes, give betting tips, wish you all the best for Chinese New Year and you give me nothing, no reply. I always ask to see you and you never reply. Today, you come. Why?"

"I didn't like the company in my apartment. What do you want?"

"First to say, thanks for not taking my phone *ah*, need that to talk to my daughter."

"Is that it?"

"No *lah*, wait first. Wanted to ask about The Indonesian?"

"Ask me what?"

"If you catch him already?"

"You know we haven't."

"Are you close?"

"I've not been working the last few days."

"Yeah, I know. That *ang moh* jump right? Idiot. These *ang mohs* always so *wayang*, I tell you, so drama. I met him before last time."

Low looked surprised. "Did you? Not with me you never."

"*Wah*, you think you were so big-time is it? You my number one? I had so many like you. That time I take Dragon Boy, I think, just to have a look around. See what these bastards doing."

"Really?"

"*Yah lah*, nothing much, usual thing, try to spy on betting, gambling, websites, all these things so old already."

"Hmm." Low wasn't listening. He was distracted, staring at the blank wall behind Tiger. "Hey you remember that one last time? The boy you said was talking to CPIB."

"Which boy? *Chee bye*, so many of you run and talk cock to CPIB, bloody strawberry generation, kids all bruise so easily one. Last time in the kampongs, much better, kids stronger, tougher. They stayed with me last time. Now got no loyalty, change jobs all the time, still never happy, always complain, complain about not enough buses, not enough space, not enough money, everything not enough. I swear *ah*, the richer we get, the weaker we get one. Last time, we had nothing and still never complain. When we were young, must work for our rice bowl."

"When you were young, you used to put pig's blood all over your customers' doors and mailboxes."

"But I was always there. I never delegate, never. Always went to every house and they always pay me in the end."

"Look, never mind, got no time for the history lesson. Do you remember that kid you thought had family inside the CPIB?"

"Family?"

"You know, the young one, your bookie's runner, we saw him after you heard someone was talking to the CPIB."

"Ah, that one *ah*, the skinny one with the glasses? *Yah lah*, bastard, had a cousin inside the CPIB some more. But he never knew. They never spoke to each other. Just pure luck. Funny, right?"

"But you still sliced him across his back with the *parang*."

Tiger closed his eyes, savouring the memory. "Owe money, pay money."

"Yeah, across his back. He couldn't lie down properly for weeks."

"Correct. But he never spoke to the CPIB again."

"He never spoke to them before. Anyway, that's not the point. What about me?"

"You? You what?"

"I spoke to the CPIB. I am the fucking CPIB. I put you here. Why didn't you do that to me?"

Tiger sat back, suddenly confused by the question. "What?"

"Why didn't you do that to me?"

"You arrested me. I was here *wha'*. What can I do?"

"You can *tekan* someone outside any time. Why you never whack me?"

"Why you care now?"

"I want to know."

194

"You want to know why you weren't punished is it?"

"I just want to know."

"Feeling guilty is it?"

"I just want to know."

Tiger smiled. He scratched the lion tattoo poking through his T-shirt sleeve. "Because I liked you."

"You liked lots of your *ah longs* and runners."

"Yeah, I never cut them either."

"They didn't put you in here."

"They just do their job. Like you. That's OK, *wha'*. Why are you asking me now?"

"Don't know."

Tiger edged so close Low could smell his breath and stare right into his perspiring pores. The old man's eyes still gleamed. He made the inspector feel old. "You want to talk about punishment? You want to know why you escape so many times, is it? You feel guilty because I'm here and you cannot solve a case, and now one of your witnesses go fly kite off the Fullerton Hotel."

"I don't feel guilty that you're in here."

"You wanna know why I never *tekan* you, right?"

"It doesn't make much sense."

"Like my phone."

"What?"

"You always say you'll take my phone. You come in here, stick your chest out, like Ah Lian in the old days, and say my phone is finished. But my phone is still here."

"So?"

"And you're still here. Cannot give it up, right or not? The old life. You miss me. You miss the fun. You miss Ah Lian. I miss Ah Lian at the Balestier coffee shop, eating *bak kut teh*, talking shit. He was a mad bastard."

"Bullshit."

195

"Admit it. Admit that you miss Ah Lian."

"I came here because you message me asking about The Indonesian."

"*Yah lah*, but I don't know much. Told you everything last time, he runs some gambling websites, money quite big, maybe he's got a syndicate already and this fucker Jimmy Chew owes him a lot of money, but you know that already. You knew that last time. But you still come."

"I come for the case."

"No *lah*, you come because you got nowhere else to go. No one likes you, you piss everybody off. Even the *ang moh* killed himself. Your only friend in Singapore is in here, me. You know that already. Look at me, old Chinaman gangster in Changi, your only *kaki*. That's why you come back. In here, you come alive. Outside, you're dead."

"Outside, I hurt people," Low heard himself mutter.

"Don't talk cock, Ah Lian. Outside, you're a hero. You save people."

"From what?"

Tiger smiled. "From old Chinaman gangster like me."

The German backpackers piled onto the battered bumboat and shuffled along the wooden benches. The chipped blue paint scratched their thighs as the boat's engine roared into life. The bumboat chugged past Low sitting in the Changi Point Ferry Terminal. Across the small inlet, a family took photographs around the adventure playground at Changi Beach Park. They lived in a different world. Low sat back on the bench and sighed. He wished he could join them.

"Eh, bugger, why you bring us here. Going fishing is it?" Tan slapped Low across the shoulder. The CPIB inspector looked down at the ground and grimaced. He hated being touched.

Chan joined the men, eager to speak. "So can we tell you the good news now? How come cannot talk on the phone?

Low raised a finger to his lips and gestured towards the immigration officers manning the security checkpoint. "Come. We get on the boat first. I booked one already."

The three officers passed through the checkpoint scanner, flashing their IDs. They tiptoed across the wobbly gangplank and ducked into a bumboat. Low nodded at the captain; a scrawny, sun-crisp Chinese man in his late 70s with brown, knotted skin like gnarled tree bark. The bumboat pulled slowly out of the harbour.

Tan watched the Changi Point Ferry Terminal shrink behind him and shook his head. "Is this really necessary? We must take a boat to Pulau Ubin to talk is it? We need to be so paranoid?"

Low eyed the whistling bumboat captain. Covered in cancerous lesions, the captain's bony legs hung beneath his billowing, baggy shorts like pieces of string. As he guided the boat towards Singapore's biggest offshore island, he paid no attention to the three other Chinese men behind him.

"Only speak in English and quietly," Low ordered. "What did you find out about The Indonesian?"

Chan's eyes widened. "Well, I checked the security cameras again and ..."

"Wait first," Tan interjected impatiently. "What is all this bullshit, Stanley? We don't see you for days. We call and call, you never pick up. Now I see you, you look like shit; you got cuts on your hand, your face. You call me and say meet at Changi Village when you finish with Tiger ..."

"You went and saw Tiger? At Changi Prison? Why?" Chan exclaimed.

*

197

Tan bridled at the childish interruption. "Eh not now *ah*? Talk about that later." He looked back at the weary inspector. "Where you been? Why can't we talk on the phone? Why can't we *makan* at Changi Village? And why are we on a boat to Pulau Ubin like bloody *ang moh* tourists?"

Low smiled mischievously. "It's close to the prison."

"Eh, balls to you. We're ready to bring The Indonesian in, got no more time to play the fool, OK."

Low gazed across Serangoon Harbour as a cargo ship cruised past. Yachts danced from side to side in front of the Changi Sailing Club. Singapore really was rather beautiful, from a distance. The truth was the CPIB officer could've discussed the case at Changi Beach Park in one of their cars. He was desperate to get away, even for a few hours, from the murders, from the dead South African, from the wretched ugliness, from the hypocrisy, from himself.

"You're right," he said finally. "Sorry for the cloak-and-dagger stuff. But I am pretty paranoid. I've been warned to back away from the case, well, not in so many words, but it's been made clear to me that as soon as the paperwork is in order and enough time has passed to stop it looking suspicious, I'll be discreetly pushed out of the picture."

"You'll be fired," Chan blurted out.

"Eh, no need to be so dramatic. I'll just be reassigned ... the computer hacking ... to be honest, they care more about online abuse than a dead *ang moh* anyway."

"How long have you got?" Tan enquired.

"Oh, I don't know, maybe a couple of weeks, at the most. But if any more government websites get hacked ... it could be tomorrow. But look, I don't care about that, really, don't give a shit. You know me, James. I'm here to talk about The Indonesian. Basically, it was made clear to me that I ... we ... should back off."

"What? We can't do that," Chan shouted over the bumboat engine and the churning waves. "We're so close. We almost got the bastard."

Tan raised a hand to gently silence his excitable junior partner. "Not so loud, *ah*? ... Who spoke to you? The director? Must be *lah*. I can understand. You had so many problems on your side."

"No, no. You think I give a shit about the director? He's an office man, a scholar. I did one year-plus undercover as Ah Lian, he knows not to touch me. No, this one from the big boss, the Home Minister told me to back down."

Tan focused on Pulau Ubin's wooden jetty in the distance. A couple of stray dogs trotted freely along the wooden planks. Suddenly, a seafood lunch and a lime juice on the island didn't seem like the worst idea. "He called you?"

"No, he came to my apartment, on his own some more."

"*Basket*," Tan mumbled.

"That's why. Turned up late, banging on the door like an *ah long*. I nearly shot the fucker."

The other men exchanged brief glances as Low spoke. They both considered addressing the gun reference, but thought better of it. Tan pushed his thick hair away from his sweating forehead. "So how? That's it then, right?"

Chan was incredulous. "What? What you mean that's it? Cannot be. We almost got him, thanks to me, we almost got him. He's a pimp. He's a ... he's a ... syndicate boss. He's obviously a money launderer and probably a murderer too."

Low smiled at Tan. "What's happened to him?"

"Ah, he got one lucky break on the case while you were away and now he thinks he got hairs on his balls. He's very excited right now; naive, but excited."

"Hey, come on *lah*, no need to patronise me," Chan

objected. "Why we must protect this bastard? He's not even Singaporean."

Low pointed towards the distant outlines of Indonesian islands dotting the horizon line. "You see over there? That's Batam. Round the corner, Bintan. We are surrounded by 15,000 of their islands. There's a lot of money over there. They give us the haze, we take their money."

"What's the haze got to do with anything?"

"Those illegal loggers can't keep their cash in Indonesia. If they don't dump it in Temasek Boulevard, they'll dump it in Hong Kong, China or even Costa Rica. It's going to go somewhere, might as well come here, right."

Tan scratched at the peeling paint on his box seat. He really liked Low and admired his tenacious police work, but he loved his country more. "Enough with the conspiracies, eh, Stanley? We're not *ah peks* in a coffee shop."

Low held up his hands in mock surrender. "OK, OK. There could be any number of reasons. His contacts with Myanmar ... his investments here ... a dodgy past, who knows? But for now, we can't touch him."

The three officers had nothing else to say. They watched the bumboat captain reverse the creaking vessel and brush its homemade tyre bumper against the jetty with an effortlessness achieved decades ago. He threw the mooring rope over a bollard. "Out," he barked.

"Wait first," Low shouted. He leaned towards the two policemen sitting on the box seat opposite. "But I'm not stopping," he whispered. "The Indonesian is involved. We all know that. We don't know how yet, but he's involved. Those two in the hotel were murdered by someone. So I'm not going anywhere. Fuck that."

"What about the Minister?" Tan asked.

"What about him? What's he gonna do? Get the CPIB

to follow the CPIB? Heck care *lah*. I've been followed by worse. And they're not here, right? So I'm going after this bastard. That's it."

"Same," Chan spluttered. The older men both chuckled. "What?" he continued in indignation. "I can't go after him? I'm the one who watched him get those women to be . . . you know . . . by those military fuckers. And I'm the one who saw him with the dead prostitute."

Low was stunned. "What?"

"*Yah lah*, he's been waiting to tell you all day, wetting his panties."

"You saw them where?"

"Security camera, Marina Bay Sands. She went into his hotel room and picked up something, just a couple of hours before she went to Richard Davie's room. So that's it. I'm in. You cannot stop me."

Low slouched back and rested his arms on the windowless, splintered wooden frames. He smiled at Tan. So did Chan. The chubby inspector shifted his gaze between the two. "All right *lah*, *basket*. My wife already wants me to retire. Now I can retire early. But we do it together, no more secrets, OK *ah*, Stanley?"

Low nodded. "Let's eat."

Tan suddenly scrambled to his feet. "Eh, the seafood here not bad."

Kevin Xavier watched the moron fiddle with the buttons on his mixing desk. He had been a music producer for 20 years, sustaining a profitable career in a country where the local scene was on its knees, and still had to suffer fools gladly. Straight-up, professional singers and hotel lounge perform-ers were always the best; self-designated artistes the worst.

Anyone who considered being an 'artiste' a legitimate occupation automatically denied themselves the opportunity of ever truly being one, and yet the TV company's cattle trucks regularly pulled up outside Xavier's recording studio and the latest herd of artistes were shepherded into a sound booth, mooing and baaing as they went. Yue Liang was different, but only marginally so. She was an independent artiste. She still couldn't sing, but at least she called the shots. Her recording sessions were not conducted by a non-creative committee, just an idiotic author whose musical spectrum began with the Bee Gees and ended with Adele. As Jimmy Chew pushed the intercom button, Xavier eased his swivel chair back into the studio's shadows.

"That was great darling, it really was, just like Adele," Jimmy gushed. "What did you think, Kevin?"

"What? Ah, yeah, was like she was there in the room. But I'm just wondering if that's the right tone for this song, you know."

On the other side of the glass panel, Yue Liang listened intently through the headphones. Whipping her hair away from her face, she breathed heavily into the microphone. "How do you mean, Kevin?"

Xavier wheeled over to the mixing desk and picked up a crumpled piece of A4 paper. "Well, the lyrics, as written here, are about a poor Hispanic kid growing up in an LA slum and how he finds the inner strength to become a successful hip hop artist. The lyrics are short and fast, they trip off the tongue, you know. So I'm not sure if singing them like a ballad will get that message across."

Yue Liang pondered the producer's words. "What if I sang in an American accent?"

Xavier held his hand over his mouth and coughed quietly. "Yeah ... yeah, that might do it."

Jimmy fidgeted at the mixing desk. He was getting impatient. "Look, that's fine. But it is only a demo, right, for us to take to LA and give them a feel for the song. That's why we're going over there, to get the song produced properly."

He shot a withering look at the producer. Xavier smiled back at the fool. He couldn't care less where they got the dreadful song produced. The track had no chance of being sold beyond their obsequious followers and he was being paid for his time either way. "Hey, you guys do whatever you think is best, you know."

"But I do think Kevin might be right, Jimmy," Yue Liang argued. We've done so many ballads already, in English, in Mandarin, Cantonese, even I'm fed up already."

Jimmy was aware that other people were listening in on their disagreement. He crouched closer to the mixing panel and whispered: "I know that, darling. But ballads sell in Asia. Ballads are safe. Singapore likes safe. Safe sells."

"I don't know, Jimmy. Hip hop and R&B sell in the US. If we're serious about getting the message out over there, it just has to be something more than a love song." Yue Liang tottered on tiptoes in her stilettos and craned her head, peering over her husband's shoulder. "What do you think?"

"I really think it's up to you. It's your voice and name on the song. You've got to be comfortable with it." The Indonesian rested against the wall at the back of the studio as he spoke, little more than a silhouette in the dimly-lit room.

"That's right," Yue Liang agreed. "I've done the cheesy love songs so many times. I can't sing *'wo ai ni, wo yao ni'* anymore. I've got to change, like Katy Perry in the jungle thing. We've got to get it rougher, dirtier. We've got to take risks."

Still leaning over the mixing desk, Jimmy became aware

that The Indonesian now stood just behind him. "Look, darling, maybe we can talk about this later. We don't want to waste precious studio time."

"Don't worry about the studio time," The Indonesian assured, smiling at Yue Liang through the glass panel. "It's more important that you get what you want."

"Exactly. That's right. I want it grungy, more hip hop, more like Los Angeles. That's what will impress the producers over there. Can you do that, Kevin?" Yue Liang gushed.

Xavier lifted his head from his hand. "Eh, sure, whatever you want."

"Great, see if you can find some hip hop beats we can lay underneath. Everybody OK with that?"

The Indonesian nodded enthusiastically. "What do you think, Jimmy?" He rested a hand on Jimmy's shoulder. The self-help guru's shoulders slumped.

"Whatever she wants."

The three officers sat inside the car, sweating. Alone in the backseat, Chan wiped his forehead. "Can we turn the air-con on?"

As he held the steering wheel, Tan glared at Chan through his rear-view mirror. "No, don't want engine on, no sound at all, OK? Bloody strawberry generation."

Low chuckled as he rested his head in the passenger seat. "That's why. They want air-con all the time, only eat in air-con food courts. Hey, Charlie, why don't you get your maid down here? Ask her to do the surveillance for you."

"Balls to you."

The inspectors laughed. Tan looked through the windows. "Good *makan* around Bukit Merah," he remarked. "Hey, afterwards we go IKEA."

"IKEA? You want to buy a book case?"

"No *lah*, their Swedish meatballs damn *shiok*."

"I thought you said you wanted to go Jalan Kayu after this for *prata*." Chan was still sulking about the air-con.

The plump inspector eyed the kid through the rear-view mirror. "Too far. I've been sitting outside this studio for one hour-plus and no *makan*. Doesn't even look like a studio anyway, looks like a chicken factory."

Chan sat up. "Hey, I heard they got an engineer from Abbey Road to design this place. They record all the National Day Parade stuff in here."

"*Wah*, must be good then."

Low grinned and then stopped suddenly. He noticed his face in the wing mirror outside. The cut under his eye was scabbing over and the rings under his eyes had darkened, deepened. He hadn't slept properly for days. He always struggled on a case unless he was undercover. Ah Lian slept like a baby. "I don't think IKEA will still be open at this time. We could go to ... they're coming out."

The three men instinctively ducked down in the car. On the other side of the road, Yue Liang and Jimmy Chew emerged from the multi-storey industrial complex. The studio looked more like a warehouse. The property was reportedly owned by a Singaporean, but managed by engineers from China; modern Singapore had infiltrated the music business. Jimmy paused to shake Kevin Xavier's hand. The producer then air-kissed Yue Liang on both cheeks before the celebrity couple hurried towards their car, keeping their heads down. Xavier turned back and held out his hand.

"I don't believe it," Low whispered. "It's the bloody Indonesian. He thinks he's Simon Cowell now."

Chan frowned. "Why?"

"Shut up. Just take some pictures."

Chan grabbed a camera and snapped quickly from the back

seat. Like a paparazzo, he held the camera above his head and snapped through the window. He continued to crouch up against the door, using the small screen at the back of the digital camera to focus. Xavier shook hands with The Indonesian before returning to the cavernous studio building. The Indonesian strolled casually along the street.

Tan started the engine. "Shall we follow him?"

"Nah, let's do *Dumb and Dumber* first."

Chapter 17

EVEN the most jaded of CPIB officers came out into the corridor to see her. They had interrogated CEOs, bankers, loan sharks, people smugglers, drug traffickers, professional footballers, actors, rappers and news presenters, but none of their interviewees ever looked as good in a cocktail dress. They knew she wasn't a prime suspect. She was still a pin-up. Flanked by Tan and Chan, Yue Liang fluttered her eyelashes and flirted with the leering men propped up against office doorways as she swept past. Like the officers around her, she was never off duty. She was always switched on. She had been a celebrity since primary school. The rest of Singapore only needed to catch up. If the prissy teachers at Katong Convent couldn't tame her, no one could. Chan blushed as he ushered her into the interview room. The inspector followed behind, dropping his folder on the table. She watched both men as they sat across from her at the table. The old, fat one wasn't interested. She would focus on the young, star-struck one.

Yue Liang addressed the wide-eyed sergeant directly. "Thanks for making this a quiet chat. Really appreciate that. Cannot have any bad media right now, you know."

"Didn't do it for you," Tan replied gruffly. "This is a delicate case. Must tread softly."

"I understand."

"No, you don't. Who was the guy with you at the recording studio earlier tonight?"

"That was my husband, Jimmy Chew, you took him to another room, right?"

Tan looked directly at Yue Liang. "You can do that once, OK, just once."

"Do what?"

"You've done it once, that's it. Do it again and you'll really piss me off. No more acting *blur* like *sotong*, OK? We're not fans asking for autographs. We're not media here to laugh at your jokes and give you a nice big story for the National Day Parade, OK. Understand or not?"

Chan noticed a change in the singer's demeanour. Her eyes darted between the two men, desperately looking for a reassuring gesture. She was terrified. She nodded and looked around the small, stuffy room. "Is no one else coming in? Can I bring someone in?"

"What for? You're not being charged with anything yet. You're helping a joint CPIB and Singapore Police Force investigation. We can keep you overnight, at least, without a lawyer present. We have the powers to detain you for as long as we like. You wanna sing-song about that?"

Yue Liang was angry at the tears stinging her eyes. She loved to control her audience, particularly an all-male audience. She craved the attention. Control was her drug. She went cold turkey without it. She crumbled. She needed to be loved. And to be loved by her audience, any audience, she had to control it. "Why are you being so mean to me?"

"Because I cannot *tahan* your nonsense," Tan growled. "Now, when you met Detective Inspector Stanley Low in Toa Payoh, you told him that your husband owed a lot of money, correct or not?"

Yue Liang scrutinised Chan's face. He was rather handsome for a police officer. "Should I have a lawyer here maybe?"

Chan smiled awkwardly. Tan tapped the table. "Oi, you can't have a lawyer here, so stop asking, OK? Does your husband have big gambling debts? Make me ask three times and you will be on prime-time news in the morning."

The singer's celebrity mask was slipping. "Yes, you know that already," she mumbled. "You saw the figures, right."

"What figures? What figures have we seen?"

"The figures ... the figures ... the figures that the *ang moh* got?"

"The *ang moh*'s figures? Richard Davie's figures, you mean? Richard Davie the *ang moh*'s figures? Richard Davie the *ang moh* you were having sex with's figures? You mean those figures?"

Chan shifted uneasily in his feet. Police interrogations unsettled him. There was seldom any legal representation in Singapore, no right of reply. Law and order pummelled them all. It was merciless. Holding back the machinery was like catching water between the fingers. Even Yue Liang had no chance, no one to turn to, not even him.

"Why are you doing this?"

"Because Richard Davie is dead. Because Richard Davie appears to have murdered a Singaporean woman, perhaps on the orders of someone else, someone who had power over him, someone who could convince him, order him, force him to kill someone. Because Richard Davie had no previous criminal record, not in Australia, not in Singapore, not even a parking ticket. His family says he never had a fight since primary school, not even a typical *ang moh* fight over an SPG in Clarke Quay, not a fight outside a taxi stand in Sentosa, nothing. So we got an *ang moh* who's never been violent, never. Suddenly he strangles a Singaporean before somebody kills him. And this happens just after he finds out that Jimmy Chew owes big money to a gambling syndicate. Money he cannot pay. Money you cannot pay. No matter how many books he sells, no matter how much you sing song, no matter how much you talk cock on TV, you cannot pay right? This is almost half a million, right or not? So you screwed Richard Davie to keep him quiet."

Yue Liang wiped the tears away in disgust. She loathed being vulnerable. "No, I like him, OK? After I met him at one of Jimmy's talks and he tells me what he does, I ask him to have a look, just have a look. I knew Jimmy was gambling. He's always gambled. He's Chinese. Of course he gambles. But I didn't know where or how much. So I asked Richard to have a look. We met again, at some Formula 1 show near the Singapore Flyer. He tells me what he's found out about Jimmy, he tells me how much money and how long, and I want to kill him."

"Richard Davie?"

"No, my husband. And I tell all this to Richard. I open my mouth like a silly schoolgirl and tell him. It was a corporate event, free champagne, everything free. As long as we pose for photos, everything free. So we're talking and drinking, and Jimmy's not there, he's at some shitty Suntec City self-help conference. And Richard is being so kind, really, so kind. He's not trying to screw me. He doesn't want anything from me. He just wants me to know that if he knows about Jimmy already, then other people will find out eventually. You people will find out. The media will find out. Find out that my husband, the business expert, the man who makes so much money, is a lousy poker player. He's nobody, nothing, just another Chinese gambling addict."

"So you slept with him so they don't find out?"

Yue Liang struggled to control the rage rising in the back of her throat. She clenched her fists under the table. "No, policeman. I slept with him because he's kind, because he feels sorry for me, because he knows my husband is a moron. I slept with him because I loved him, OK? I loved him. I loved everything about him. And when I wake up next to that disgusting, weak gambler every day, I think about Richard, and how much I miss him, how much I miss talking to someone who doesn't speak bullshit, who doesn't talk about book sales and stocks and shares and profit projections . . . and all that other money-making crap. I miss a man, a real man. And you say I'd want Richard dead? Please *lah*. You've got no idea. I wish I had been involved, OK. Then Richard would still be alive and Jimmy would be dead."

Chan closed the door and sat beside Low. As instructed, he whispered in the inspector's ear, melodramatically cupping a hand to his face to cover his moving lips. On the other side of the table, Jimmy Chew thought about his darling wife being grilled in the other interview room. He loved her dearly. And he wondered if he trusted her. He certainly loved her. He knew for certain that he loved her. He thought he trusted her, but he definitely loved her. He tried not to think about his wife by focusing on the strangely familiar face. He waggled a finger in front of the younger officer's face.

"I know you. I do know you, isn't it?" Jimmy declared, slapping his hand on the table. "Charlie Chan. That's you, right? Detective Charlie Chan. I signed a book for you in . . . er . . . Toa Payoh . . . that was it, at a family fun day. Detective Charlie Chan. That's it. I knew it. I never forget a face."

"It's Charles actually," said Chan, unable to conceal his irritation.

"Yeah, he gets very sensitive about his name," Low

interjected quickly. "Now, Jimmy, I like you. Well, actually, no, I don't like you or your books or your seminars. I think you're full of shit and I should know. I deal with shit for a living. This job is one long swim through shit. But I wade through it. That's the job. And then, just when I think I'm done for the day, I must come in here and look at you, a big, steaming pile of shit all over my desk. You haven't got a shred of decency, *ah*? Cannot be honest, cannot tell the truth. I'd take financial advice from the auntie who cleans our office before I'd take it from you. You steal from poor, gullible, superstitious, uneducated Singaporeans, right or not? The only person who gets rich from your self-help rubbish is you, and you're not even rich anymore, are you Jimmy?"

Jimmy loosened his tie, only a little. He was nervous, but the interview room wasn't particularly stuffy and presentation was essential in the pursuit of professional perfection. It was a popular line in his seminars. Alliterative lines always were. They were easier to remember. Besides, he genuinely believed in keeping up appearances. "Why are you antagonising me? I didn't do anything wrong."

The inspector pushed a spreadsheet across the table. "Well, that's not entirely true is it, Chewie? Do you mind if I call you Chewie? Tough shit if you do really. You see, Chewie, there is a list of all your recent transactions concerning a particular website. A website called ..." He tilted his head, for dramatic effect. "Poker Plus. There it is. Poker Plus. Man, you love that website, don't you? You're on it for hours. If you spent as much time writing books as you do gambling, you could retire. You could write *Fifty Shades of Shit Poker Playing*. Look at that figure there, 50K in one night."

Jimmy Chew scratched at the table with his manicured fingernail. "It's my money."

"Ah, that could be an admission of guilt right there.

212

You see, gambling is not permitted in Singapore unless it's licensed. But it's tricky, you see, like a legal minefield. These laws predate the Internet, so remote gambling is a loophole that the Government is looking to close. Still, you, a prominent Singaporean placing bets with unlicensed gambling operators. We don't like that. We want your bets placed with licensed gambling operators. So you give your money to Singapore Pools so we can build hospitals and theatres. Or you keep it in your pocket. You took the third option, which means you're fucked."

"You're going to charge me with gambling outside? You'll have to arrest half of Singapore."

"We love a high-profile scapegoat here at CPIB, Chewie."

"Can I get a drink of water?"

"No. Poker Plus has been traced to Macau. As far as you're concerned, it's an illegal, offshore gambling and betting operation with links to major crime syndicates, and you break the law every time you type in your credit card number. You want to go to jail, Chewie? *Wah*, I'm sure your get-rich-quick seminars will be damn popular in the exercise yard when you're playing basketball with the *ah longs*, the drug dealers and the pimps. How long you think you can survive? You think your wife is pretty now. When you come out, she will look like Maggie Q. And even then, she won't be your type anymore. Everything will suddenly feel a bit too ... loose."

"You really are an asshole."

"And you'll be seeing plenty of them soon enough."

Low nudged his junior partner for a reaction. The inspector's spiteful goading always made the younger officer deeply uncomfortable.

Jimmy coughed nervously. "Can I get a drink of water please?"

"Fuck you. This is CPIB not the Fullerton. You drink when we tell you. You piss your pants when we tell you. Now, you owe this website—just this website—300,000-over dollars. And there are other websites. But I'm only interested in Poker Plus, Chewie, because Poker Plus is—we think—owned by the man who was at the recording studio with you tonight. Now, I ask you. How the hell is that possible?"

Jimmy scratched harder at the tabletop. "He's helping to finance the recording sessions."

Low knocked the self-help guru's hand aside violently. "That scratching is driving me fucking crazy. What did you say? He's paying for your wife's new record?"

"No, just a demo to take to the US."

"Ah, fair enough. Now it makes perfect sense. You're free to go."

"Really?"

"No, idiot. Why is the man who you owe $300,000—a prominent Indonesian businessman who practically lives at Marina Bay Sands—why has a man like that decided to help you and your wife now?"

Jimmy dropped his hands in his lap and sat back in his chair. He sighed and appeared to smile to himself, as if in on a joke that no one else understood. "Because he wants to have sex with my wife. They always do."

As Chan re-joined Tan, the senior officer drummed his fingers against the scratched tabletop. Yue Liang glared at his ugly, scarred, chubby fingers. The fat policeman had perspiration rings under his armpits. His ill-fitting, greying white shirt was dotted with curry and coffee stains. He disgusted her. He was precisely the kind of rotting middle manager that had her pining for LA. She wouldn't encounter such grotty little men

214

in California. She could forget fat, greasy detectives. She could forget about Richard Davie. The deliberate, incessant finger drumming was driving her crazy. She crossed her legs tightly. Tan welcomed her irritation, her loathing, her discomfort. There was no identity crisis on his side of the table. He knew what they both were. Only one of them was hypocritical. He stopped drumming suddenly and balled his hand into a fist.

"Here's what I don't understand, Yue Liang. You are obviously an attractive woman. You wear nice clothes. You keep your hair nice. And you are sleeping with Richard Davie. *Wah*, the *ang moh* cannot believe his luck, right or not? You are definitely not an SPG. No way. You are a supermodel compared to SPGs. He cannot get a woman like you back in Australia in a hundred years. He cannot get a woman like you anywhere. That is obvious."

Yue Liang smiled vaguely. "Yah, so?"

"So, if he's got champagne like you waiting at home, why does he go out for cold *kopi*?"

"What?"

"Come on man, if he was having sex with you regularly, why did he have sex several times with a Singaporean auntie before killing her?"

Tears sprang from Yue Liang's eyes like stinging beads of fury. She felt the bile rise. She wanted to spit it out, watch it dribble down the inspector's grotesque, flabby face. "You son of a bitch."

"There had to be a reason for him swapping champagne for cold *kopi*, and then paying to drink the cold *kopi* at Marina Bay Sands some more. And then strangling her. What kind of a man does that? No man does that. Only an animal does that. Was Richard Davie an animal?"

"No, he was ... he was ... kind and gentle and ... and ..." Yue Liang's voice vanished as grief overwhelmed her.

"But cannot be, right? He had sex with her more than once, you understand or not? His semen, no one else's semen, only his semen was found all over her body, do you understand or not? In her vagina, in her mouth, in her anus—in her anus, Yue Liang—his semen, everywhere, do you understand or not? He held her over the bathroom sink and squeezed her neck until she was dead, you understand or not? He squeezed her neck so hard that when we found her, her neck was covered in red and blue bruises, blue fingermarks, his fingermarks, understand or not? We think he was having sex with her while he was killing her, do you understand or not?"

Tan was on his feet and standing over the weeping Yue Liang. He was shouting. "Well, do you understand or not?"

Chan grabbed his arm and eased him back into his seat. "It's OK, boss. Let's give her a drink or something. You want some water or something, Yue Liang?"

"He told him to take her there." Yue Liang sobbed so loudly that she was barely audible as she wiped the snot from her face. Tan took a deep breath.

"Who told him?"

"You know who. He called Richard and told him to meet him and a friend—the prostitute—in the lobby, take her to the hotel room. He said the girl had some connections that would help. He said they would meet and settle everything."

"Settle what?"

"What else? That moron in your room next door. Jimmy's gambling debts. Richard knew how much Jimmy owed and who he owed it too. He called me and said he had found a way to settle Jimmy's debt for me. He was going to meet The Indonesian and settle the debt for me. For me."

"And then?"

Yue Liang gazed beyond the two unattractive interrogators, her red, puffy eyes searching for a lost, happy memory.

Through her tears, she found a smile. "And then, I was going to leave Jimmy."

Chan gently shouldered the door open, balancing a cup of *teh tarik* in each hand. Rather elaborately, he eased the cups down on the side of the table away from Jimmy. Low sipped slowly from his cup, never breaking eye contact with the esteemed author. "Ooh, damn *shiok*. I love *teh tarik* at supper time."

Jimmy no longer had the heart to even pretend to play along. "Can I get some water please?"

"You get fucking nothing. Did you know The Indonesian was going to have Richard Davie killed? Why do you think he would do that?"

For the first time, the self-help guru looked afraid. He jolted slightly in his chair, as if fear had suddenly seeped into his brain. "What do you mean?"

"Why would your new music producer *kaki* have a betting data expert and a prostitute murdered?"

"He killed them? Why would he kill them? I mean, that's ... Christ ... is this really true?"

"No, he's really Santa Claus. Of course it's fucking true. And since their murders, he's been seen with you and your wife on at least two occasions by us, which from this side of the table smells a lot like aiding and abetting."

"No, no, you must believe me. I didn't know anything about that, really. Oh god."

"Then why, Chewie? Why would you spend time with a man who you owe so much money?"

Jimmy hung his head. He could no longer face them. "He said he would clear my debts, help me build my business ... if I introduced him to my wife."

"So you pimped your wife? You pimped out Singapore's

most successful pop star to Indonesia's most successful money launderer? *Wah*, you really are the self-help king."

Jimmy pushed his chair back as if to get up. Chan rose to his feet. "Sit down, Mr Chew."

"How dare you?" Jimmy snapped. "My wife would never do that. She would never sleep with a man like *him*, not a man like *him*. He's disgusting. She would never do that, not to me ... not to me." He turned his nose up. The thought appalled him. The Indonesian was a repugnant individual.

Low registered the disgust. The bastard betrayed some sort of wounded pride, a warped code of ethics. "So she wouldn't sleep with him because ... why? He's a money launderer? He runs a syndicate? He's Indonesian? He wears bad clothes? He orders the murder of two people in a hotel room? What?"

"She wouldn't sleep with him because she promised me she wouldn't." He started weeping. "She thinks I don't know. She really thinks I don't know. I knew everything. I knew about Richard Davie. I even knew about his bloody South African business partner. And the others, the record producer last time, the CEO on the TV side when she was still an 'artiste' working in the TV factory, whoever she needed at the time. She thinks I don't know, but it's OK, I've understood all along. Her career comes first. Look at me. You think she'd be with me? Look at me. She doesn't want me. She needs me. She needs my followers. She needs my business contacts. She needs their endorsements, their sponsorships. She needs to be loved. So she needs to be famous. I understand that."

Low finished his *teh tarik*. "You have no idea what you are talking about, no idea what she sacrificed for you, what she lost for you. She tried everything she could to settle your fucked-up gambling debts. And she lost everything. For you."

"I'm still here. We've still got each other."

"Whoopee-fucking-doo. She'll be so happy. I might finish you now as a point of principle," Low rubbed his face repeatedly in exasperation. "Look. Last chance. Do you think The Indonesian could have killed Richard Davie and the prostitute Wong Yu Lin?"

Jimmy ran his hand through his hair. His head drooped onto his arm. "Yes," he mumbled into his armpit.

"What?"

He lifted his head and exhaled loudly. "He probably killed the *ang moh*. The Singaporean girl, I don't know."

"Why?"

"Because the *ang moh* was monitoring his gambling sites, he knew how much income was coming in, how he was avoiding tax and all the rest of it. The daft *ang moh* bragged about it to my wife, trying to get her underwear off, asshole."

"And that would get him killed?"

Jimmy leaned across the table. "About three or four months ago, I said I couldn't pay. I just couldn't pay. I basically said, 'Screw you, do you know who I am?' The next day, I get back to our house and two Chinese men, China Chinese men, were sitting in my living room. I don't know how they got in. I don't know why my burglar alarm didn't go off. They must have waited for the maid to take the dog for a walk. In Mandarin, they just said, 'You're right. We do know who you are. We know what you do. We know where you live.' And they picked up a photo of my wife, beside the TV. They nodded at it and smiled. And they took the photo with them. I knew what they meant. I get it all the time."

"What?"

"He wasn't really interested in me. He was only interested in my wife. He knew I didn't have any money, just my wife.

This man . . . he got them into my house. He can do anything he wants. He can take anything he wants."

"Why didn't you come to us then, before all this shit happened? You might have saved their lives."

Jimmy smiled at the memory. "I didn't want to hurt my wife."

"It's a bit fucking late for that."

Chapter 18

AS he strolled quickly though the opulent lobby of the Marina Bay Sands Hotel, Low listened to Chan on the phone. The breathless sergeant was reporting their prime suspect's movements. "Suspect getting into Mercedes, boss ... he's pulling out of the VIP car park ... turning left into Marina Boulevard ... stopping at traffic lights ... he's indicating to turn left ... looks like he might be heading onto the ECP."

Low cut in, "Yes, OK, Charlie, that's great. Appreciate the enthusiasm, but no need to tell me every time he turns left or picks his nose. I can read your report later. Just tell me when he's on his way back to MBS ... Ah, Pierre ... Charlie, I got to go."

Dressed impeccably as always with his hair effeminately lacquered, Pierre Durand waited for the irritating inspector outside the lift lobby. The hotel manager held onto the Singaporean's hand far too firmly and for far too long. It was a long-held law of the corporate jungle; the higher up the ladder, the more aggressive the handshake. But Durand's physical intensity was not lost on the undercover specialist, nor was the film of sweat around his neck collar. Low always snuck a peek at neck collars. In Singapore's cool, air-conditioned bubbles, they were his entry point. The

Frenchman had failed the first test. He was nervous. Low followed him into the lift and waited for the doors to close. "So you're going to let me see The Indonesian's suite?"

"You know I can't do that, detective."

"It's Detective Inspector Low. Don't waste that patronising shit on me. Or I'll start calling you the concierge. You are letting me into that suite, Pierre, you personally. Or I'll bring a CPIB team back here to check your guest list again, particularly our friends from Myanmar. I'm sure they had extra, non-paying guests staying overnight, didn't they?"

"I think the gentlemen you're referring to are no longer here."

Low stepped towards the hotel manager. Durand instinctively retreated and bumped his head on the lift wall. The gentle thud echoed around his temporary metal prison. The Singaporean eyeballed the Frenchman, standing so close he could count the blood vessels streaking across the whites of the other man's eyes like a spider's legs. He revelled in such moments. He felt alive. Positivity flowed through every pore. He was unstoppable, untameable, untouchable. He was an energy field, his batteries fully charged, a force for good in perpetual motion. He had no weaknesses, no pressure points, no inferiorities. Low was gone—back in the apartment, lost in the bedroom, wallowing in self-loathing, pointlessly flailing around like an upturned cockroach. Ah Lian had taken charge—a gung-ho gangster with a police badge. He would get whatever was required from this pants-pissing Frenchman. He would mock him, insult him, ridicule him, horrify him and crush him if necessary. But he would prevail. He pushed his nose against that of the quivering hotel manager.

"No more bullshit. There isn't enough time. You're gonna show me his hotel suite, now. You're gonna do whatever

222

I tell you to do. Or I am gonna kill you, right here, right now, in this fucking lift. I'm gonna kill you and your family right now. I'm gonna make a call, cancel your employment pass, pull your wife out of her yoga class, pull your kids out of international school. And then I'm gonna arrest you for obstructing my enquiries. You won't get a job in a Geylang brothel after this. So what's it gonna be ..."

The lift bell dinged and the doors opened. Waiting outside, a middle-aged American couple gasped. Low backed away and smiled broadly at the confused couple. "It's OK, we're old friends. He just lost a lot of money in the casino. Enjoy your stay in Singapore. Make sure you try the chilli crab."

The plump American, wearing a Hawaiian shirt and shin-high white sports socks ushered his gawping wife into the lift quickly as Low led the hotel manager into the corridor. The inspector waved enthusiastically to the tourists as the doors closed. "Now, take me to his room."

Durand danced in the doorway, craning his head back and forth as he desperately tried to monitor both the infuriating inspector's flagrant trespassing and the hotel corridor for any unexpected and most unwanted visitors. "I could get fired for this, just for letting you into this suite. This is a Straits Suite."

"I could get you fired if you didn't let me into the room. Now stand there and shut up."

"But he could return any minute."

"No, he won't."

"How do you know?"

Low dashed through the rooms, navigating his way around the ostentatious opulence—the piano beside the full-length windows overlooking Marina Bay, the KTV lounge, the sunken marble bath, the private gym, the full kitchen, the office, complete with 24-hour butler service—all the obvious signs of an Asian businessman's affluence; all in one extraordinary hotel suite. The inspector turned to face the jittery hotel manager and held up his mobile phone. "Because I know exactly where he is. Now, you're telling me there are no interconnecting doors here, no private internal staircases."

"Of course not. This is a hotel, not Alice in Wonderland. Our guests' privacy is critical. We are finished without it."

Low smiled. "Of course it is. If you don't close one eye, they all go to Macau, right? Over there, they close both eyes."

But he was flummoxed. The Straits Suite offered no insight beyond the man's wealth and value to the casino. He ambled over to the window. The view was undeniably spectacular. Historic Singapore was dwarfed by hubristic Singapore. Money trumped memories on the mainland. The facing skyscrapers overshadowed the Boat Quay shophouses in every sense. Only the grand old lady of the Fullerton Hotel emerged with her dignity intact. Age could not wither her. She hadn't turned to seed from being endlessly fed casino chips. She had retained her colonnade curves and her ageless beauty. Low made out the small, curved balcony on the Fullerton Hotel roof and thought about Leonard Viljoen. And then he remembered unzipping the suitcase and discovering Wong Yu Lin's body; two dead bodies on opposite sides of the same bay. If he had to die in either hotel, he'd pick the grand old lady. She was less dazzling, but softer. The inspector realised he was drawing the outline of the Fullerton Hotel roof on the window. He stepped back suddenly and examined the frames. "Do these windows open?"

Durand shot him a withering look. "We're on the 51st floor."

"Yes, all right, and there are definitely no internal staircases anywhere to switch between rooms and floors."

"Detective, please."

"Inspector. What do you do in a fire then? You must have a fire drill, a safety procedure."

"Of course, we have an internal stairwell and we evacuate, if the lifts are disabled."

"What if people were trapped up here on the 51st floor?"

"We have common access windows at the end of each corridor that are marked with red triangles. They are firemen's access windows. Those windows can be smashed in the event of a fire. These windows cannot, under any circumstances, be opened."

"Look, how would someone get from one room to another room in an emergency? There must be a way. There has to be a way. What if there was a fire inside this hotel room and the guests couldn't get to the corridor?"

"Then we contain the fire."

"Yeah and let the bastards burn."

"I never said that. I said we contain the fire, stop it spreading to other rooms and floors."

"You let the bastards burn. That should be your corporate pledge."

"I'm sorry, I cannot help you and I really must get back to work."

Low noticed the manager's agitation. "What exactly do you keep looking at in the corridor?" The inspector brushed past the fidgeting Frenchman and followed his eye line. "You're looking at the camera aren't you? Why do you keep looking at the CCTV?"

"I'm not. I need to get back to work."

"It's the camera, isn't it? That's the only incriminating evidence. That's the only thing that will show someone leaving this room and going down to room 4088 on the day of the murders. That's the only way someone can get from room to room in this place, unless the rooms are next door to each other. It's up there, isn't it?"

Low wagged his finger at the camera and continued, "You've done it, haven't you? You've somehow doctored the tapes. You've cut the footage of him leaving this room and heading down to the other one. You've cut it out and spliced empty footage together. Haven't you?"

Durand examined this pathetic Singaporean. He almost pitied him. "Inspector, I can't even begin to ... they'd have to go back down to the lobby, walk out into the lobby, change lifts, go back up to the 40th floor, with a hotel room card key. There are cameras everywhere, in all those places. Look, if what you're saying was even possible, would I still be standing here talking to you? Would I still be in Singapore? You say you have the power to kick me out of the country for not showing you a hotel room and I believe you. Really. But what do you think the Sands owners would do back in Vegas if I risked jeopardising their close relationship with the Singapore Government with such an overt, illegal act? What would your government do if I changed security footage of Marina Bay Sands? We cannot advertise the casino. We cannot take coach parties to the casino from the housing estates. We cannot mention the casino on TV. We get fined for any and every minor mistake and misstep. We cannot even have signs around Marina Bay directing guests to the casino. The Government needs us to be invisible. We want to be invisible. We cannot cross the road from the hotel to the casino without the Government watching us. And you think I have the power to order MBS security to wipe CCTV footage on heaven knows how many cameras? Do you think I would even try? Surely you, of all people, are not that naive, inspector?"

Low didn't speak at first. He divided his gaze between

the omnipresent eye in the hotel corridor and the lecturing hotel manager. He was playing head tennis, but his opponent wasn't breaking. He had never met a liar he couldn't bluff. He was a masterful liar. Ah Lian was the most belligerent of bullshitters. He didn't just hear lies. He could smell them. Durand was probably telling the truth.

Low realised he was smiling. "I'm sick of this place. You got a bar downstairs, one out on the bay?"

"Why? Are you going to interrogate the bar staff?"

"No, frog's legs, I'm going to get pissed."

Chan rushed out of the hawker centre holding a cup of coffee. He balanced the coffee on the roof of his car, above the driver's seat, and grabbed his phone.

"Hey boss, he's just had lunch ... No, he had it at Bedok Corner of all places, very quiet ... *Yah lah*, opposite the army camp, good Malay food inside ... Just a couple of guys, don't know who they were ... I think I got some photos, might be a bit *blur* ... OK, suspect is heading back to his car ... Sorry, sorry, I won't call him 'suspect' anymore ... No *lah*, we been in East Coast the whole time."

The bar owner dumped a fresh beer beside the empty glasses on Low's table. "You want me to clear them," she drawled in an Australian accent defiantly undiluted by her time in Singapore.

"No thanks, I'm working on a collection." The inspector was developing a slur. The snarl usually came later. "Tell me, what made you leave Australia to set up a bar here?"

Low nodded towards the bay in front of them. The bar squeezed itself snugly in the middle of Marina Bays Sands' Event Plaza promenade, not far from Pangaea, one of the world's most profitable nightclubs. On a quiet night, Pangaea made more money than the inspector did in two years. He didn't understand his country anymore. He didn't even recognise it. The Australian was more at home in Marina Bay than he was.

She shrugged her shoulders as she wiped down his table. "Ah, I dunno. It's like Melbourne without the danger, you know. You got the multiculturalism without the tension. You got the nightlife without the crime. You got the beer without the sports jocks. Yeah, nah, Singapore's perfect."

"Oh, it's perfect all right, just fucking perfect."

The bar owner was shocked by the sudden invective. She checked his eyes. A reddish tinge was developing. He was on the way. "Do you think you might have had enough, mate?"

Low produced his police ID and dropped it on the table beside his empty beer glasses. "I'm a detective inspector for the Corrupt Practices Investigation Bureau. Do you know what we do?"

"I've got no idea."

He raised his glass. "We get drunk on duty."

The bar owner smiled and stopped wiping the table. "So what's that like then?"

"Being drunk?"

"No, I mean being a copper in Singapore. I imagine it must be quite dull at times. In Melbourne, we've had the Italian and Greek crime gangs, Chopper Read, the whole *Underbelly* thing, loads of gangland shootings over the years. Yeah, nah, running a bar in Melbourne, you never feel completely safe, you know what I mean?"

"Of course I do. You're right. Very smart one. It's the easiest job in the world; a policeman in Singapore, damn solid. All we do is sterilise cats in the housing estates and march in a straight line at National Day Parades," slurred Low, trying to point in a straight line. "It's easy. You could do it."

"No, thanks. I'm ambitious."

"Yeah, right."

The bar owner turned to leave the inspector to drown his sorrows in peace. He raised a glass to her as she headed back into the Singaporean sanctuary of air-conditioning. In another life, he might have fancied her. But he didn't have another life. He was stuck with this one. He stepped down from his stool and wandered towards the promenade. The alcohol had given him a taste for melodrama. He wanted to join Marina Bay in toasting his failure. He wandered along the narrow jetty, with the floating, glassy crystal pavilion beside him—another architectural acknowledgment of the bay's success and direction. The pavilion housed a Louis Vuitton store.

Low ambled past a pair of gabbling Chinese tourists clutching shopping bags and stopped at the water's edge. He raised his beer glass to the omnipotent skyscrapers that circled the bay he no longer recognised. He spotted the Fullerton Hotel and turned his back on the bay. He threw his head back and downed the beer. The unremitting glare scorched his eyes. The unforgiving sun stung his cheeks. But he didn't feel worthy of shade. He was in the mood for masochism.

As the cool, soothing beer flowed, he tried to open his eyes. He wasn't sure why, to stare down the sun, to force tears in public. His narrow squint offered slits of shelter from the sunrays. There was something swinging, rocking from side to side. A pair of silhouettes, dropping; dropping and swinging, dropping and swinging, between the gaps in the gently swaying palm trees. The silhouettes couldn't be there, he convinced himself. His drunken eyes were betraying him. They couldn't be there; suspended in the sky, scaling the vertical sides of Marina Bay Sands' three monolithic tributes to money.

He narrowed his eyes further, his eyelids almost touching as warm tears wriggled free to escape the blinding sunlight. The silhouettes were still there, descending further and faster, gaining momentum; dropping and swinging, dropping and swinging. Low stood up suddenly and wiped his eyes. Using his hand as a sun visor, he craned his head again and stepped back to take in the panoramic vista; three packs of cards knitted together by the SkyPark, always threatening to collapse at any moment. Low scanned all three towers. There were more of them; dropping and swinging, dropping and swinging.

The inspector ran back to his table at the bar. His shaking hands reached for the phone, but instead knocked his beer glass off the table. Customers mocked the mad Chinese man stumbling around outside in the midday sun. The smashing glass had made them jump. The bar owner tilted her head in exasperation. Low mouthed an apology and then smiled as he dashed back onto the Event Plaza promenade with his phone. He surveyed the glassy facade of Marina Bay Sands and began nodding furiously. "Ah, James, it's me. Listen, we need to get an address and get over there right now. I've got it. It's the bloody window cleaners."

Chan pulled over quietly, a safe distance away, in Changi North Crescent. He was in the middle of an industrial estate, surrounded by factories filled with cheap labour in gloves and hairnets packing airline meals. He checked over both shoulders before reaching for his binoculars on the passenger seat. The Indonesian pressed a buzzer at the entrance of a nondescript, boxy building beside a bus stop. The building was at least 50 metres back from its perimeter fence. There was a patch of grass between the two, but no garden to speak of. The building itself was only a few storeys high, perhaps two or three, and appeared to be windowless, from the outside at least. Chan struggled to tell. The building was covered in a green skin, almost an eco-friendly membrane, perhaps to keep the sun out or the privacy in. The unimaginative, rectangular building literally camouflaged itself, withdrawing from Changi North Crescent and merging with its grass field; just another functional, unremarkable building in a street filled with functional, unremarkable buildings.

When The Indonesian had finished speaking into the intercom, the gates opened and he swept through quickly. The gates closed behind him immediately. Two men in dark suits, perspiring heavily in the equatorial sunshine, greeted him enthusiastically, shaking his hand. They ushered him along the gravel drive, chatting amiably and laughing loudly at his comments before disappearing into the building. Chan thought he'd better get out. He trotted briskly along the deserted road. During work shifts, Singapore's industrial estates were ghost towns until everyone clocked off and poured into bus stops and onto the backs of trucks like armies of ants desperately searching for a grain of something sweet. If he was spotted, he knew he had the convincing cover of the bus stop beside the building's entrance. He had to find an answer for Low's inevitable question later. What the hell was a syndicate boss doing, wandering around Changi's industrial park?

Tan struggled to keep up. He watched his younger, marginally fitter friend march ahead of him, weaving his way through the Chinatown crowd. They left Neil Road and headed into a side street of restored shophouses. The properties once housed car mechanics and food stalls; now they housed Ferrari owners and boutique businesses. Low knocked aside a couple of dithering tourists and sprinted up the staircase of a shophouse. Tan paused to offer a breathless 'sorry' before trudging wearily up the staircase. He passed a gold nameplate beside the doorway. It read: *A Touch of Glass*.

As Low slalomed his way through the confined office space, further restricted by bookcases and cluttered desks, a petite Chinese girl blocked his path. "I'm sorry, do you have an appointment? Mr Samy is very busy."

"Get out of the way." The inspector sidestepped the apprehensive secretary and pushed open the door to a separate glass-partitioned wall at the back of the office. An Indian man, in his early forties and dressed smartly in a white shirt and dark tie, rose from behind his chair. Low gritted his teeth and pointed at the swivel chair. "You. Sit. Now."

Samy puffed out his chest. An Indian businessman didn't become successful in Singapore by kowtowing to the voice of the majority every time. "You can't come here into my office, into my company and tell me ..."

Low flashed his police ID. "I'm Detective Inspector Low and I'm CPIB, which means I have a licence to do whatever the fuck I want. Now sit down before I knock you down."

Samy sat down slowly as a red-faced, huffing Tan joined them.

"What's this all about? I haven't done anything. I know I haven't done anything."

Low pointed at a large company logo of a gleaming chandelier above the words "*A Touch of Glass*" on the wall behind Samy. "You clean windows right?"

"Well, we don't just clean windows. We also install ..."

"Do you clean the windows at Marina Bay Sands. Yes or no?"

"Well, yes."

"And you don't use a ... what do you call it?" Low cupped his hands and faced his colleague.

"A cradle," Tan interjected.

"Yeah, a cradle, one of those platforms."

"Er, no, we use the rope access model."

"Correct. And how does that work?"

"It's, er, well, it's the same techniques used in rock climbing. We anchor the ropes to a fixed point and the cleaner abseils down the side of the building. Why?"

"So you fix the ropes where? To the Marina Bay Sands roof?"

"Yes. There are anchor points at the top of each of the three towers. Why? Why are you asking me these questions? These are issues that I think you should ask Marina Bay Sands security."

"I'm asking you. So you send teams of cleaners over the side? And they come down floor by floor?"

"Yes, usually in pairs, sometimes in threes or fours. I prefer to have the cleaners close to each other, working in tandem. They clean the windows faster and they can help each other."

"Those are the windows on the Marina Bay side, where it's all glass. I've seen those guys. But on the other side, the side facing the sea, are all balconies. How do you clean them?"

Samy eyed the policemen nervously. "We, er, just go through the hotel rooms, like the regular room cleaners, and clean the balconies that way."

"So you don't swing down the building on those ropes?"

"No need. It's all balconies. We don't need to and besides we couldn't; it's not a straight, flat glass surface. We don't need to use the ropes to clean that side of the towers."

Low smiled and nodded. "Yeah, that's what I thought. There's no way you could use ropes, and even a daredevil cleaner is not going to climb down a dozen balconies. Even if he was stupid enough, he'd be seen by the thousands of cars going by. So you don't clean the windows using ropes on that side of the hotel towers?"

"No, I said that already. We just go through the hotel rooms and clean the doors on the balconies."

"That's not true is it, Samy?"

The cleaning company owner fidgeted with a pen on his desk. "What do you mean?"

"I went and had a look at the back of those towers. There are windows that must be cleaned, windows that can only be reached by rope access. There are windows sticking out from those suites in Tower 1 and, more than that, there are common corridor windows at the sides of each tower that run all the way from the top floor to the lobby. Isn't that right, Samy?"

"Er, well . . ."

"They can only be cleaned by cleaners coming down on ropes. Isn't that right, Samy?"

"Yes."

"Yes, it fucking is. Do you know, Detective Inspector Tan, that there are rope anchors on the roof of Tower 1, practically on top of the Straits Suites and only 15 floors above room 4088? I've watched these cleaners. They're like commandos. They can drop down floors in seconds. And room 4088 is almost in the corner of the tower. It's right in the corner. It's right beside those common corridor windows. Those cleaners control their ropes, their . . . what do you call it?"

"Their slack," Tan offered.

"That's it, their slack. If they make the ropes just a little bit loose, they could move past the windows, along the wall, turn, and step into the balcony of room 4088, couldn't they, Samy?"

"I cannot speculate on something like that."

"Yes, you can speculate. Could those cleaners come down the side of Tower 1 and just reach around into the balcony of room 4088?"

"How do I know? I wasn't there. Marina Bay Sands is such a big cleaning operation for my company, my biggest contract. It's 57 floors across three blocks plus the shopping centre. Have you got any idea how many windows that is?"

Low rested his elbows on the table and glared at Samy. "You employ all foreigners to clean the windows right? Filipino supervisors, is it? Bangladeshi minions? A few Indians and China guys, right? All on the correct employment passes are they? I'm sure you pay them the correct salaries so they meet the tougher wage requirements for the new employment pass right? You want us to check? You want me to call the Ministry of Manpower? You want us to find cleaners on the wrong work visas? You want me to fine you for any we don't like? And I will find them. You want us to take away your licence? Because I will. I'll take it today. You won't be allowed to clean the windows of your own fucking condo by the time I'm finished."

"Yes," Samy whimpered.

"Yes what?"

"Yes, they would have enough rope to reach the nearest balconies on that side of Tower 1, the ones nearest the common corridor windows," Samy sighed loudly.

Low heard his heart pumping. Adrenaline surged through his body and raced towards his nerve endings so quickly, his skin tingled. Euphoria would soon consume him, but revelation came before delirium. The highs focused his thoughts. They harnessed him. Ideas flooded his mind. All he had to do was hold on, stay afloat and not go under. The mania would do the rest. "How often is Marina Bay Sands cleaned?"

"Oh, once every couple of months. Depends on the time of year ... rainy season ... haze ..."

"Were those corridor windows along the side of Tower 1 cleaned on the afternoon of the murders?"

"What murders?"

"Don't. Just don't. Not now. Were those windows cleaned on the afternoon of the murders?"

"I'm sorry. I can't say. I'd have to ..."

Low leapt across the desk and grabbed Samy by the throat. "Were the fucking corridor windows cleaned on the afternoon of the murders?"

"Yes."

The inspector released the spluttering Indian, who flopped back into his executive leather seat clutching his throat. Low looked down at the coughing fool. "Of course they were. Because you already knew this didn't you? Because I've checked with MBS security. Your cleaners, like all other non-essential staff, had to stop work while we carried out our preliminary investigations. You couldn't carry on with your window cleaning on the other towers. You had to stop. And as soon as you heard about the murders, the first thing you did was check your work rosters didn't you? Didn't you, you sneaky bastard? You checked who was cleaning what and where, didn't you, you little shit?"

Samy refused to make eye contact. "Yes."

"And did it?"

"Did it what?"

"Did the roster show that the common corridor windows near room 4088 were scheduled to be cleaned on the day of the murders?"

"Yes."

"Yes." Low glanced across at Tan. He smiled and nodded. Low went on, "So, we are left with three possible scenarios, only three, Samy. One, they cleaned the windows on the same day—the same day—did nothing wrong and it was just an insane coincidence. Two, they cleaned the windows, saw something and no one from this company thought about

236

letting us know. Or three, they were involved. They reached the balcony using your rope access method."

Samy said nothing. There was nothing to say. His self-made business, his lifetime's work, was crumbling. His proud empire was collapsing.

"You have a roster, right? So you know who cleaned the windows that day, right?"

"Yes."

"Would they have also cleaned the windows of the 51st floor that day?"

Samy looked up suddenly. He was confused. "What?"

Tan stepped forward. "Answer the question."

"Were those common corridor windows on both the 40th and the 51st floors cleaned on the same day?" Low shouted, leaning belligerently over Samy's desk. "The floors are near to each other. I saw them fly down the windows on the Marina Bay side, it wouldn't take long."

Samy collapsed back in his chair. He half-smiled. "Yes," he whispered.

Low calmed the screaming voices in his head long enough to hear himself speak. "What was that, Samy?"

Samy straightened his tie. "Yes, same guys, same day, different floors." He released a deep sigh before continuing, "Do you know I spent 15 years building this business, started with some shophouses around here, Chinatown, got some jobs from old *kakis* cleaning their restaurant windows in Race Course Road. And then I got the MBS contract, was the happiest day of my life. My father sold *prata* for 10 cents each in Jalan Besar and I got the contract for one of the biggest hotels in the world. And after this comes out, it'll be all gone. And the worst part is, it's not even my fault."

"When did you realise?"

"When they disappeared, without being paid, a day after

the murders. They hadn't been with us long. I only hired them as a favour. They didn't even look like window cleaners; too big, too smart to be window cleaners, too clever, and they never complained. Never. The others always complain. The Filipinos, the Bangladeshis, something always makes them upset—their salary, their hours, their accommodation—but these guys never said anything, never complain. In Singapore, everyone complains. That's how I knew something was not right, even before. When they disappeared, I checked the roster and I knew. I should've called you guys, I know that."

"Yes you should. This might be considered obstruction, withholding information. You're going to have to give us everything now, and I mean everything—work rosters, employment records, IC numbers, flight details, accommodation, pay slips, everything."

"I know. I know. I'm going to lose everything now, right? I should never have hired them. I should've been tougher. And now I've got to live with that. I'll never forgive myself."

Tan crossed his arms. "Why?"

"They weren't like my other cleaners. They didn't fit in. My guys are usually from Bangladesh, the Philippines and maybe Myanmar. These three guys were different. They were from Indonesia."

Chapter 19

LOW pursed his lips and held onto the dashboard as Tan overtook a car in the middle lane. They still had time before rush hour reduced the traffic to a crawl, but the East Coast Parkway was always busy. The rows of palm trees along the beach merged into a green blur as the inspectors sped towards the Changi industrial park.

"Come on, we're not in a funeral," Low shouted over the engine. "Accelerate *lah*."

"I'm going *lah*, *basket*." Tan changed lanes again, weaving between the taxis and cars heading for Changi Airport, everyone pulled towards the green dome of the air traffic control tower. "Eh, we got enough to charge him?"

"We got enough to hold the bastard. We got sobbing Samy's work rosters. Three Indonesians open his window, grab a needle, some tablets, swing across to Richard Davie's room, give him the needle in the balls, job done."

Tan honked his horn at a taxi hogging the overtaking lane. "*Eh*, move *lah*, bastard. You want a ticket? ... Hey, OK. So we got three Indonesian Spidermen swinging across Marina Bay Sands, but how they get inside the room? How they open the balcony door? You think they're Tarzan, is it? Come on man."

"I don't know. Richard opened for them? Maybe they said

it was an emergency? Heck care *lah*, we'll find out when we arrest the bastard. It doesn't matter. We got enough for me to bluff the Minister while we hold him. We got the motive. Richard Davie was investigating his gambling syndicate. And we got the means—three of his *kelong* bastards drug Davie and throw the prostitute in the case."

"It sounds ridiculous."

"They clean their windows on the day they were killed and then skip the country the next without being paid. You don't think that's fucked up?"

"I don't know."

"Exactly. Now hurry up *lah*."

Chan had been sitting at the bus stop for more than an hour. No one else had gone in or out of the building behind him. As the bus stop served only one bus service, every driver had stopped to let him on, and then swore at him in Mandarin for not moving. He had waved them away quickly, not wishing to draw attention to himself. He stood up to stretch his legs and peered through the fence. Apart from a couple of security guards wandering around the grounds, the property was eerily quiet.

Low pressed the phone so hard his ear throbbed. He slapped his other hand repeatedly on the dashboard. "Come on, James, come on, let's go, man ... Ah, Charlie, we're on our way, what's happening? ... He's still inside?" He checked the clock in the car. "But that's more than an hour. What's he doing in there? ... No, I know you don't know. Are you sure there's no other exit, no back door or anything ... How can you be sure? ... It backs onto the airport? Charlie, where exactly are you? What's the name of the place?"

As Low listened, he appeared to freeze. His eyes glazed

over. His jaw loosened. He felt his lips drying. He dropped the phone and began punching the dashboard. "You're a fucking idiot," he raged, the veins at the side of his forehead snaking through his skin.

Tan took his hand off the wheel and grabbed his colleague's shoulder. "Whoa, whoa, whoa, what are you doing? Get your hands off my car."

Low clenched both fists and unleashed a primal scream so violent, so powerful, it unnerved the veteran policeman. "Do you know where he's been for the last hour? Do you know where he's been? Inside the Singapore Freeport."

Tan absorbed the information slowly and carefully. Then he slapped his steering wheel. "Shit. Shit. Shit. What a fucking idiot."

Their car mounted the pavement and screeched to a halt beside the bus stop in Changi North Crescent. A couple of factory workers sitting beside Chan jumped back, terrified. The inspectors charged out of the car, leaving their doors open.

Low reached his junior partner first and grabbed him by the scruff of the neck. "Do you have any idea what this place is, you idiot? Didn't you check first?"

Tan pulled him away. "We haven't got time for that now. Move."

Beside the Singapore Freeport sign, Tan buzzed the intercom repeatedly. "This is Detective Inspector James Tan. Open this gate now."

"This is a private storage facility," a voice crackled through the intercom. "Do you have a warrant or official permission?"

Low was out of patience. "I've got a big gun. When I shoot you with it you'll know this was official police business. Now open the fucking gate."

Low flashed his ID badge to the CCTV camera positioned above the gates. Finally, there was a buzzing sound, and then the gates wheezed and creaked before slowly separating. The CPIB inspector squeezed through first, drawing his Beretta and dashing along the gravel drive. Still clueless, Chan pulled his standard issue Taurus Model 85, desperately hoping he wouldn't need to use it. When the gates had parted enough, Tan chased after them.

They ran quickly as the tension lifted their legs. They were so close. It was almost over. At the checkpoint, the two tubby security guards waddled down from their post. "Eh, hang on, cannot go inside," the elder, senior guard said meekly. "Cannot, not without a warrant."

Low swivelled and shoved his gun in the security guard's face. "Eh, Billy, don't be a hero, OK. Not now. I got enough bullets to shoot you and the guy inside. So sit down, shut up and drink *kopi*, OK."

"Now, what's the problem, here?"

The detectives turned to face a suited Singapore Freeport employee that Chan had spotted earlier through his binoculars. The tall, well-groomed man offered a hand to Low. "I'm Kim Siang Yi and I'm the manager ..."

"I don't care if you're Kim Jong-il. Where's The Indonesian?"

"I'm sorry. Where's who?"

"Chinese guy, mid-forties, quite handsome, grey hair above his ears, wearing black trousers and a white Ralph Lauren shirt," Chan said matter-of-factly. "He came in here exactly 75 minutes ago. You stood at this exact spot in front of the security post there. You shook his hand and then you went inside."

"Oh, that guy," Kim exclaimed, as if recalling a distant encounter. "Yes, of course. Yes, well, he's gone."

Low's face twisted as if wracked with pain. Tan nodded ruefully. Chan glanced furtively at both senior officers like a little dog lost. "He's not gone. He can't be gone. He's inside. I saw him go inside. He never came out."

"He's gone," Tan sighed.

"How can he be gone? I've been sitting at that bus stop over there, getting an itchy backside for nearly two hours and no one came out. So where the fuck did he go?"

Low lost it. He pulled Chan by the arm, squeezing him tightly as he dragged him along, down the side of the building. "You see that there? You see it? Right in front us, that's the private runway for private jets. And our man is up there, right now, flying away, free as a fucking bird. Isn't that right, Kim Jong-il?"

Kim began, "Now look . . ."

"No, you look," Low interrupted, releasing the junior officer and pointing his gun in the Singapore Freeport manager's face. "Me and Detective Inspector Tan have been doing this a long time. We know what you do here and we will make sure—I will make sure—that the last face you see before the judge sends you away is mine."

Chan thought he was going to cry. "So, what, this guy has helped The Indonesian escape? I don't understand what's going on here."

"Come on, Charlie. Singapore Freeport is where rich people buy and sell rich things, almost tax-free, no one asks any questions," Tan explained. "It's like we bring a little bit of Switzerland to Singapore and stick it in front of Changi Airport. *Towkays* come, get off their private jet, this *basket* has a limo to pick them up from the runway, give them champagne, take them to see a nice Van Cock painting, and then they buy it. That's it. No need to waste time filling in so many tax forms because they never leave the airport. Then they have another glass of champagne and get back on the plane. And no one knows they were even in Singapore. Not their wife, not the taxman, not their country, not anyone. Right or not, Mr Kim?"

"We are a prestigious storage facility of luxury items offering a discreet service to VIP guests . . ."

"Balls to you," Tan shouted. "You are a Singaporean bastard. You exploit our tax system to make rich people richer and poor people like me poorer. You make me embarrassed to be Singaporean."

The portly inspector found himself clenching his fist and stepping towards the smarmy, squirrelly, Singapore Freeport employee. Low intervened, stepping between the two men. "Eh, enough with the flag-waving already, where is he?"

"I'm afraid he didn't tell me."

"You had to get your limo to drop him off in front of a plane or a gate, right."

Kim stifled a giggle. "It's not like regular airlines where you line up at a departure lounge."

Now Low's eyes bulged. The veins danced around his neck like boiling spaghetti. He grabbed Kim by the throat and pushed his stubby, Beretta pistol into Singapore Freeport manager's nostril. The gun muzzle protruded through the skin of Kim's nose. "Don't fucking patronise me. Your people dropped him off at the steps of his plane. Where did he go?"

Chan gently grabbed his senior officer by the elbow. "Hey boss, no need *ah*. No need to do this. We can check with Changi Airport where he is?"

"Get the fuck off me," Low roared, shrugging his partner away. "Now, tell me, or I'll send your nose over to Indonesia to join him. Where is he?"

Kim held his shaking hands up, a pitiful act of self-defence. "I don't know. He never told me. He doesn't have to tell me."

Low pulled the pistol forcefully from his nose, ripping the flesh open. Blood flowed from his nostril and covered his teeth. This time, the inspector forced the barrel deep into his mouth. "Where is he now?"

Tan edged towards his old colleague. "Stanley, that's enough."

"No, this doesn't end when that fucker says it ends. It ends when I say it ends. Where is he now?"

Kim started to heave. His eyes watered. He was choking on the gun barrel. "He got on an MBS plane. That's all I know. That's it. He got on an MBS plane. We're not even allowed to ask where they're going, especially the casino planes. We can't ... please ... I can't breathe."

Kim retched violently. Low ripped the gun out of his mouth just before the vomit spattered against the Singapore Freeport manager's shiny black shoes.

Low was out of the car before the engine had stopped. He realised he was running, sprinting; fury and frustration pumping his legs like pistons. The garden gate creaked loudly as the inspector kicked it open, loosening the hinges in the wooden post. He passed the Japanese-themed garden, with its Bonsai trees, stone pagodas and koi carp pond. Water cascaded down a sheet of glass and flowed into the pond, an expensive but artificial and tacky indulgence common among the landed properties that ringed the Bukit Timah forest. Singapore's wealthiest found tranquillity and privacy among the dense foliage. They had to put down the native monkey population to maintain their tranquillity, but a few dead macaques were a small price to pay for an undisturbed view of such natural splendour.

The inspector pressed the doorbell continuously. He craned his neck up at the monstrous three-storey house. A pair of Chinese guardian lions sat on marble bases jutting out from the second floor. They were cast in bronze. The symbolism was ostentatious but fitting. In Singapore, this was a modern Chinese imperial palace. Money oozed from the ghastly property. Low toyed with the idea of throwing a rock at the bronze beasts, but he already knew the outcome. He would barely scratch the surface.

He kicked the oak-panelled door. His toecap left a scuffed dent at the base of the door. "Open this door now or I will kick it down. I don't give a shit who you are."

He booted the door again, harder this time, leaving wooden splinters in the grooves of the pebbled path. "Open this fucking door now."

Low heard the door handle turn. The door opened slowly and deliberately.

"You tipped him off didn't you? Admit it. You told him we were after him."

The Minister for Home Improvement opened the door a little wider, but still no more than a crack. "Who are you talking about?"

"Really? You want to do this now? Really?" Low took a step towards the door. The Minister instinctively recoiled. There was something in the policeman's eyes; something he rarely saw among his constituents—fearlessness.

"Look, there's no need for any unnecessary aggression on my doorstep."

"All right, I'll come in."

"No, no, no, we can chat here. That's fine."

"When did you tell The Indonesian we were coming for him?"

"Inspector, I don't know what you're talking about. And I really don't like what you are insinuating."

"I don't give a shit what you like. He was here while

we were putting the case together, we get a breakthrough and then he's out the Changi Airport back door, through the Singapore Freeport back door, where all your neighbours keep their fancy paintings. You know Singapore Freeport. You know what it's for, who it's for. You opened the bloody thing. You were the only one who could've warned him."

"Now, look, I appreciate all your hard work and respect your track record at CPIB, but have you forgotten who you are talking to. I could ..."

"You could what? Stop me from interviewing a murder suspect? Take me off the case? You still want to move me over to cyber-terrorism? You want me to oversee hacking? You want me to explore the mechanics of hacking? You want to give me the tools to hack government websites? You're supposed to be the genius here."

The Minister opened the door wide and stood firm. He had earned his political stripes, working his way through the stat boards and the permanent secretaries to avoid being bullied. He did the bullying. He was never bullied. It was not a reciprocal agreement in Singapore. "Are you trying to blackmail the person who oversees your employers?"

"Is this the point where I shit myself? You go back to your ivory tower. I'll go back to the street. Let's see who does the most damage first."

The Minister smiled. "I can see why everyone at CPIB rates you so highly."

"No more bullshit. We will monitor every Marina Bay Sands flight into this country, every private jet. Immigration and customs will check every passport. I'll get in touch with Indonesia, Macau, Vietnam, Hong Kong. I know them all. We will catch this bastard. And if you warn him again, I'll have every hacker in Asia telling this story. I'll give this story to Human Rights Watch, Amnesty International, everybody."

"Some might call that sedition."

"Sedition? I try to arrest a foreigner for killing a Singaporean woman and it's called sedition now?"

"I told you before, calm exteriors. We're not too worried about the size of the boat. It's all about the motion of the ocean, remember?"

"OK. You waste my time with *cheem* Confucius talk. Your job is the bigger picture, fine. My job is to catch killers."

"Definitely."

"Right, then. Bring me The Indonesian or I will leak the whole fucking story."

The Minister closed the door without either man saying goodbye. Low picked up a loose pebble on the path and threw it at one of the bronze guardian lions. He missed.

The bedroom was cavernous, but surprisingly minimalist. Apart from a king-sized bed, a built-in wardrobe and a couple of paintings hung either side of the flat-screen TV, the room looked more like a show flat than a real home. Standing over his bed, the Minister held his phone, nodding impatiently. "No, I think everything will be fine ... Yes, he's gone ... Get the other one reassigned first ... No, don't put him on cyber-terrorism ... Yeah, exactly, we can worry about that later ... Look, I've really got to go, got to make another call ... Yeah, OK, bye."

The Minister threw the phone onto a pillow and stared at his bed. He smiled. "You really are a pretty little thing, aren't you?"

"Thank you."

Yue Liang rolled onto her back and adjusted her black bra. She knew the Minister was a breast man. He had told her so at a recent family fun day. When she was satisfied with her cleavage, she started to roll her panties slowly down her slender thighs. She stopped halfway and grinned coyly at the middle-aged politician.

"If my LA trip doesn't happen, I will be allowed to do the National Day song this year, right?"

"Of course," the Minister replied, unbuttoning his shirt. "You're a Singapore icon."

Chapter 20

YUE Liang rolled over in bed. She felt violated. She watched him fiddle with his unfashionable, *ah pek* underpants beneath the sheets. She loathed what she was doing, despised the calculated hypocrisy. She sold feminism to her fans through her songs. She sold herself to pay for the studio time. She had only really loved one man in her life and he was dead. There was nowhere left to go. He turned on his side and faced her.

"Where were you today?"

"Oh, nothing much, went shopping."

Jimmy Chew knew his wife was lying. When she sighed, she sounded sincere. She pretended to pay attention to her husband. She played the good wife. When she had nothing to hide, she had no reason to disguise her indifference. He knew he was a weak, pathetic partner, but he had come to prefer the lies. She granted him eye contact when she lied. She acknowledged he existed when she lied. He swallowed hard. He tried to suppress the ball of pain rolling along the back of his throat.

"So, er, did you buy anything nice?"

"No, they didn't have anything that suited my new feminist look, you know, the street look for LA. What have you been up to?"

"Oh, I've been on the computer most of the day, trying to organise some big conference talks."

Yue Liang knew her husband was lying. He always came up with the most mundane of admin tasks to explain away hours wasted at a poker table in cyberspace.

"Did you get any bookings?"

"No, it's very slow right now, the school holidays are coming. It's never a good time for seminars and signings."

Yue Liang nodded. He had obviously lost heavily again. "Maybe we should look to do a few events together again, focus on rebuilding our family brand. That always sells the most, right?"

"Yeah, it does." Jimmy hoped his forced smile was convincing. "But we're OK, right? You're OK now, after the police interview?"

"Yeah, of course, fine. You?"

"Yeah, fine, fine. We're on a pedestal. We're there to be shot at, but we'll get through this."

Yue Liang grabbed his hand and squeezed tightly. Her nose brushed against his. Her beauty was breathtaking. "Of course we will. We can only send out a positive message."

"That's right."

"Oh, and it looks like I might be singing the theme song at this year's National Day Parade."

"Ah, that's great, really great."

Jimmy hugged his wife and kissed her neck gently. He didn't want her to see him crying.

Sitting in her executive chair, Dr Lai checked her watch again and tutted loudly. The fricative hung in the air of her otherwise silent office. She picked up the phone on her desk and dialled. She sighed at the recorded voice message. That inspector had done it again. She grabbed a pen and scribbled through the name "Stanley Low" in her leather-bound diary. When it came to incorrigible, irredeemable, bipolar patients like the obstreperous inspector, she truly didn't know why she bothered. In such rare, reflective moments, she secretly questioned the value of her profession. Stanley Low would never be a positive endorsement for the great strides taken by modern psychiatry. He was adamant his greatest weakness was still his greatest strength. He was a bloody waste of time.

The three policemen watched the fishermen examine their live bait. The hawker centre at Changi Village was usually filled with craggy, wrinkled, sun-ravaged anglers making their catch predictions before lugging their rods and reels onto a bumboat. Serangoon Harbour offered decent fishing just before sunset. Low envied their contentment. A rod, a reel, a packet of chicken rice and the dusky, breezy sea air offered tranquillity and a sense of personal fulfilment. They belonged. Low belonged everywhere and nowhere. His condition controlled him. If only his mood swings shared the reliable consistency of Changi's tidal patterns. He found peace only in the shadows of dark souls. He lived to catch crooks. Bad people completed him. He struggled to function in a world without criminals. He knew he was fucked up. He also knew there was nothing he could do to change that. He wasn't sure he even wanted to. Besides, there were always short-term remedies for the pain.

He raised his glass. "Right then, here's to the Singapore Government. May they continue to give shelter to money launderers, gambling syndicates and shit gamblers. And may they make it hard for us to catch them."

Tan and Chan chinked glasses in their mock toast before banging them down again on the table. "We will get him," said Tan. "I'm not like you, *basket*, I cannot *tekan* my country."

"Yeah, we will catch him," Chan concurred.

"Love the optimism, love it, but it's not gonna happen. He's half the world away."

Low reached for the ice bucket filled with bottles of Tiger Beer at the middle of the table. He topped up his glass. "We've got two murders we can't solve. And for that, I'll probably get demoted or maybe even pushed sideways for fucking up the case."

"*Wah*, so *wayang ah* this one," Tan interjected. "They're not going to move the CPIB golden boy."

"They already are. I'll be doing cybercrimes before you know it."

"Cybercrimes?" Chan echoed.

"Yes, Charlie Chan, I'll be chasing people younger than you, hiding in their parents' apartment, wearing Guy Fawkes masks and thinking they are Julian Assange. Idiots. Upset 'cos cannot get a decent job, so they terrorise from their bedrooms. Will be a waste of time. But that's modern Singapore. Our '*Gahmen*' more worried about a few blogs than a couple of murders. What to do?"

Chan scratched at the damp label on his beer bottle. "I feel bad for the woman."

"That's why. Bloody sick, sadomasochistic *ang moh basket*, got no sympathy for him, but why did she have to die?"

Low shook his head. "I still cannot understand why she was even there. Richard Davie was shagging Yue Liang any time he wanted. He could've gone to Orchard Towers and picked up a nice Filipino half her age and twice as pretty."

Chan sipped slowly from his glass. "*Yah lah*, was the same in Balestier. All the girls say they cannot understand why she go with this one. They said Rosie had her clients and she told them about them, but she never mention this *ang moh* before, must have been her one and only time, so sad."

Low sat up suddenly. "Wait, wait, wait ... who's Rosie?"

Chan looked nervous. "What? Rosie. That's what some of her friends called her."

"Her name's not Rosie. Her name was Wong Yu Lin. We checked her IC, passport, NTUC card, everything. She was never called Rosie. She never had a western name."

"I don't know. Her friends just called her Rosie, must be a nickname or something."

Low tried to focus on the ice bucket of beer on the table, but the bottles were floating. He was light-headed. His legs shook under the table. The incessant hum of coffee shop chatter was overbearing, deafening, disorienting. Sweat trickled through his reddening cheeks. "Rosie ... are you absolutely sure?"

"Yah, Rosie, so?"

"They called her Rosie? A prostitute from Balestier called Rosie?"

Tan touched his colleague's arm. "You OK?"

"It wasn't just about him, it was her. It was about her," Low was rambling now, speaking quickly and repetitively. "It wasn't only the *ang moh*, it was her. It was her. We were looking in the wrong place, bloody got excited over the big shot *ang moh*, but it was her. Rosie. We were looking in the wrong place. She was meant to be there. She wasn't random. It wasn't just about him, it was her. It was Rosie. She had to be there."

"What? What was about her?"

Low jumped to his feet. He knocked his bottle over. Beer flooded the table. "Fuck, fuck, fuck, fuck!" he shouted. "It wasn't The Indonesian. I know exactly who it fucking was."

*

254

The door flew open. Low stormed into the room and pointed at the uniformed officer leaning against the opposite wall. "You. Out. Now."

"But I was told . . ."

"Out."

The officer closed the door behind him. Low turned to face the killer. "You bastard."

"*Wah lan eh*, been waiting so long already."

Tiger leaned back on his chair and rested his arms behind his head. He stretched his legs out under the table, as if sitting in a first-class cabin rather than the Changi Prison interview room. His black trousers were neatly pressed and his white vest revealed his tattoos. He chuckled at the sweat-soaked, jittery inspector. "*Wah*, Ah Lian you looked much better last time."

Low's adrenaline wouldn't let him sit down. He stood opposite Tiger, eyes piercing down at his former mentor, rocking gently from side to side. "Why did you do it?

"Do what?"

"Come on, *lah*. Rosie. Fucking Rosie. You always talked about Rosie last time. I never met her, but I know she worked for you. Rosie. She was your girl, your favourite one. Your Balestier KTV lounge for the bookies, the gamblers last time, she was your girl before. No way she worked for anyone else."

Tiger smiled at the memory. "Ah, I did like Rosie. Very sweet, that one. You know she actually retired at one point, but then she came back, just for me."

"You think it was her, right?"

"I think it was her, what?"

"You think it was her who set you up. I went back and checked the file. When you were arrested, you were with a girl. It's on the file. You said you were with a prostitute. They questioned her last time and then they let her go. You never had sex with your girls last time, you were too careful, except one you said, the older one. Rosie. She was with you when they arrested you. So you think she set you up."

Tiger lowered his voice. "She did set me up."

Low leaned on the table and eyeballed the old Chinese gangster. "No, she didn't. I did. I set you up. Me. No one else. Just me. I tracked you. I fooled you. I caught you. It was my operation. I don't even know this Rosie. I never met her. You never let the other bookies and *ah longs* meet her. You didn't trust them. I didn't know her. We didn't expect you to be with anyone when we picked you up. She didn't set you up."

Tiger registered his surprise. His eyes narrowed as he sat up slightly. "Really?"

"Of course. You were finished. I had everything. Voice recordings, betting slips, bookies runners, website addresses, overseas contacts; I brought down the entire fucking syndicate. Me. Not some retired *xiao mei mei* from Balestier."

Tiger's eyes widened. "Hey, she was never a cheap *xiao mei mei*, OK? She was a good girl, Rosie."

"Whatever. She wasn't involved. It was me. Just me. You were under surveillance for weeks. We didn't care if you were with a woman that night. It didn't matter. Everything was synchronised. We were going in."

"So she never spoke to CPIB about me, never help your case?"

"What for? I followed you for more than a year. There is an entire room at CPIB just filled with your shit. What would I need a prostitute for? She died for nothing."

Tiger digested the news slowly and carefully. He appeared to shrink slightly. And then he shrugged his shoulders. "Ah, what to do?"

"How did you get Richard Davie involved?"

Tiger smiled and pointed at the inspector, suddenly

animated again. "Ah, now that one really was your fault. You got the *ang moh* bastard all excited."

"What?"

"You go to him for help *wha'*. You want data on this syndicate, that syndicate, gambling websites, and he starts to help you, helps the *'Gahmen'*, helps Interpol, Europol, every *chee bye* poll. He gets a big head, suddenly he *hao lian* everywhere, thinks he's in the CIA, starts giving you stuff about me, fucker thinks he's big time."

"He was just doing his job, like me. You told me after the trial that I was just doing my job, and you respected that."

"Of course. That's why you're still here. But Richard Davie didn't do his job."

"Yes he did."

"Your head *lah*, he worked for me." Tiger thumped his chest defiantly.

The inspector shook his head in disbelief. "What?"

"You think I set him up to watch me? Please *lah*, I set him up to watch my competition."

"You set up an online sports betting surveillance firm to protect you?"

"Mus' know about my competition *wha'*. Where you think a *blur* Aussie gets money like that to set up such a big company? What kind of Aussie sets up this kind of company to check on football betting? Aussies and football, forget it *lah*. You see. You look like Ah Lian, but still think like *blur* policeman. You never learn from last time. The *ang mohs* always easy. Just give them skinny, brown legs and good sex, finish already. You remember last time? I give them all long black hair and olive skin, and that's it. Your *ang moh* was the worst. Can never say no to Asian girl; his big weakness, likes the dirty-dirty stuff. Cannot go to his wife for these things, so he go to the Asian girls, he go to me. After that, easy. I

257

give him girls. He gives me what I need. But then the fucker forgets about me. He thinks he's Robin Hood. He helps you, he helps that pop star. He helps every bastard except me."

Tiger tapped the table with his index finger. "Idiot thought I was dead in here. But you know from last time, right? Handphone enough already."

"So he killed Rosie . . . for you?"

"For me, for his family, for love, he was a mess. I told him, 'Finish Rosie at the hotel and I'll finish everything. Tell your singer that the hotel thing was that Indonesian bastard's idea. And then, that's it. No more debt for Jimmy Chew, you can screw Yue Liang and be happy.'"

"And he agreed?"

Tiger laughed. "Of course not, *lah*."

"Then how?"

Tiger scratched his shoulder blade with a real air of indifference. "Ah, that one, very simple. I told him one of my bookies will go down and rape his wife in front of his little girl. After that, no problem."

Low sat down and stared at Tiger. He couldn't find the words. The gangster smiled at him. His former apprentice found himself smiling back. He didn't like Tiger, but he understood him. That's what made him ill. That's what made him so good at his job. "The Indonesian insulted you, didn't he?"

Tiger became animated. "*Wah lan eh*, finally. Now you get it. Now you understand. You see this? Look at this?"

Tiger slapped the tattoo of a lion on his bicep. "You know what that is, right? That's the Singapore Lion. That's me—the King of *Kelong*. Even in here, I am the king. You cannot stop me. One handphone, I control everything. I fix everything. Cannot touch me. It's mine. And this Indonesian fucker think he can take over? Cannot. You want money, gambling, women, *kelong*, you come to me, OK? You don't go to some Indonesian bastard in MBS, you come to me. I am like Changi fucking Airport; number one. This is mine. Foreigners cannot come to Singapore and take it. Cannot."

"You're saying you did all this out of . . . patriotism?"

"Singapore is mine, OK? I am the *Kelong* King. I will die the *Kelong* King."

"So the window cleaners . . ."

"*Yah lah*, of course. Three bookies from Jakarta, *wah*, those guys *ah*, proper gangsters last time. The Indian. The window cleaner, big business, thinks he's a big gambler. Forget it *lah*. Lousy gambler, owed me so much money. He told me what day they clean the windows. So, I tell Rosie do this one last thing for me, then can retire, finish. Take the *ang moh* to the hotel, tell everyone she works for The Indonesian, even knock on his door first, just for fun, ask if he wants special service; smile for your camera. Then Richard do his job and wait for them at the balcony."

"Richard Davie opened the balcony door and let them in?"

"I tell him they would take Rosie's body away. He was an Idiot. Just like The Indonesian. They think I'm finished in here. They try to take my balls in my own country. I fuck them, Ah Lian. I fuck them all."

Low sunk into his seat. There seemed to be nothing else to say. He was exhausted.

"Why?" he asked finally.

Tiger shrugged his shoulders. "Three birds, one stone, just nice. Rosie, the *ang moh* and that Indonesian bastard. He's finished. Cannot come back. That's it. You all know already; cannot close one eye. Plus, I wanted to give you something to do . . . OK not you, *lah,* the other one. The real one. Ah Lian."

"What?"

"Admit it *lah*. You enjoyed it, right? A little bit? Seeing me again, talking cock, Ah Lian back on the street, giving everybody shit, just like last time. It was fun, right?"

The younger man didn't answer. He didn't need to. They both knew the answer. Tiger leaned across the table and smiled warmly. "They cannot *tekan* you now, right? I made you a hero again, second time already. No one can mess with my Ah Lian now."

The old Chinese gangster gently patted the inspector's hand. They would miss each other. Low felt his vocal chords tighten.

"They'll hang you for this. You know that, right?"

Tiger nodded slowly. "What to do? Changi Prison cannot make it. Their *bak kut teh* damn lousy."

Glossary of popular Singapore terms and Singlish phrases (In order of appearance)

Angmoh: A Caucasian (literal Chinese translation is "red hair").

Lah: Common Singlish expression. Often used for emphasis at the end of words and sentences.

Wah lau: A mostly benign expression that can mean 'damn' or 'dear me' in Hokkien.(See *wahlaneh* for a more vulgar variation.)

Kakis: Buddies or mates.

Ahlong: Loanshark (in Hokkien).

Kelong: A colloquialism for cheating, corruption or fixed, oftenused in a sporting context. (In Malay, *kelong* is a wooden sea structure used for fishing.)

Stylo-milo: Local term for fashionable, trendy.

Talkcock: To speak nonsense.

Makan: To eat (in Malay).

Garang: Brave, reckless; powerful (in Malay).

Towkay: The big boss or leader (in Hokkien, towkay means head of the family).

Teh-c: Tea with evaporated milk and sugar.

Charkwayteow: A popular flat-noodle dish in the region.

Nasipadang: A regional dish of steamed rice served with fish, meat and vegetables.

Bao: A Chinese delicacy, a steamed bun usually filled with meat.

Siewmai: Traditional Chinese pork-filled dumplings.

Kiasu: Singaporean adjective that means "scared to fail" (in Hokkien). There's no direct equivalent in English, underlying its unique value to Singapore.

4D: A national lottery organized by Singapore Pools. But 4D has become the shorthand description for lottery games.

Teh tarik: A popular tea in Singapore, particularly at roti pratastalls. Literally translated as "pulled tea", the hot, milky drinkis poured into a cup from a considerable height, giving it afrothy,bubblyappearance.

Duakang(ortuakang): In hokkien, *duakang* translates as "big hole", a popular description on forums and blogs to describe someone who tries to "big up" himself.

Sotong: A popular seafood dish. Sotong is Malay for squid. But it's commonly used to describe an idiot, often by saying, "blur like sotong".

Wah lan eh: A naughty relative of *wah lau*. In Hokkien, it means "oh penis" or even "my penis".

Kaypoh: Someone who is nosy, a busybody. In Australia, the equivalent would be a sticky beak.

Ahpek: An elderly man.

Wayang: A Javanese word for theatre, particularly puppet theatre.Someone who is *wayang* is melodramatic, over the top or pretending.

Chee bye: One of the filthiest and most popular terms in

Singapore. It's the rudest interpretation of vagina and is heardin coffee shops, building sites, school playgrounds and living rooms. But authorities and censorship boards will always insist it doesn't exist in Singapore.

Tekan: A Malay term to hit or whack someone, but not always in the literal sense. *Tekan* means to abuse or bully. An abusive workplace might be accused of having a "*tekan* culture".

Kopi: The Hokkien word for coffee (*kopi tiam* means coffee shop).

Kana sai: Loosely means "like shit" (in Hokkien), suggesting something is poor or inadequate.

Kena whack: To get hit or criticized. In Malay, *kena* means 'to get' and often precedes something negative (e.g. *kena* whack, *kena* scolded).

Gahmen: What began life as a Singlish mispronunciation has now become a common gentle jibe when referencing the Government.

Kan ni na: A strong contender for the most abusive phrase in Hokkien.It can mean 'fuck you' or 'fucking' (e.g.*kan ni na angmoh*.)

Chickens: Slang for prostitutes.

Xiao mei mei: In Mandarin, it means "little sister". On some rather strange websites and blogs, it can also refer to attractive women and prostitutes.

Ah Lian: An *ah lian* is a common name for a stereotypically unsophisticated girl, usually Chinese, uncouth and loud, sometimes tattooed and always with an *ahbeng*.

Ahbeng: The male equivalent of an *ahlian*.A popular stereotype, an ahbeng is often depicted as a scruffy, skinny Chinese guy who favours Singlish and Hokkien vulgarities.Loud, bright clothes can be popular, along with squatting in public places and betting heavily on football matches.

LoHei: The tossing of a rawfish salad at Chinese New Year – known as the Prosperity Toss – in the hope of spreading wealth.

Cheem: A Hokkien expression used when someone or something is deep, profound or particularly clever.

Bakkutteh: The Chinese translation literally means "meat bone tea". It's more commonly known as pork rib soup. Popular bakkutteh stalls are found in Balestier Road in central Singapore.

Tahan: Malay expression meaning to take or endure (e.g. cannot *tahan* roughly means cannot take it.)

Sarong Party Girl: A derogatory term used to describe Asianwomen who go out with Caucasians and adopt Westernaffectations.

Keropok: Deep-fried crackers, popular in South-east Asia.

Gorengpisang: Bananas in fried batter, a cheap snack food.

Shiok: A fantastic, wonderfully pleasurable feeling.

Prata: A fried pancake usually served with a fish or meat-based curry.

Kosong: Malay for zero, often used when ordering prata or tea to explain that nothing should be added (e.g. two *kosong* would mean two plain prata.)

Wo ai ni, wo yao ni: In Mandarin, the sentences mean, "I love you, I want you." Listen to any Chinese ballad. The lyrics will be belted out at some point.

Haolian: Arrogant (in Hokkien).